MONSTER FIGHT
AT THE O.K. CORRAL

Also Published by Tule Fog Press

Anthologies
Swords & Heroes
A Fistful of Hollers
Monster Fight Volumes 1 & 2
While the Morning Stars Sing
Residential Aliens Volume 1

Collections
Pale Reflection: Tales of Dark Fantasy by Gustavo Bondoni
Fragments of a Greater Darkness by Michael T. Burke
Tule Fog Tales: Speculative Fiction from Lyndon Perry

Individual Works
Razored Land: Books 1 & 2 by Charles Gramlich
The Sword of Otrim by Lyndon Perry
Christ of the Abyss by Joel V. Kela

Residential Aliens Magazine

MONSTER FIGHT
at the O.K. Corral

An Anthology of the
Weird & Wild West
~ Volume Two ~

Edited by Lyndon Perry
Published by Tule Fog Press

Monster Fight at the O.K. Corral ~ Volume Two
Lyndon Perry, Editor and Publisher
Vega Baja, Puerto Rico

This collection © 2023 by Tule Fog Press. All rights reserved.
Individual stories in this collection are copyrighted by their authors.
Cover and graphic design is copyrighted by B. L. Blankenship.
All other illustrations are copyrighted by their creators.

AMAZON ISBN: 9798864851494

Each story is a work of fiction. All characters and events portrayed in this anthology are the creation of their respective authors. They are fictitious; any resemblance to actual events, locales, or persons, living or dead, is entirely coincidental. Any historical references are used fictionally.

No part of this publication may be reproduced, stored in a retrieval system, or transmitted in any form or by any means without prior written permission from the publisher, except in brief quotations in printed or online reviews. Email TuleFogPress@gmail.com for information.

DEDICATION

TO ALL WHO RIDE
THE WESTERN STRANGE

A Witch's Brew

TABLE OF CONTENTS

Introduction ~ Lyndon Perry	1
Water Talks to Water by David Powell	5
Riding Out With a Dead Man by Shawn Phelps	15
Only One Color Matters by Aaron C. Smith	25
Silverlake by John M. Floyd	41
The Watch by Jonah Buck	49
Trail of the Black Coach by Tim Hanlon	63
Entrails West by Gregory Nicoll	77
The Cost of Gold by Henry Herz	89
A Day's Ride from Tarabuco by Gustavo Bondoni	99
The Hills Had a Heartbeat by Trevor Denning	113
Birds of Prey by Stoney M. Setzer	125
The Price of Gold by Su Haddrell	135
Light in the Mine by Marc Sorondo	149
One Shot, One Sin by Jason M Waltz	163
Final Words by B. L. Blankenship & L. B. Stimson	175
Afterword & Acknowledgments	186
Our *Monster Fight* Contributors	187
Copyrights: Stories and Illustrations	192
The Stories of *Monster Fight Volume 1*	193
Support Our Authors & Advertisers	194

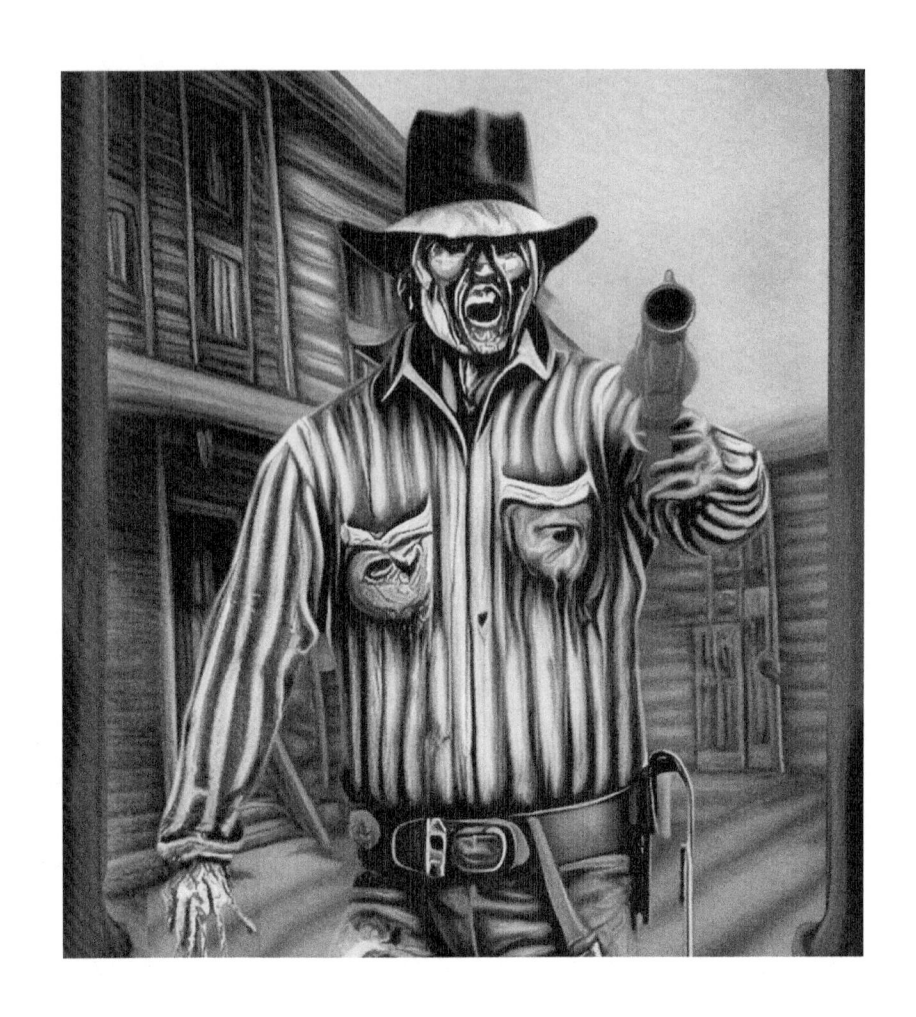

The Gunman

Introduction
Lyndon Perry

This project is a result of a crowdsourcing campaign. And what a boon such platforms are to writers and editors! I'd accepted thirty stories for my *Monster Fight at the O.K. Corral* anthology and knew I'd need to fund two volumes to house these strange tales 'straight outta' the Weird Wild West. In the Acknowledgments I list and thank those 'super supporters' from Kickstarter that helped make this project come to life.

What I want to do here, though, is tell you how some of these stories came to be a part of Volume Two of the antho. This second set of fifteen weird westerns seemed to work well together in my mind. Looking over my spreadsheet, I noted a number of common tropes. There were werewolf stories, of course, and vampires, too. A few cryptids showed up, an alien or two, along with the walking dead. The question was: How to present them?

I could clump all the were-critter tales together, sure. Same goes for all the other monsters that filled my in-box. But that might get a little tiresome, unless I specifically advertised a themed anthology. So I tried to sprinkle a variety of creatures throughout both volumes, mix it up a bit.

Now one recurring plotline emerged and became obvious, and that was the 'monster in a cave' trope. I hadn't realized it at the time, but by the end of the sub window I'd accepted five or six stories set inside a mountain! And I thought, why not? They're different enough in style and antagonist, let's just put them together and let the reader enjoy the ride.

So as I was dividing up the various pieces into each volume, creating a kind of *storytelling flow* for the table of contents, a general overall theme developed. If you've read Volume One, you might note that vengeance plays a prominent role in many of the stories. In Volume Two, it's greed. Not every tale, of course, but it is a common thread, and one worth exploring. So, yeah…monsters, mines, gold, greed, vengeance. Let's do it!

To start us out, though, we're going with a handful of tales that just struck me as different. The style, the subject matter, the *oomph* with which each of these three weird western tales left me — well, I knew I wanted you to read them at the outset. Any one of them could have opened this volume and done this project proud.

First up, then, is David Powell's 'Water Talks to Water.' It's Old World meets the Old West in an understated faerie drama that is as much western adventure as it is horror. I like the mashup and think you will, too. The ending is not a foregone conclusion but it is satisfying.

The next story, 'Riding Out With a Dead Man' by Shawn Phelps is a mournful, poignant tale of loss and heartbreak, for what hope does a dead man have except to die (again) with dignity? But in the aftermath of the Civil War, such a request being granted to Johnny Reb is far from certain.

'Only One Color Matters' by Aaron C. Smith is also set in the aftermath of the War of Northern Aggression. It strikes, as one might suspect from the title, powerful notes of duty and justice. Throw in vampires, a werewolf, and some strange magic and you have one weird and wild western.

While many of the tales in Volume One ended in violent tragedy, I wanted Volume Two to have a different tone. Not that we'll end up with a collection of 'happily ever afters', but one or two are surely welcome. Maybe 'Silverlake' by John M. Floyd is one. Maybe not. Read it and find out.

Desperate times call for desperate measures, and in 'The Watch' by Jonah Buck our hero does all he can to protect the love of his life. But there are some evil mysteries in this world that one cannot prepare for. That's when you're happy just to make it out of those desperate straits alive.

The protagonist in Tim Hanlon's 'Trail of the Black Coach' confronts the netherworld in his quest to face the embodied evil shrouded in a certain black coach. It's a quest that explodes in a heart-thumping gun fight and leads to the precipice of life and death, the outcome uncertain until the end.

Monsters in the night stalk an army regiment in 'Entrails West' by Gregory Nicoll. In this gruesome tale of western horror, the tension mounts as a troop of Buffalo Soldiers takes a shortcut across land even the local Native Americans avoid. They learn their mistake a little too late.

Continuing the army on the western frontier setting, and beginning our 'cave monsters' section of the antho, is 'The Cost of Gold' by Henry Herz. No surprise, greed is front and center when gold is in the offing. But some things are more powerful than the lure of gold. More powerful indeed.

Ever wonder where Butch Cassidy and the Sundance Kid settled once they escaped to Bolivia? Well, Gustavo Bondoni writes that they ended up just 'A Day's Ride from Tarabuco.' Yep, and in a cave looking for treasure. Of course, they discover a lot more than gems and rubies when they disturb the crypts of the spirits that inhabit that lonely mountain. Fortunately, the Pinkerton man who tracked them down was able to, er, help them out.

In 'The Hills had a Heartbeat' by Trevor Denning, a bounty hunter captures a man who is simply more than he can handle…because he's not just a man. But a monster seeking revenge is just the distraction our hero needs to escape something worse than the criminal he originally caught.

'Birds of Prey' by Stoney M. Setzer scratches the cowboys vs dinosaurs itch that I had when I first imagined this collection. I like the setup and I especially like that Stoney brought back one of his great characters, Obadiah Riddle, a kind of 'Old West/Testament' prophet. Better heed his warning!

Yes, there's another story in this anthology with a similar title, but Su Haddrell's 'The Price of Gold' offers a different slant on that ubiquitous vice of greed. Here, a gang of criminals stumble on a dangerous mystery yet they fight on. Maybe the tale's moral is that love (of gold?) conquers all?

Not only did I want a western dino story in this collection, I also wanted to include a cowboys vs aliens tale — and got one in 'Light in the Mine' by Marc Sorondo. Experiments on cattle and sheep are one thing, but when it comes to family, well, there's nothing stopping a man from getting revenge.

Wrapping up this second volume are two supernatural and spiritually themed stories. Jason M Waltz brings us 'One Shot, One Sin', a creative take on the 'bad guy seeking redemption' theme…except this bad guy's a fallen angel; for every sinner he 'redeems' he's one step closer to heaven. Until the Lord of the Underworld takes notice and this rollicking tale turns into a 'this-town-ain't-big-enough' shootout. Exciting and diabolical.

'Final Words' by B. L. Blankenship and L. B. Stimson is the final story, fittingly enough. A dark and disturbing tale of death, loss, guilt, confusion, deception, and madness. When a man's sole reason for living is stripped from him, he has nowhere to go but to the Lord in prayer. But when that fails? The temptation to turn elsewhere for answers is great. Sin begets sin, and the result is truly horrific. This is the kind of cautionary tale that sticks with you long after you close the book.

In fact, I hope all these stories stick with you for a while! To find out more about the authors, check out their short bios in the back. And if you like their contributions, please support their work — drop them a line, even. I know, as a writer, that I'm super stoked when I get an email or message via social media that someone liked what I'd written.

Oh, and be sure to check out Volume One! Thanks for reading!

Lyndon Perry, August 2023
Vega Baja, Puerto Rico

Water Talks to Water
David Powell

I watched the river spirit rise up and cursed that I'd got this reputation as a fixer. I only wanted to escape my husband Nechtan's wrath and make an honest douser's living. West Texas made a perfect hiding place — huge, dry, and remote. No preachers howling to string up the witch, no nickel-dick sheriffs trying to tax my earnings. The law can't abide a single woman with means, but out here water matters more, and I can always find it.

All water's connected, though — that's my trouble. Springs talk to creeks, creeks talk to rivers. Pretty soon a new well outside San Antone recognized me and spread the word. Now here I stood facing down Chalchi, my sister spirit. Two hundred miles north of where she belonged, but she'd blocked Madera Springs to draw me out. Nechtan's doings, no doubt. Nothing to gain but spite.

Chalchi reared up and straddled the creek fork soon as she heard my voice, twenty-five feet tall if an inch. That's a lot of water muscle for dry country like West Texas, but I had muscle of my own. Comanche and Apache drummed and danced on the north bank, joining their war songs into a union that put the Mexican spirit off balance. On the south side, Tonkawon drums gave a beat to the Second Regiment bugle corps, while the proud (if flea-bitten) boys of the Texas Mounted Rifles fired cannon charges. What a glorious racket! Nobody looking to shoot, capture or scalp anybody, because everybody needs water.

Chalchi cowered under the noise; she's made to bless springs and rivers, not to make war. She gave up her height and spread her watery feet to overrun the banks, threatening to sink them all in a marsh. Bluffing, mostly. The dry rock ran too deep to hold water on the surface. Kids ran out with skins and woven thatch, covering the ground so the braves and soldiers could stand dry and keep up the music without losing a note. I didn't have to do that, but the kids loved it, and the tribes had a slightly harder time hating each other, watching their kids play together.

Before her serpent headdress sank out of sight and the spring flooded free again, she reached out to me. I'd won the battle, but she didn't brand me an enemy. Water talks to water.

Colonel Banks threw a party afterwards. I was this close to getting a cute Comanche boy to pronounce the goddess' whole name, *chalchiuhtlicue*, when the Fort Davis scout flailed into the camp and bellowed my name.

"Bo-anne!"

I tried to duck down where he wouldn't see me, but too late. The young brave spooked, stood up, and Chief Toshaway dragged him away from me. I don't speak the language so good, but I'm pretty sure he yelled something like, *What the hell's wrong with you? Leave that damn witch alone!*

The scout saw the commotion and slid off his sweaty roan before it could stop.

"Bo-anne!" Wild-eyed, dust-covered, and out of breath. This couldn't be good.

"At least say my name right! It's Boan, not Jo-ann with a 'b'."

"Don't matter what your name is, long as you're the one unblocked the Pecos. There's ten dead at Howard Springs. Colonel Nelson says it has to be you."

Kelpie could outpace that roan for the six miles to Fort Davis even after a battle, but I didn't push her. I tucked the new silver pieces into my saddle lining and followed the scout down Wild Rose Pass.

The body, mangled under squabbling vultures, lay where the shallow draw from Howard Springs met the pass. I spurred Kelpie alongside the scout.

"You telling me a water entity did that?" I asked.

He didn't look at me. "Just you wait," he said.

The regiment's survivors sat in the dust, dabbing grease on the carriage of a 12 pounder, their carbines stacked in a circle like a tee pee. They looked up at me like I was their daddy, come to give them a whipping. Wishing like hell they were man enough to knock me down and leave home.

Colonel Nelson squatted beside them, sorting through a case of shells that looked left over from the Mexican war. He squinted up at me, champing the last three inches of a stogie.

"Boan."

He said it right, blending the vowels and sliding over the "n." His people skedaddled west from Ireland, same as me. I nodded at the howitzer.

"Thought that did ceremonial duties only, Colonel. Think it's safe to fire it?"

"If we lose Howard Springs, won't nobody be safe. You see what was left of Private Dolarhyde?"

The soldiers fidgeted, some no older than eighteen. They probably watched Private Dolarhyde torn to pieces.

I looked up and down the deserted commons. The upstart Union never intended Fort Davis as a fortress. Sixth Regiment delivered mail, calmed tribal wars, re-supplied west-bound gold hunters. They had no stockade, and one crusty howitzer. Families lived here. Two doors down a curtain moved and a kid peered out. A woman in faded gingham pulled the curtain closed.

I plopped down cross-legged beside the soldiers and fished a plug of tobacco out of my pocket, cut a piece, offered it to the men. They just stared.

"Who can tell me what happened?" I asked.

Silas, a veteran with a wrinkled face tanned to leather, cleared his throat. "Reckon I'll take a chaw," he said. I pitched him the plug and he took his time wiping his knife blade on his britches before carving off a piece.

"Lieutenant Echols got orders to find a better trail through the mountains." He nodded west. "Like they ain't enough of our bones bleaching out there already."

A lifetime of contempt in that voice, and I couldn't blame him. Easy for them to send soldiers out to die. The Comanche hunting trail veered east, away from this wasteland, but the Union didn't want to hear how smart Indians were.

"We meant to top up the water barrels and let the mules drink their fill. Turned 'em loose at the pool, and while they were drinkin' the water level rose up, ran over the rim. Something comin' out of that water. Something *big*."

He stuck the chaw in his mouth and chewed a minute, then looked at me. I waited. He had the cadence of a master storyteller and wouldn't be rushed.

"You ever seen a alligator?" he asked.

I nodded. "In Louisiana. Never in West Texas."

"This thing came out of the water looked like a gator, a bat and a eagle had a baby. Fifteen foot if it was a inch. Picked up a man in each claw and chomped those teeth down on Echols. Bit him in two just like that" — he snapped his fingers — "innards trailing down like fish guts. Bunch of us fired but it didn't seem to notice. Then we were just runnin', fastest I ever saw mules move. Didn't stop till we reached the pass. We got behind some rocks and re-loaded, men still screamin' up the draw, and a minute later

Dolarhyde comes sailin' out of the air and plops down right by the trail. Like warnin' us to stay out."

Colonel Nelson stood, casting a long shadow in the afternoon sun. He snapped his suspenders and watched me, waiting.

"Colonel, that's no water wraith. You don't need me; you need a paladin. Hell, you need a paladin *brigade*."

"They're all tied up in Lake Pontchartrain, keeping little people off the railroads," he said. "That's all guv'ment cares about these days. Nobody gives a damn about Fort Davis."

I didn't argue that point. Once the Union got that railroad across the plains, they'd forget about West Texas entirely.

"I'm sorry, Boan, but you're all I've got."

"Boys," I said, "I just spent two hours pushing Chalchi out of Madera Springs."

Silas' eyebrows went up. "This far north?"

I nodded. "Something's bothering the ground water, clear down to Mexico. Think now. You say the water rose up. Anything else happen right before the monster came out?"

Silas spat and turned his head away. A boy hardly old enough to shave looked up, frowning.

"Lieutenant stayed with the mules. I don't know, petting them and such."

"He babies the damn things," Silas said, "like he's got to inspect every sip they take."

"He walked round and round," the boy said, "singing that song. The one that says, 'Come to the well, Colleen.'"

My heart started hammering in my chest. "Which direction did he walk in?" I asked.

The boy frowned. "What you mean?"

"To his right? Counter-clockwise?"

He nodded.

I fought to keep my breaths even, tried to look thoughtful, not scared to death. Dammit, my husband Nechtan had conjured his way across the ocean. All the way to this hellish dry country. I should have seen it coming. I'd ripped the Well of Wisdom from his grasp, and he couldn't stand to look powerless.

How could I explain that Echols' luckless German ass had blundered into an Irish curse?

"Colonel, pitch those shells and see if you got any grape shot. We need a barrel of black powder, too. Get your best wranglers to round up all the rope they can. And every piece of wood you can spare."

He turned on his heel, already barking orders. Somehow his speed alarmed me even more.

~*~

Nechtan is jealous and domineering, like all husbands, but his arrogance even outstripped the Romans, back in the day. He hid knowledge away in *Tobar Segais*, the Well of Wisdom, allowing no one to approach it but himself and his cup bearers. Knowledge is wasted on those three fools, barely smart enough to hold up a chalice so their mighty god can get drunk.

The land suffered, as it always suffers whenever fools hoard wisdom. If West Texas suffered in drought, Ireland languished in ignorance under Nechtan's tyranny. But knowledge, like water, belongs to all, and I broke his hold by walking against the sun's direction, three times around the well. The gigantic wave he sent chased me to the coast, where I came apart in salt water, but the ocean's deep trenches allowed me to heal myself. I chose this shape to move about on land, embraced the rough language and manners of this upstart Union, and hoped Nechtan would lose track of me. But water talks to water. Bastard got Chalchi to find me and dispatched his elder beast to trap me here in the drought land.

~*~

Light had faded by the time they rounded up what I asked for; evening chill seeped out of the gathering dark. I scratched a diagram in the dirt while they built a cook fire and explained the plan. Taught the guys some words to chant.

Go tobar an eolais, lig do gach cur chuige. 'To the well of knowledge, let all approach.'

The words did nothing, but these boys had watched their comrades torn apart; they needed something to stiffen their spines. If I told them the true story, they'd never believe it, in spite of what they'd seen.

We set off for Howard Springs well before dawn. I wanted the sun shining when the dragon poked out of the water. Entities travel, but like humans they tend to settle where they feel comfortable, drawing strength from the land. Howard Springs belonged to the dry heat of the sun, and Ollipeist sprang from freezing northern waters. More heat, more fire, might hurt him.

Kelpie high-stepped along the path, sensing the fight to come. She's the gamest little pinto I ever saw. She'd rather charge in and die than give up a fight.

The eastern sky glowed a velvet gray by the time we reached the draw. About twenty Plains People sat their mounts, motionless. Comanche on one side of the pass, Apache on the other. They needed Howard Springs, too. Driving Chalchi away had boosted their courage, and the fragile peace between them still held. The People had covered Dolarhyde's body with stones and built a cairn at his head.

"Well, shit," the Colonel said. "How many battles we got to fight?"

"Look close, Colonel. Nobody's painted for battle, and they respected Dolarhyde's body. They just want the water to flow."

"They willing to die for it?"

"Are you?"

Colonel Nelson turned and spat into the dirt, and I nudged Kelpie forward. Ekoka, the Comanche's translator, met me beside the cairn. I scratched my diagram into the dirt and explained the plan, watching Ekoka's face to see if he understood. He studied the ground, betraying no emotion.

"Many beasts, Patsabi," he said.

Most of the Plains People called me Tutsu Puha, witch, but the Comanche saw me a different way. Patsabi, Water Spirit, was closer to the truth than they knew.

"You think I brought them," I said. "You're right. This one came for me."

"We give you to him, he goes away."

"Or he takes me and decides to stay. What happens to your water then?"

Ekoka walked back to the chief, who stared at me throughout their conversation. I met his stare without blinking.

"Patsabi nayapu," the chief said. *Water Spirit sinned*

"I stole knowledge," I said, "because *knowledge* belongs to *all*!"

Foolishly shouting, passion flooding my voice, because this sin was no sin. Knowledge belongs to all, as water washes both good and evil, wise and stupid, innocent and guilty.

The monster's shriek split the air, echoed down the draw and sent stones tumbling. My emotion had cost us the edge of surprise; Ollipeist knew my voice.

I swung to the ground and held Kelpie to stop her charging between the ridges. I had a high-risk plan, but I needed to look sure, or my mongrel army would lose its nerve.

I planted feet on my diagram, face to the sky, thinking it through. Arms outstretched, palms up, I turned around three times clockwise. Ollipeist is fierce and deadly, but simple in understanding. If my luck held, breaking my spell of transgression might confuse him.

His shrieking receded into a locomotive chuffing, angry but uncertain.

I knelt to touch the stones, mind racing. Ollipeist moved freely in air and on land, but he hadn't followed the soldiers out of the canyon. My husband must have spun a protective charm that held him to the pool, thinking that was close enough to strike me. If poor Echols hadn't blundered so, my guts would be splattered across Howard Springs now.

I took some stones from the pile and stood, mumbling the words I'd taught the soldiers as I worked.

"Go tobar an eolais, lig do gach cur chuige."

I placed stones on the diagram where ropers, brush fire, shooters, and howitzer would go, hoping to convince them. Hoping my performance would be enough to unite Army, Comanche, and Apache long enough to slay a dragon.

~*~

I went over the timing again with Colonel Nelson and Ekoka while People and soldiers studied my diagram.

"Don't get any closer than twenty-five feet. He'll stay in the water, but he can throw boulders and flap those wings. He'll raise up high as he can, so wait till those wings clear the water. Soon as they spread, throw true and pull tight. Be ready with that howitzer before he can pull the ropers down. Stop up your ears. That scream can sap your will to fight."

Wranglers circled wide around the shallow canyon and eased into position above the pool left, right, and center. Everything depended on lassoing the monster's head and arms as soon as he showed.

The fire detail piled mesquite, creosote, and every piece of timber Fort Davis could spare just out of the monster's reach. They poured black powder over everything, piling it thick over the driest brush. We didn't want him to see fire till time for him to roast.

"Make it big," I told them. "Big enough to barbecue a dragon."

I couldn't risk Ollipeist hearing me again, so I hung back while they took their positions. The People could move quietly, but the soldiers with their spurs and canteens would rattle and clank in the rocky draw, and the twelve-pounder's cart would make a racket. The biggest risk, though, I completely forgot about. The remains of eight companions still littered the poolside, and as soon as the men saw buzzards feasting on their fellows, they lost control and started shooting.

Kelpie just needed the slightest cluck. She leapt up the draw, ears flattened and nostrils flared, seeming to glide over the rocky ground. We rounded the last bend as the pool bulged upwards and the dragon's eyes rose from the pool like twin green moons, water sluicing between enormous teeth.

Wranglers twirled rope round and round, loops widening with each turn.

"LET HIM RISE!" I triggered my hidden voice, the thunder of waterfalls, startling both men and monster. The dragon's ear fins fluttered. Kelpie pawed the ground and roared with the joy of battle.

Ollipeist rose, water glistened along his scaly length, wings and absurdly short arms set to unfold. He would leave enough body in the water to hold steady, crucially off-balance for seconds. Colonel Nelson gave a piercing whistle, and the wranglers sailed their ropes over the beast, catching one arm, then two.

"PULL TAUT!"

Soldiers and braves together pulled left and right, digging in their heels. Ollipeist threw back his head in rage, and the third loop dropped below his chin, neat as roping a steer.

"FIRE!" I bellowed.

They tossed a torch and black powder sizzled, then *fooshed*, belching white smoke above a glare blinding as the Texas sun. The brush exploded in flame as Ollipeist began to spread his bat-like wings.

"HOWITZER!"

They touched flame to fuse and stepped back, half expecting the cannon to blow apart, but it still had some fight left. It gave a deafening *whoom* and grape shot tore through the monster's right wing, shredding the membrane to tatters. Ollipeist gave a shriek that would have been pitiable, had it not been followed by a fearsome roar.

"PULL RIGHT!"

The damaged wing had him off balance, but he righted himself by sheer rage. He pulled with all his strength, and the ropers slid forward, boot heels digging at the rocky ground, then the left side wranglers whipped into the air like dead leaves in a windstorm. One brave soul managed to seize a twist of ripped wing, swinging wildly while he scrambled for his Colt, but the dragon plucked him free with his teeth, tossed him up, and swallowed him head-first. We could still hear him screaming as his boots disappeared down the monster's gullet.

"EYES!" I yelled, and Comanche bowmen let loose, three arrows finding their mark, sinking into the glittering green, and this time Ollipeist couldn't roar for the cowboy stuck in his throat.

The right and center ropes stayed taut as men shifted position to keep the tension. Soldiers fumbled to reload the howitzer, but I had my eye on the brush fire. We needed to topple the monster now, at the height of the blaze, before he figured out he could sink into the pool and drag the ropers with him. Two of the left-side wranglers lay crushed on the rocks, another struggled weakly in Ollipeist's claw, and the slack rope slid this way and that as the monster tossed its head.

It had to be now.

I clucked to Kelpie and loosened the reins. She reared on her hind legs, squealing, as if to say *about time, witch,* and galloped, hoofs crunching on dry rock, reaching the pool, plunging in up to her stomach mere feet from the monster — crazy, beautiful girl — and snagged the slack rope with her teeth, turning to scramble out of the pool. I held onto her mane, grabbed the wet rope, and looped it around my saddle horn.

"GO KELPIE!"

The pinto galloped straight toward the brush fire, stopping short as the rope thumped taut against the monster's weight, and I whispered a silent prayer that the wranglers would figure out my move. Kelpie strained forward and I held her mane, shouting encouragement, then one rope went slack, then the other, and my pinto leaned into the weight like a draft horse three times her size. She side-stepped the fire just barely, flame licking out and singeing the ends of her mane. Bows twanged and the howitzer whumped, and I could feel the monster's weight displacing air as he lost balance and fell. I flung the rope aside and kicked heels into Kelpie's ribs, turning just in time to see Ollipeist, mangled wing fluttering, crash into the fire.

Carbines popped as the army put load after load into the monster and Plains People piled sticks onto the fire. The howitzer detail pushed the smoking twelve pounder off its wagon and rolled that into the blaze, too.

I rode back to the pool, alarmed to see so much of Ollipeist's tail still in the water. Thrashing, scrambling for purchase, seeking leverage to roll out of the fire or pull back into the pool.

But count on the Irish. Colonel Nelson, bless him, ran to the pool's edge with his saber raised above his head. A ceremonial blade but sharpened to a clean edge that flashed in the morning sun as he landed a blow with a wet *thwack* on the monster's tail, two feet thick near its tip, so two blows, three, and the wriggling stump thrashed apart, bloody scales flying.

Another soldier moved in with a rope, looping it around the severed tail so they could drag it all the way out, breaking Nechtan's spell. The razor-sharp tail fin whipped over their heads, scraped the dry rock, and they stood well back, watching the monster's death throes.

Shrieks gave way to shuddering groans as the fire died down. People and soldiers joined forces to pile stones for two reasons: to make a mass grave for their dead and divert the river of blood from the monster's body away from the pool. Keep the water clean for all.

Fort Davis would host one hell of a barbecue tonight. Peace would last as long as bellies were full. Silas would sharpen his story, shamans would sing. I hoped they'd keep the witch in the song, but fat chance. Each tribe would claim the victory for itself.

Water talks to water, and eventually my arrogant husband will know his elder beast is dead. He'll think twice before trying to reach around the world again. It might be safe for me to return to my green homeland, but I've gotten used to this desert and my new friends. Maybe I'll stay. Maybe this wasteland could turn into a paradise.

Riding Out With a Dead Man

Shawn Phelps

For Joe R. Lansdale

"I know it sounds incredible, Mart," the President said. "That's why I need you to investigate. I don't want to commit troops, or cause a panic, if there's no substance to these rumors."

President Ulysses S. Grant took a deep drag on his cigar and looked across his desk at me. He tugged at his shirt collar, loosening his bowtie. When I had fought beside him, he'd been General Grant and he had seemed more comfortable in a soldier's uniform.

"The entire business about these people may be hokum," he continued. "But they're causing a ruckus down at the border. Been giving the Mexican government fits. They call them *Los Purgatorios*. Say they're caught between heaven and hell. Claim they can't be killed, despite being shot full of holes."

Seeing my expression, he poured me a tumbler of whisky. A cloud of cigar smoke escaped from his lips and obscured his features. His beard had more grey woven through it, but his hands were unchanged, still rough and workmanlike.

"Some Southerners can't accept that they lost the War Between the States; these *Purgatorios* refuse to even concede they *died* in the war," he said. "We killed them once, but now they've come back and are forming a militia down at the Mexican border. I'd appreciate you going down to see if they pose a threat to the Union."

I took a sip of the whiskey and let it swirl over my tongue. My old suit was shabby and out of place in the President's grand office. The whiskey soothed me some, but my soul felt as threadbare as my clothes.

I had been wounded in the war and seen my brother cut down by rebel bullets. Sleep eluded me most nights. Though I survived, I often envied my brother's fate.

Ulysses and I had fought together to preserve the Union, but afterwards our paths had diverged. After the war, Grant's star had continued to rise; my own trajectory had been more like a meteor plummeting to earth. Upon my discharge, I returned to Illinois. There I had a career as an unsuccessful farmer, failed husband, and apprentice drunkard.

"Mr. President," I said, "I am no longer the man you knew. I'm not fit for much anymore. These days, *this* is my primary occupation." I raised my glass and drained the whiskey.

Grant looked at me from beneath his heavy brows. He set his cigar in an ashtray and placed his hands flat on his desktop. After studying me intently for some minutes, he resumed speaking.

"Mart, your country needs you again. I need you. There were times during the war that your advice saved me from grave missteps. No other man will do. Now you go shave and take a bath. Everything you'll need has been assembled. The train to Texas leaves in two hours."

We shook hands and I left. I had never been able to refuse a request from Ulysses. It was a character flaw that had frequently landed me in trouble.

~*~

Three days later I stepped off the train in Brownsville, Texas. A heavy rain had turned the streets into a sea of mud. The brown waters of the Rio Grande threatened to overflow and drown the city. A pontoon bridge, built across the river connecting Brownsville and Matamoros, Mexico, swayed in the current. Some Federal soldiers of the 114th Regiment guarded it. They capered like children in the rain and were constructing toy boats out of paper. They dropped them in the river and hooted with delight as their playthings raced downstream.

I wore a new suit of clothes and had a fine pistol strapped to my leg. Grant had sent a trunk filled with clothes, maps, ammunition, and a box of his own cigars. In my breast pocket was a letter from the President requiring cooperation of any citizen, or soldier, of the United States in the prosecution of my mission.

Planks had been thrown down in the street's mire to form a crude sidewalk. A man I'd hired at the depot brought my belongings in a wheelbarrow. He tottered along the planks, stopping finally before a mud-spattered building of pale wood called The Rose of Texas Hotel.

Outside the hotel, a single man sat on a covered porch that ran the length of the building. His face looked like it had been carved from whalebone by a Nantucket scrimshaw master. He was petting a ragged, one-eyed tabby cat that perched on a table beside him. I nodded to him as I shook the water off my hat. He continued scratching the cat's head and stared into my eyes. He did not smile.

Inside the front door was a bar and several tables. The smell of bacon cooking came from the kitchen. A heavyset bartender sat reading a newspaper. He occasionally shooed a fly away from his face, but was otherwise motionless.

"I'd like to ask you a question, sir," I said.

"Are you buying anything, or just asking questions? This is a place of business," he replied, not looking up from the paper.

"Since you ask so politely, I'll have a glass of beer and I need a room for the night. There's a trunk outside that will need to be taken to my room."

He grudgingly rose, slapped the newspaper on the bar, and poured my drink. Perhaps it was my Northern accent that put the man off.

"Now for my question. Have you heard or seen any of the men the Mexicans call *Los Purgatorios*?" I asked.

Taking out a pocketknife, he began to clean his nails.

"Bunch of them rode through here a few weeks back. Not one came in to buy a drink, which I thought peculiar. Just watered and fed their mounts. Camped one night outside of town and the next morning were gone."

"None of them stuck around?"

"One did. You passed him sitting out front on the porch." The bartender slammed his fist on a bell and a frightened boy appeared. "There's a trunk out front. Get it up to room twenty-two," he barked.

As the lad passed, the bartender slapped the back of his head. I sipped my beer watching him berate his young employee. When I had finished, I set my mug on the bar and returned to the porch.

The man was still there stroking the cat in an absentminded fashion. It was early evening, the rain had let up, and masses of purple and orange clouds filled the sky. His face, devoid of any coloration of its own, absorbed a weird, shifting hue from the clouds.

"Sir," I said, "my name is Major Martin James. I'd be grateful if I could ask you a few questions."

"I bet you would be grateful. But I didn't fight, and die, to jump whenever some Yankee whistles," he replied.

"Well, I been sent here by President Grant to gather information about the men known as *Los Purgatorios*. I can show you the letter he gave me if you like."

"You keep that letter in yer pocket. It don't mean a thing to me. Grant ain't my president. He got no more authority here than the man in the moon."

He drew out a Colt Navy revolver. The pistol held six .36 caliber bullets. I had seen men knocked out of their saddles by the force of that firearm. He held it a few inches above the table and then let it drop. It struck the wood with a heavy thud that startled the cat. It leapt from the table as if scalded and darted away.

The weapon gave off an acrid whiff of gunpowder. Unlike his threadbare clothes, it had been carefully maintained. The gray barrel and dark wood grip gleamed in the setting sun.

"That sidearm appears to have seen some action," I said.

"It certainly has, sir. There's many a man come to grief because of it. If you walk away now, you don't have to share their fate. But any more talking I do will be with this pistol."

"I was hoping it wouldn't come to that."

"I am sorry to dash those hopes, sir, but as you insist on pestering me, that's exactly what she's come to. Let's you and I walk out in that street and do our talking. To be fair, as you're a fellow soldier, I'll let you know that I cain't be killed."

"That was precisely the subject I was interested in discussing," I remarked.

He rose from his chair and stretched. He motioned for me to precede him down the steps to the street.

"Time for talk is passed. I offered you the chance to walk away. You would have been wise to oblige me. I'm going to walk to that end of the street and you go down yonder. We'll face each other and see who walks away."

He stopped some distance down the main street and turned to face me. His legs were spread and his right hand hovered over his holstered pistol. Then the gun was in his hand and he fired. When they heard the shot, the soldiers guarding the pontoon bridge bent at the waist and ran for cover.

The pale man wasn't particularly fast clearing his sidearm. Faster than me, but it didn't matter. His bullet went wide. After you have faced a thousand angry rebels in a field, one man with a gun is not so terrible.

Pulling my pistol from under my coat, I raised it, and sighted along the barrel. A couple more of his shots went past me. One made my coat jump as it passed through the fabric. I exhaled and pulled the trigger.

The bullet took him in the right knee. His leg came apart and he went down in the dirt. He lost his gun and began to crawl through the mud searching for it.

I walked toward him and took aim again. This time the bullet struck his outstretched hand and took off some fingers. He reached his other hand towards the gun, but I was standing next to him and kicked it away.

He rolled on his back and stared blankly up at me. His wounds were ragged, but there was no blood.

"Are you in pain, soldier?" I asked.

"Naw, it don't hurt. I don't feel much of anything these days. Getting around will be a mite inconvenient though."

"How about we stop shooting and have a talk. Just two veterans having a sit down."

"I suppose that would be alright. Could you kindly help me up?"

Having a leg and some fingers shot off seemed to have made him more amenable to reason.

~*~

I walked down to the bridge where the two Federal soldiers were hunkered down behind barrels.

"Thanks for your support boys," I said.

In their flight, they had lost their caps. They looked ashamed and sullen.

"We ain't obliged to get involved in any crazy gunplay betwixt private citizens. Our job is to protect this here bridge. You got no right to chastise us," one of them said.

"I certainly hate to interrupt two brave men such as yourselves from carrying out their duty. As far as my rights, you are mistaken, sir. I am Major Martin James on special assignment for President Grant. You best snap to attention."

I pulled Grant's letter from my pocket. One of them slowly read the document aloud. It seemed to require extraordinary concentration on his part and his lips quivered with the effort.

"Get your caps on and follow me. Conduct yourselves like soldiers and I won't feel obliged to report your boat building activities," I said.

The three of us returned to the injured man, who sat calmly in the mud. Shaking his head, the hotel bartender watched the proceedings from the porch. He aimed a kick at the tabby cat, missed, and returned indoors.

Following my instructions, the two soldiers lifted the wounded man from the street.

"Major, would you do me the courtesy of gathering up my leg and those fingers?" he asked. "I hate to be separated from them."

I thought it a bit late to be worried about being parted from his limbs, but agreed to his request. I put the fingers in my pocket and the leg under my arm. The four of us made quite a picture walking into the hotel's dining room.

"I don't want you bringing him in here," the bartender said.

I placed my pistol on the bar, the business end pointing at his gut. Grabbing his shirt front in one hand, I backhanded him with the other. He staggered and clutched his bleeding nose. I pulled Grant's letter from my pocket and spread it out on the bar.

"That's a document from President Grant giving me wide powers to accomplish a mission here. One of those powers includes being able to command any local Federal soldiers. If you prove uncooperative, I'm walking down to the 114's garrison and bringing back a dozen men to tear this building apart and burn what's left of it."

He stepped out from in front of my gun barrel and moved down the bar.

"You got the wrong idea, sir..." he said.

"No, you fat turd, I don't. Now get a room ready for this man. Get him a bath run and some fresh clothes. If you treat that soldier with anything less than the respect he deserves, I will horse whip you in the middle of that street. I might just let that boy you been pushing around get in a few licks, too. Now move."

After the wounded man was cleaned up, I sent one of the soldiers to get a doctor. Twenty minutes later he returned with a young man, certainly not yet thirty, wearing a waistcoat and pocket watch on a chain. Mud stained his boots and pant legs.

His hands were nimble and he quickly sewed a flap of skin over the man's wounded knee. The same was adroitly done to the hand where the fingers had been blown off. I complimented the doctor on his skill.

"I did my medical training in Boston," he said, rolling his sleeves back down. "But I perfected my craft on the battlefield." He turned to his patient and said, "Well, sir, other than not having a pulse, you seem to be in stable condition."

"Is he fit to ride tomorrow?" I asked.

"I was only contracted to sew him up. Though I'm curious, I won't pry into his habit of not breathing or having a heartbeat. But, yes, he can ride. I'll bring a crutch by in the morning."

"What do we owe you sir?" I asked the doctor.

"No charge. Not to a fellow soldier. Wouldn't feel right."

As he left, I gave him one of Grant's cigars.

"That's a gift from Ulysses S. Grant for your service, sir," I said.

He stared at it, then wrapped it carefully in a handkerchief, and placed it in his breast pocket. Nodding to us both, he left. After he had gone, I posted the two soldiers as guards outside the room's door. They sat in chairs and smoked a couple of Grant's cigars.

An oil lamp illuminated the room, making shadows flutter on the walls. The soldier studied his right hand, of which only the thumb and two fingers remained.

"What's your name son?" I asked. "How did you come to be here, I mean in this condition, neither alive nor quite dead. Were you killed in the war?"

"My name is Isaiah Morgan. I don't recall much of my soldierin' days now," he said. "Just wisps of feelings. Being cold. Hungry. Always afraid. Don't even know where I was when that Yankee bullet found me. Some field with poplar trees at its edge, their leaves fluttering. I was watching those leaves when something slapped my chest. Then…darkness."

He paused and asked if I had any more smoking tobacco. I handed him a cigar. He smoked for a bit and then continued.

"When I woke up, I was on my back in a pine box. The first thing I saw was Spanish moss waving from a tree limb above me. It was dark and the moonlight made that moss look just like sheets of lace. I could smell muck, wood smoke, and swamp water. I later learned we were in Louisiana, not far from New Orleans.

"I sat up and saw I wasn't alone. There must have been a hundred other boys sitting in coffins. We just sat there like a bunch of silent owls looking at one another.

"A black witch woman, naked as a jaybird, was dancing around the fire. She had some symbols painted all over her. Waved her arms and screamed all sing-song, like a preacher at a tent meeting.

"There was a creek nearby and mist was rising out of it and swirling about the coffins. I heard a splash of hooves and saw a rider coming across the water towards us. He wore the uniform of a Confederate General. His left sleeve was rolled up and pinned. That side of his face was also blasted like a tree that's been lightning struck.

"His horse wanted nothing to do with us. It reared up and its eyes rolled like two white marbles. The man pulled up hard on the reins and gave that horse his spurs. Then he began to ride amongst us. 'Boys', he said, 'The Yankees say we're beat. But you have been called from your rest to fight again.' His voice buzzed like a nest of mad hornets. Whatever ruint his face and arm must have done something to his throat, too.

"I'd done my share of fighting. Having died once for the South, I figured I'd given my all. Decided it was time to go home. I climbed out of that box and started walking away. A few others did the same. The General didn't make no attempt to stop us, or convince us to stay.

"He saluted us as we left. 'You'll be back, boys. We'll be waiting here for you.' I walked out into that dark and thought, 'Like hell I'd be back.' But he was right. We weren't the first bunch that was brought back. He knew what awaited us at our homes.

"My wife and little girl were in the yard when I stumbled back to Kentucky. Sally took one look at me and her legs nearly gave out. She turned white and grabbed a fencepost to stay upright. My little daughter screamed and buried her face in my wife's dress.

"'You cain't be here, John,' she said. 'You're dead. I got the letter in the house. Bill wrote me, said he helped bury you. It ain't right.' She wailed and tears rolled down her face. My old dog tore after me and tried to bite my horse.

"A man came out of the house and called to her. I recognized him, he used to run a hardware store before the war. He came down carrying a shotgun. 'You all right, Sally?' he asked. He looked at me and his eyes 'bout popped from his head. 'You git,' he said. 'You got no business here any longer.'

"I could have killed him, or pled with Sally to take me back. The fact is, I knew he was right. I turned and rode off. Ended up back in the company of the General. We all rode down here to form a militia. The General plans to march north as soon as we get enough guns."

We both sat quietly and smoked a bit. I asked if he was hungry, but he said food no longer appealed to him. He didn't feel hunger or thirst. Heat and cold no longer disturbed him. Pain was unknown to him now.

"Isaiah, I need to find this General," I said. "I want to stop another war from happening. Will you help me?"

"I think I could lead you to him. Be dangerous, but I could do it. There's a favor I'd want in return."

"I got the resources of the Federal government at my disposal. If it's in my power, I'll grant whatever your favor happens to be."

"I want you to help me die," he said. "For good this time. You see what little effect bullets have on me."

"I suppose fire might do the job," I replied.

"Sir, I done studied on that. I believe a hot enough fire might work. But I can't do it. I got enough on my conscience as it is. Bible says self-murder is a sin."

"You want me to do it?"

"Yes, in exchange for taking you to the General. But you'd have to be willing to take on the sin," he said.

"There are so many black marks against my soul, one more on the ledger won't make much difference," I told him. "I'd be proud to help you, Isaiah. The fact that you're already dead might give me some leeway as far as sin goes."

"Major, you think I got any chance of making it into heaven? After all the killing I done in the war?"

"I feel certain you'll be forgiven, son. Jesus told his disciples they should forgive up to seventy-seven times."

"Well, that would be about one forgiveness for every man I killed in the war. I guess I might could be covered." He thought a moment. "You suppose the Lord will put me back together if I make it to heaven?" he asked. "Stitch my fingers and leg back on?"

"Isaiah, you ever heard how angels play harps in heaven? Making that kind of music calls for ten fingers, so I think putting you back whole will be a necessity."

"That does make sense. I never did think much of harp music though. You think I could play banjo instead? I was a fair hand at the banjo before the war."

"Isaiah, I believe an exception might be made."

The next morning the weather was fine. As promised, the doctor brought a crutch. Isaiah hobbled downstairs and said goodbye to the tabby cat. The bartender never looked up from his paper.

I telegraphed Ulysses and told him of my plan to search for the General and *Los Purgatorios* in Mexico. The soldiers brought us two horses and helped Isaiah mount. They wrapped his severed fingers and leg in canvas and tied it behind his saddle. His horse was nervous, jumped a bit, but finally settled.

Our horses' hooves were loud on the pontoon bridge as we left Brownsville. The two soldiers had taken up their posts again and they saluted us as we passed. We stepped off the bridge and into Mexico.

It was strange. I was in the company of a dead man, searching for a crazy Confederate General, and hoping to stop a second War Between the States. Yet, I felt the best I had in years.

It was good to be riding out with a fellow soldier. Even if he was dead.

Only One Color Matters
Aaron C. Smith

The second I felt him moving about behind me, I knew I should've just left the dead man where I found him. Who knew why he'd been strung up? Safer to just leave him there and ask when I talked to the locals about serving the warrant I carried for a murdering thief named Vincent Stagg.

Thing was, I'd seen the postcards from down South, people treating a lynching like a picnic. The swinging man's face hadn't been on any wanted posters. My role as a Deputy U.S. Marshal meant keeping those top of mind.

So, I cut him down, figuring he could receive a Christian burial in town. Now, the dead man repaid my charity by refusing to stay dead.

I slashed the ropes securing the body and my horse reared. Trotting back a few steps, I traded the blade for a short-barreled shotgun.

"Please."

The word was faint.

Most things that can take a hanging see you and me as their next meal. *Most.* Some don't. I didn't shoot, though my finger rested on the trigger.

The hanged man started to stand.

"Hey now, you just stay there. Got me a barrel of silver shot and a barrel of iron shot aimed right at you. What the devil are you?"

It was my standard load. Between the two, they'd do for any humans and most monsters. Time with the Cherokee and Creek taught me what really roamed the land, and I carried a medicine bag next to a cross. My preacher might have some words about that, but they both kept me safe. Good Lord couldn't begrudge that.

The hanged man took a few seconds before answering, but that'd likely be more from his just coming back from being dead than conjuring up a lie.

"Werewolf," he admitted, with a faint German accent. "Water?"

"Pack around here?" I asked, looking at the tree line and tossing him a canteen. If others stalked me, seeing me be friendly wouldn't hurt.

He drank deeply. "I am alone."

That was almost certainly a damn lie and my finger tightened on the trigger of the shotgun. "Don't much hear about lone wolves."

"You do not often hear of colored lawmen," he replied.

"Fair point." I was the first United States Marshall of my race posted west of the Mississippi.

I almost shot anyway, but wolves weren't born evil, like fairies or skinwalkers. They'd been cursed and they made choices, some of them pretty savage. "How do you get hearts?"

His kind required a human heart each month, ripped out of a body by their own hand. I couldn't hold the need against him. How he fulfilled it? That I could. My finger kept tight on the trigger.

"I hunt the sort you do."

He looked me in the eye. I pride myself on reading men and the things that look like men. My trigger finger loosened, but I kept the gun aimed dead on.

"How'd you come to be stretching?"

"I was ambushed. I assume that it was the gang I was tracking."

"You could rip a gang of men apart."

"They moved quickly. Very quickly."

The story made just enough sense that I didn't fill him full of shot. Yet.

"Who you hunting?"

"A man named Stagg and his crew. They stole a load of Katy's dynamite."

The Missouri, Kansas and Texas Railway Company did not take kindly to thieves.

"Stagg tried selling it back to the railroad. Then he shot the railroad's representative and kept the money they sent intending to buy the powder back."

"Now they sent you to buy it back?"

The werewolf smiled. "I will not be giving Mr. Stagg any funds when I retrieve their property."

"And you saw Stagg?"

"I saw his ring. Do you believe many people around here attended West Point?"

He made an excellent point. "Well, I've got paper for him," I said. "I aim to bring him to see justice."

He smiled. "I would never disrespect the law. Now, I must ask you a favor."

I saw this coming but waited.

"I could make it into town myself on four legs, but I would be noticed at some point."

True, especially since he'd have to leave his clothes behind if he transformed into a wolf. Naked men caught folks' eyes.

"My friend, I have heard they say skin color does not count for much in Opportunity, but I still believe you will take the attention from me."

I laughed.

With no reason to doubt the story, leaving him didn't seem Christian. Besides, the medicine bag hanging around my neck would provide me an edge if he meant me harm.

"You have a name, Mr. Wolf?"

"Erik Prinz. And I have the pleasure of meeting?"

"Bass Reeves."

~*~

Built by folks from Louisiana looking to better their horizons after the war, Opportunity Missouri, sat between two of the Katy's lines. One ran north-to-south, the other east-to-west. The town offered people moving goods between lines supplies and a night of rest.

Opportunity was still a baby. General store. Saloon. Hotel. A few houses and outbuildings. Not even a church yet.

As the sun hung low, few people walked the street. The town was going to bed. Hopefully, the sheriff didn't set out early as everyone else in town. We rode to his office and walked inside.

A tall blond man sat at a desk; an unlit cigar clamped between his teeth. He looked at us, eyes narrowed.

"Gentlemen, welcome to Opportunity. I am Sheriff Henri Lyon." He set his cigar down and gave us a smile that didn't meet his eyes. His voice carried a New Orleans accent. One of Opportunity's original founders, it seemed. "Is there something I can help you with, Marshal, or are you just passing through?"

"Depends," I said, introducing myself and shaking his hand. He watched Prinz with studied detachment.

I handed him my warrant for Stagg. A West Point graduate, Stagg joined up with Nathan Bedford Forest in Tennessee during the war. He'd led men at Fort Pillow. Survivors said he and his boys'd taken to killing surrendering Negro soldiers with abandon. After the war, they'd taken a page from the James boys and turned bandit.

Stagg said his men were Klan. I wanted him alive to see if he could name names, help stamp out the terrorists. "You seen any of these men?"

Lyon took his time with the papers, then shook his head. "We have heard rumors of this group. They call themselves 'the Hangmen' and camp in the woods, leave the occasional victim hanging from the trees as a warning."

"If you're willing to gather some men, I could telegraph St. Louis, ask for troops to help."

"We left the war behind. Neither renegades nor Federals are beloved here. We have kept the Hangmen from interfering with us. We do not need help in this regard."

"They interfered with me," Prinz said. "Just outside town. They left me nothing, save the matches in my boot."

"Then, Monsieur Prinz, you are incorrect."

"What do you mean?"

"Perhaps they were not the Hangmen. After all, they left you your boots. And, apparently, your life."

"I suppose they did, Sheriff. Tell me, the hotel next door? Does the establishment entertain wagers of feats of skill? Strength?"

Lyon nodded.

"Then I believe I shall attempt to regain my fortunes."

"With only matches?"

"And as you said, my clothing. And my life." Lyon watched as Prinz left the building.

"Mind if I stick around, talk to some folks?" I asked.

"I am never one to send custom from our humble town," Lyon said. "Besides, it is dark, and, apparently, our woods are not as safe as I assumed."

"Question, Sheriff."

"Yes, Marshal Reeves?"

"You talk about leaving the troubles, but is there going to be a problem with me getting service next door?" I asked, nodding toward the hotel.

Lyon smirked. "You should feel welcome there. Only one color that matters in this town."

"Silver?"

The sheriff nodded. "Of course. Silver."

~*~

Nobody noticed as I entered. Behind a bar, a tall man with chocolate skin dried a glass. He smiled, flashing a gold tooth.

No wonder Lyon knew I'd be welcome.

Most of the patrons surrounded a table where Prinz arm wrestled a bald man who wasn't quite a mountain of muscle, but was certainly a large foothill.

Prinz's tight face showed a decent portrayal of effort. He could throw the man across the room. Prinz's arm fell back an inch. Then two.

He sold it well. More people cried out bets.

Then the werewolf closed his trap. The man's wrist slammed against the table with a shotgun crack. The winning bettors cheered, and the rest filtered away, mumbling. Prinz collected his winnings.

He caught my eye and, with no other challengers, joined me at a table.

"A bracing exercise," he said.

"Could've made more money if you hadn't shown off."

He shrugged. "I now have enough for a room, a meal and drinks. After a few hours, and more drinks, people will convince themselves that they could do better. Besides, we still have an audience."

A trio of women watched from the stairway leading to the rooms upstairs. They wore what my preacher'd call night clothes, except most people didn't wear arm's length gloves to bed.

Two of the women wore blue dresses and white gloves, their facial features marking them as sisters. They stood slightly behind the third woman, who wore a white shift with black gloves. These three would remember what Prinz did. Their kind remembered everything. I needed to speak with them.

The feeling seemed mutual. The woman in white stared at me and I smiled. She accepted the silent invitation and walked to our table.

"You gentlemen occupied?" she asked, smiling at Prinz. I took no offense at being ignored. A colored man running the bar didn't mean there couldn't be trouble. Lyon might have been laying the tolerance here a bit thick.

Prinz smiled politely but did not speak. From what I heard about his curse, he couldn't have relations with a human woman.

With a professional reading of his disinterest, she turned to me. "I'm Belle," she said with the same accent as the sheriff and held out a gloved hand.

"Bass," I said, bringing the gloved hand to my lips.

"*Encenté.*"

A shadow fell across the table. Foothill. The man stood tall and tried not to rub his wrist.

"You're in the wrong place." His twang told me he was a visitor.

"Excuse me?"

Belle stood, hands raised. "We don't need violence here, *cher*. One of my girls—"

"Passing a whore off to me doesn't mean I'm going to sit here and let some darkie buy a white woman."

"But you had no issues with the gold toothed gentleman at the bar selling her?" Prinz asked, happy to stir the pot.

Foothill ignored the werewolf. He didn't want to chat with me, either. Instead, the bald man telegraphed a powerful haymaker with his good arm.

I leaned in close enough to make it look like he connected, feeling the wind from the punch on my cheek. Then I wrapped my arms around his chest, dragging us both to the ground in a tangle of arms and legs.

Foothill did the smart thing, the obvious thing. The thing I wanted.

A head butt to my face.

I felt nothing, but Foothill's nose and cheeks shattered as the force he tried using against me hit him. I'd pay a price later. Right now, I drove my knee between his legs. I pushed myself up as he howled, looking at the crowd that gathered around us. I kicked him in his damaged face.

"Move it on! Move it on!" a familiar voice called. "You be moving now." Sheriff Lyon and a pair of men forced their way through the crowd, ax handles in hand. "Trouble, Marshal?"

Belle pointed at Foothill and spoke. "That one wanted trouble, *Cherif*. He found it."

Lyon turned to his men. Foothill tried to stand, but the lawman lashed out with a kick. Two more followed. "Take him." He turned to the crowd. "Remember folks, this is a nice town. A fun town. A town to do business in and tell your friends about. We welcome most anyone. But we do not tolerate such *merde*." He nodded. "Carry on. Lafayette, a round on me."

The crowd mobbed the bar.

"That was…interesting," Prinz said, his tone making me wonder what he saw. Before I could try to find out, he joined the others at the bar.

"It was *exciting*." Belle made the last word sound like a sentence all its own.

"It is at that, and I'd like to buy a moment of your time, if I may," I said.

"We only have one cowboy staying here tonight." Belle said. "There're plenty of rooms upstairs, for an hour or all night. Whatever *you* want, *cher*."

"It would be my pleasure, but I have another sort of proposition for you." I showed her Staggs' wanted poster. "Seen him around?"

She looked at the papers and pushed them back. "No, Marshal."

I slid a silver dollar across the table. "Keep it. If you, or any of the other girls, hear anything, there's four hundred and ninety-nine more of these waiting."

She smiled at the coin, taking it in her gloved fist. "You've seen how the *Cherif* deals with trouble. Bandits are smart enough to keep clear of here. I'll tell you what, Marshall. I feel like a cheat taking your money for nothing. Are you sure you don't want some time upstairs?"

I sighed. "I seen flesh bought and sold. I don't take part in it."

"You think we are owned here? We are rented, at rates we set."

Huh. I'd assumed Gold Tooth at the bar ran them.

"*Cherif* Lyon stood with Grant and the Federals. He did not see so much of a difference between the men his family owned and those who walked free. He could not start a town on his own, so he led us here."

I nodded. "Only one color matters."

"Our motto."

"Keep my coin."

"I believe we are owed drinks."

I nodded and walked towards the bar.

Gold Tooth was shorter than I thought — and he stood atop a trapdoor bolted down with a lock that looked like something the Pinkertons would envy.

"Two whiskeys," I ordered.

The bartender nodded and reached up.

Then I saw the ring, the kind you earned at West Point.

Back at the table, I slid a drink to Belle. "Bartender's friendly."

Her eyes became hooded. "Lafayette lost his tongue before the war."

I doubted the man had attended the military academy.

~*~

Crack.

The wet sound vibrated through my skull. My teeth slammed together, shattering. Blood gushed from my nose. Each breath was a struggle. It might be blasphemy, but it felt a bit like Christ on that cross.

Time didn't help. The pain never became something steady, like a stone in my boot that could be ignored. Each blow was a fresh blast of pain, of the horror at knowing how damaged I was.

My belly filled with lead. It was coming again.

I tried to speak, but blood just bubbled.

Nellie…

~*~

Knock.

Knock.

Knock.

The light noise woke me from the medicine bag's price. It allowed me to avoid the force of Foothill's attack. However, I suffered the pain in exquisite detail as I slept.

Thank God I woke up. Not everyone did. Sometimes, the pain was just too much to bear. That's where my Nellie came in. She and our children were my reason to endure the pain and come back.

The knock might be Belle or another whore, coming to collect my reward.

Or it could be gold-toothed Lafayette. Five hundred silver dollars earned by just rolling a man could be an awful temptation.

I cocked my revolver's hammer and cracked the door open.

The wood plank flew back, slamming into me. The gun flew from my hand as I peddled backward.

The creature that came in looked human, except for how it didn't. Its eyes burnt with red fire, fingers stretched into talons. One eyetooth was lengthened and curved, the other was missing, like a gold tooth had fallen out.

Vampire.

Arrogant bastard made a mistake throwing me back into the room instead of just yanking me out like a gopher from its hole.

I'd landed near my shotgun. The creature moved quick. I did too, aiming in its direction and pulling the trigger. Silver shot took it in the chest.

Vampires regenerated from most damage. Silver was an exception. The creature crumpled to dust.

I staggered into the hall.

"The hell is going on?"

The question came from the cowboy staying in the room next to mine. He held a pistol in his hand. Clawed hands lashed from the shadows, twisting his neck until it cracked and hung limply to the side. The monster flung its victim aside.

Another vampire, like Lafayette. Or almost like him. This creature's sagging breasts swung as it moved towards me. It reeked of rotten meat. It grabbed me by the throat, slamming me against the wall. Its skin looked paper thin but felt like leather.

The same force hit it in the chest, knocking it back as the medicine bag did its thing. I aimed at its head and pulled the trigger. The shot was iron. Wasn't silver, but vampires didn't handle decapitation well. The creature went to dust as iron pellets shredded its head.

A light clapping rewarded my performance.

"Very good," Prinz said. His clothes appeared to have been slashed and wet with his blood. "Though I dispatched the ones they sent for me more quickly."

"Coulda lent a hand."

He shrugged. "You are unharmed and do not appear the sort to need or appreciate handouts," he said. "Is there perhaps a reason *I* should fear *you?*"

"Nope. I'm just a simple human with some not so simple friends. I don't look for trouble."

"We seem to have found it."

He pointed at a gold locket on the ground. "One of Belle's friends."

I tossed him the gold tooth and ring I'd collected in my room.

"I would really like to see what is inside the basement," Prinz said.

Man after my own heart.

I got dressed and reloaded my shotgun, loading my pockets with extra shells. We took our time going downstairs, waiting to see if anything else was coming. However, we only heard our own footsteps echoing in the dark until we were behind the bar.

Seeing the trapdoor and its fancy lock, I reached into my pocket and withdrew a set of picks.

Prinz bared his teeth in something approximating a smile. "Allow me." He positioned his claws between the hatch and floor and ripped up. The wood splintered and Prinz tossed the trapdoor away.

A foul wind blew from below.

"You don't want to go down there." A female voice.

I spun, shotgun out. This time both barrels held silver. "Ah, Ms. Belle. Couldn't decide whether we would see you tonight or not. Don't know if your kind pray or not…"

She stepped out of the shadows. Tonight, her arms and neck were bare. In the moonlight filtering through the saloon window, the scarred flesh of her neck and arms looked like melted candles.

"Not all of us here from home are…like them."

"They feed off you?" Prinz's question had a clinical aspect to it.

"They used to, until people came. That's why they built this place. Strangers coming in and out. Who notices a few missing here or there?"

"And if they did, there are always bandits to blame," I said, thinking of Gold Tooth's ring. Now it made sense how the Hangmen had overpowered the wolf.

"Did you know what was here?" Belle asked.

"Nope. Was hunting a man, like I told you. But I can telegraph someone who can send us help."

"There's no telegraph in Opportunity," Belle said. "We have to leave. And you have to take me with you."

"She will slow us down," Prinz said.

"We've killed three of them. How many more vampires did Lyon bring?"

"With those you killed, you still face over a dozen."

"There you go, Prinz. She has valuable information. And she's human."

"But I am not," he reminded me.

I looked into Prinz's hard eyes. There held no compassion, only hunger if you looked just right. I've killed men but hadn't lost my humanity.

"You can come with us," I said, speaking to Belle without taking my eyes off Prinz.

Moonlight illuminated Belle's shy smile.

I reached out, taking her hand in mine. She squeezed.

Then she screamed, jerking her hand back. The silver dollar I'd palmed clattered to the ground.

Belle lashed out with the heel of her other hand. But for the medicine bag, it might've hurt. It sure as heck caused the vampire to tumble back a few steps when her power turned back on her. My shotgun boomed. Belle's face showed surprise and anger as she turned into dust.

"Clever," Prinz said. "I had been concerned that you were thinking with your heart. Or something else."

"She only showed herself when we prepared to enter the basement. Found that interesting. She wanted to know about our intentions. I wanted to know how many suckers were in this town. See what patience can achieve?"

"You believe she was telling the truth?"

"You lie to the folks whose hearts you take?"

The werewolf snorted. "Let us see what she wanted to keep hidden."

Nearing the hole, putrid wind smelled damnably close to death.

"After you," I said, pointing at the stairs leading down.

I stepped aside to let Prinz walk down first. There was going home to Nellie and my family to think about.

At the bottom of the stairs, Prinz found a lantern and lit it. It wasn't bright, but when you're going into hell, any bit helps.

There was no doubt that the bottom of the stairs emptied into the pit. A half-dozen men lay in the dirt, chained to the wall. Most sat in silence, but one snapped awake.

"My God. Please help me!" The voice was thick and wet.

Foothill.

There wasn't a smidgen of blood on his face. I didn't want to think how they'd cleaned him.

The only color that mattered in this town wasn't silver.

Foothill recognized me and damn if he didn't look at me like Jefferson Davis and Jesus Christ rolled into one. "Please. Please. Please help me. Please, God, help me."

As honest a prayer as any I'd heard.

Prinz moved the lantern light to see the other prisoners and the tunnel that lay beyond. The wind blew from there.

I recognized the other prisoners.

Stagg and his men. Unlike Foothill, the bandits had been left long enough to sit in their own shit and piss. Old wounds covered the bandits. However, despite the discomfort they had to be feeling, they just stared ahead, like men in opium dens.

"Their saliva carries a narcotic," Prinz said. "It keeps victims compliant for the feedings, addicting them."

"Shackles seem like overkill."

"Not when they are fresh, like your friend there," Prinz said. "Why remove the chains later?"

Feet stomped above us.

Lyon. Or at least some of his followers. There was no way to know how many.

"We have dispatched some of their kind. They will likely not wish to come down those stairs."

"Fighting up seems like suicide."

Prinz pondered for a moment. "We cannot simply wait down here," he said. "However, there is another way."

He explained his plan.

Stagg and his men would die badly. Thoughts of Fort Pillow didn't inspire many tears.

Foothill, though, I didn't know him. He might've been willing to ride with Stagg. Then again, he might've just been a drunk asshole. That wasn't a dying offense, and I said as much to Prinz.

"I had thought you harder of heart than that, Marshal."

"I kill what needs killing. Not gonna let a man die to save my skin. Now can you pull the chain out of the wall?"

Prinz waited a few moments before responding. "Yes. However, that will require embracing more of the beast. Do you understand what that means?"

"Do it," I said.

Prinz walked to the prisoner, growing and twisting with each step. His back arched, forcing his head and shoulders forward as his upper body thickened. At the same time, his legs bent to look more like a wolf's hindquarters.

He stood over Foothill and raised an arm now roped with terrible muscle. It looked like an ax, ready to chop down on a chicken's neck.

Then I realized my mistake. His humanity had faded into the background. The predator didn't see a man who needed rescue.

Hell, I'm just a normal person and Foothill's fear stink hit me. He had to smell like a steak to the werewolf.

I brought the hammer back on my shotgun. "Hey now!" I called.

Prinz turned, face flowing into a snout covered in black fur. Amber eyes glowed as the lantern splashed him with light. The werewolf snarled and stepped towards me, protecting what it saw as its kill.

"Mine."

"No," I answered.

"MINE!"

"Not prey." I stepped towards him, the shotgun at chest level. "Not prey."

Prinz leaned his head back and let loose an ear-splitting howl. Damn if there wasn't some part of my brain that didn't want to find a hole, hide in it, and pull the hole in after me.

My shotgun stayed steady.

"Not. Prey."

The monster screamed again and swept its claw down towards the prisoner.

My finger tightened on the shotgun's triggers.

The clawed hand gripped the chain and ripped it from the wall.

Prinz wheeled around.

"Run." The word rumbled like a train. Prinz loped into the tunnel.

"You heard the man!" I yelled. "Get off your ass and go."

I focused on my part of the plan, dipping a rag into the lantern's reservoir and lighting it. I wrapped the burning cloth around my shotgun.

I tossed the lantern onto the stairwell. It shattered, burning oil enveloping the wood in flames.

Then I hightailed it, passing Foothill in his irons. I'd done my part in shaming Prinz into freeing him. He could save himself.

The tunnel had not been carved with someone of my height in mind. Couldn't quite run but wasn't crawling either.

Light and heat from the blaze followed us until we plunged deeper into the passage. The clank of Foothill's chain told me he was still behind me.

If that chain stopped rattling, I'd know the vamps were in the tunnel and catching up to us.

Prinz would be proud of me seeing such a use in a death.

The werewolf's breaths echoed from in front of me.

Another coldblooded thought crossed my mind. Prinz's deciding to turn and run down the tunnel instead of eating us had been close. What the hell would he do when we finished running, his blood up?

In this tunnel, if I pulled the trigger, the shot would at least cripple the werewolf. I stopped, raising the gun and tightening my finger on the trigger.

Foothill's chain rattled behind me.

Prinz hadn't needed to free him, to show that mercy. I owed him the same.

"Come on!" I yelled behind me. "Run."

The chain stopped rattling, replaced by a scream.

Turning, I sighted down the flames on the shotgun. Was that movement in the shadow flickering fire or what took Foothill? Two blasts down the tunnel seemed appropriate.

A wooden ladder led out of the tunnel and into a storage room filled with boxes and barrels. I followed the path of destruction and found Prinz near a pair of barn doors. Sitting before it was a wagon loaded with even more boxes.

"Found my dynamite," he said, his voice husky as he looked at a box he had torn open. He was still not human but far less wolf. "Railroad has to give me money."

"We get out of here, Prinz, I'll help you get your money."

Prinz knocked open the front door.

The hairs on the back of my neck stood up. I'd seen the lock on Gold Tooth's trap door. No way would the vamps leave their prizes sitting in an unlocked building.

"There," Prinz said, his words a low rumble. I couldn't see the vamps but trusted the monster. His body quivered, ready to leap out to battle.

The vamps moved forward in a wedge, with Lyon at their point.

"There was no reason for this. I told you. We run a smooth town. We only cull from the troublemakers."

"You hung me," Prinz said.

"And look at the trouble you have made. I now offer you a choice. Walk outside and we make your death quick. Force it and my people are going to want to play with their food."

"What if I made a proposal?" I asked.

Lyon laughed. "What would that be?"

"You and yours ride out. Or we slaughter y'all to a man."

They laughed. *Well, I'd given them a choice.*

I lifted a bundle of dynamite from the wagon, touching the fuse to the last bits of flame flickering on the shotgun's barrel.

I threw the explosives at Lyon. He moved fast, plucking it out of the air like a baseball.

"Nice try, Marshall Reeves," the sheriff said, tossing it back at me.

The explosives rocketed toward me as the short fuse burnt down. I stood pat.

The explosion roared out for the blink of an eye. In that same blink, the force and flame of the explosion stopped. Then it thundered back towards Lyon and the other vamps.

They flew backward, becoming dust in the night.

I fingered the medicine bag next to my cross and smiled grimly at Prinz. After tonight, my dreams were going to be hell.

Silverlake

John M. Floyd

Joe Rainey saw the graveyard before he saw the town.

That wasn't unusual. This one, like most cemeteries in these parts, was perched on a low rise beside the trail, a scattering of stone and wooden markers. What was unusual was the number of fresh graves — at least half a dozen. Rainey studied them a moment, then clicked his tongue to his horse and continued down the slope toward a wide cluster of buildings and fences.

The weathered sign at the edge of town said SILVERLAKE, the name barely visible in the fading light. Beyond it were tree-shaded stores, houses, sheds, pens, and corrals. The odd thing was, Rainey saw no people and no livestock. The only movement — and the only sound — was a creaky windmill above one of the outbuildings. The only light he could see was a strip of pale yellow from the window of a home at the end of the main street. Rainey stopped in front of it, tied his horse to a gatepost in a picket fence, and climbed the steps to the porch. The glass in one of the front windows, he noticed, was broken. He rapped on the door.

The young blonde woman who answered his knock stood in the doorway and looked him up and down.

Rainey took off his dusty hat. "Good afternoon."

She didn't reply with *Who are you?* or *What do you want?* or *May I help you?* Her reply, after her eyes flicked past him to the darkening street, was a correction: "Almost evening." She looked back at him and said, "Come inside."

He stepped through the door and watched her swing it shut and lock it behind him.

"Forgive me," she said. "There've been some strange happenings here lately. After dark."

Rainey didn't know how to reply to that. He found himself looking at the two front windows, which he figured was a result of some of these happenings. Both were covered with thick boards nailed to the living-room wall on each side. One of the boards on the broken window had been recently cracked and bent inward, and he realized it was through that gap between boards that he'd seen the glow of lamplight from the street. Solemnly the young woman waved him to a chair and took a seat facing him. When she said nothing he cleared his throat and said, "My name's Joe Rainey, ma'am. I'm a cowhand on my way north and looking for a place to stay the night. Everything seems to be closed up."

"Not closed," she said. "Empty. Everyone's gone. My pa and me are the only ones left."

Rainey blinked. "The only ones in town?"

She nodded. "We waited too long to leave. Pa's sick, and we got no horses left to pull our wagon."

"What happened to your horses?"

"Same thing that happened to the rest of the town," she said. "They're either dead or run off." She paused, her hands clenched and tense in her lap. "It's a long story."

Before he could reply, she rose, walked to the front door, and opened it again. "I'm Clara Logan, Mr. Rainey. You are most welcome to stay the night. I know you'll want to see to your horse — there's a well out back, and a barn with plenty of hay. When you're done, be sure to latch the barn door behind you." She stepped aside so he could go out. When he did, and turned to look at her, she said, "It's almost full dark. Come back quick."

~*~

Ten minutes later he tapped on the back door of the house. Clara Logan let him in, her eyes again looking past him. Looking for danger, he thought. Off to the west, the flatlands were black as the bottom of a well, the sun long gone. When she'd locked and barred the door behind him he followed her back to the front room carrying his saddlebags, rifle, and bedroll. Once they arrived there, she turned to face him.

"I know how strange I'm acting," she said. "I owe you an explanation."

"I'm the debtor here," he said, piling his gear on the floor, "and much obliged to you. But yes, I'd like to know what's going on."

So she told him, standing there in a well-arranged room except for the two boarded-up windows. As it turned out, the story *was* long, and scary as well. When she was done, Rainey wasn't sure he believed a word of it. What he did believe was that *she* believed it.

After a long pause he took a chair and sat there a minute, thinking about her words and choosing his own. "Begging your pardon, Miss Logan…a wolf just can't do what you say has been done. I've seen one take down a full-grown horse, but they don't break into houses and barns like you described, and they don't attack towns or groups of people. A bear might, I guess, but I doubt it. Certainly not a wolf."

"I didn't say wolf," she replied. "I said *were*wolf."

Rainey blinked. "Excuse me?"

"You know about them? Werewolves?"

"I guess. What I mean is, I've heard the legends. Stories of hairy manbeasts, long ago, in Europe." In a careful voice he added, "Tales told to scare little children."

"I would've thought the same, a month ago." She sagged into the chair facing him. "But something has killed nine people here, Mr. Rainey. Mangled and ate them — and cattle and horses, too. You probably noticed the latest graves as you rode in."

"I did. But—"

"And this isn't hearsay," she said. "I've seen the beast. With my own eyes."

He frowned. "You what?"

"Leland Carter shot it, there in the street, three nights ago. Shot and hit it twice with a new rifle, from twenty feet. I was watching from that window. The bullets did nothing. The thing turned on him, and he ducked inside his house, but it smashed against his door for ten minutes afterward. His windows too, but they were boarded shut like ours. Leland and his wife packed up and left town the next morning. So has everyone else who could."

The room had gone dead quiet. Rainey couldn't help glancing at the windows. Finally he said, "What'd it look like?"

"I told you. A wolf. A really big one, and black, with teeth" — she held up a finger — "this long. And when it was pounding on Leland's door it stood on two legs, like a man." She swallowed, and shivered a bit. "I know how that sounds — but I swear I'm telling you the truth."

He stared at her for a long time. Finally he nodded. "I believe you." And he did. As crazy as all this was…somehow he knew she wasn't lying.

"I'm grateful to have you here, Mr. Rainey," she said, "but I'm sorry for you that you came. I should've sent you away, but I couldn't…" Tears welled in her eyes.

"I'm not going anywhere," he said. "Tell me the rest."

She took in a shaky breath and let it out. "It came here last night. The front and back doors are thick and strong, but it broke one of our windows there and almost got through the boards I'd nailed over it." She wiped her eyes. "I think it'll come again tonight, when the moon's high, and when it does we'll probably die. There's no way to kill it."

Rainey was shaking his head. "You're wrong. There has to be."

She studied him a moment. "You have a silver bullet?" she asked. "That's the only way."

"I keep several in my saddlebag. With my set of golden knives."

Even she had to smile a little at that, which made him smile too.

"Again, I've heard the legends, Miss Logan. Maybe regular bullets *can't* kill it. But I do have a Colt and a Winchester both, right here, and I'm a good shot. I promise you I can hurt it. Maybe enough to run it off."

"Maybe so," she said, but the skepticism was clear on her face. She was probably right to doubt him, he thought. He hadn't seen the thing up close. She had.

"I know one thing for sure," he said. "If we *can* manage to hurt him, turn him away, then tomorrow we can hitch my horse to your wagon out there and drive you and me and your pa away from here. You hear what I'm saying? There are soldiers at the fort we can send back here, to take care of this thing once and for all. They hit him with one of their cannons, there'd be no need for a silver bullet."

She stayed quiet for several seconds, studying his eyes. "You'd do that? You'd help us get out of here?"

"Of course I will. And if this wolfman of yours does come tonight, well — like I said, we'll try to hold him off."

She shook her head slowly and frowned at the door and windows, probably picturing what might happen. "Who knows?" she said. "We've been saved once before — maybe it'll happen again."

"What do you mean?"

Clara Logan sniffled and looked down at her hands. "Another long story. My pa used to be the town marshal here. One time, twelve years ago — I was just a little girl — two bandits came to town, shot the place up, murdered a storekeeper. Then they left, said they were coming back the next week with their whole gang to kill the marshal and rob us all.

"The day before they got here, a stranger showed up out of the blue, a former Texas Ranger and a man he called his partner. They stood with Pa in the street the next day, and the three of them shot and killed all eight bandits. If he'd been alone Pa wouldn't have had a chance." She shrugged. "That convinced me that miracles do happen. Maybe one'll happen tonight."

Rainey nodded. He wasn't sure he believed in miracles, but half an hour ago he hadn't believed in werewolves, either.

"Where *is* your pa right now?" he asked, as the thought occurred to him.

"Sleeping, in the other room — he hasn't been well. And before you ask, there are no windows there."

Rainey took his Colt from his holster and said, "Best he stays where he is, then." He checked the load in the revolver, put it back, and did the same with the rifle. "When the moon's high, you said?"

"Yes. That's when it usually comes." She looked at the wall clock. "Not long now."

"Don't be too sure. Since it couldn't get in last night, maybe it won't try again."

She thought that over. "No. We're the last humans in town," she said again, "and tonight there are three of us here instead of two. It'll smell us — and it'll come."

Rainey nodded. He thought she was right.

Clara smoothed her dress as if all this wasn't happening and looked around. "What should I do?" she asked. Her voice was trembling a bit.

"What did you do last night, when it tried to get in?"

She pointed to a shotgun leaning against the wall. "Aimed that at the window. And waited."

"Well, do that again, if worse comes to worst." He had another thought. "Maybe it'll try first for my horse. The barn'd be easier to break into than the house."

She shook her head. "It won't, not since we're close by. Otherwise, it might."

"You're saying it prefers humans."

"I'm saying it seems to, yes."

Rainey let out a lungful of air. "I'm liking this thing less and less." He rubbed a hand over his face, rested the Winchester across his thighs, and scanned the rest of the room. Two practical chairs, a small table with a lantern, two cabinets of some kind, a rug on the wooden floor, and a heavy desk in the corner with framed pictures and what looked like mementos lined up on it: a miniature locomotive, a brass paperweight, a five-pointed marshal's badge, a single cartridge standing upright on its end. And, of course, the two board-covered windows.

For some reason, he felt the need to try to offer some comfort to this small, brave lady. That was stupid, he knew, and probably even a bit insulting. She understood the position they were in better than he did, and had already shown him she was tough. But even still...

"Silverlake," he said. "Seems an odd name for a town. I didn't see any lakes out there, or even a pond. And for sure no silver."

She forced a smile. "Me either. It's not a bad place to live, though. At least until lately."

So much for lightening the mood. He stood up, walked to the window that was broken, and tried to peer through the gap into the dark. "Where do you think it came from, this beast?"

"No idea. Pa says he never heard of anything like—"

Something hit the outside wall between the door and window. Hard. Rainey sprang back so fast he almost fell down. A low, rumbling growl came next, followed by more thumping noises. Rainey levered a shell into the rifle and aimed at the window, and Clara grabbed the shotgun, cocked both hammers, and did the same. The pounding and snarling continued.

Rainey felt he'd wandered into another world. To hear about all this was one thing; to witness it was another. He was sorry that at first he'd doubted her.

"Don't shoot yet," he said. Still pointing their weapons, both of them moved slowly to the back wall and crouched together beside the desk. The lamp painted long, stark shadows across the room. The only sound Rainey could hear, except for the thudding and growling from the porch, was the rasp of Clara's breathing and his own pulse thundering in his head. His hands were slippery against the stock of the rifle. He glanced again at the desk beside him. Should he tell her to hide under it?

And then he had a thought. A crazy but blindingly brilliant idea.

"That bullet there, on the desk," he hissed. "Where'd it come from?"

She frowned. "The stranger I told you about, who helped us. He gave it to Pa before he left. Why?"

Rainey felt a dizzying surge of hope. "He wore a mask, this stranger, didn't he? Rode a white horse."

"What?"

"And his partner — the partner was an Indian. Right?"

"Yes. How do you know that?"

He started to say *We have legends of our own, here*, but never got the words out. At that moment one of the windows exploded inward, followed by the splintered boards covering it, and the beast's head and shoulders burst through and into the room. Rainey heard the double blasts of Clara's shotgun and heard her scream, but he'd already turned away. He dropped the rifle, drew his revolver, and was diving onto the desk when the monster struggled the rest of the way through the window, roared, and charged.

In the next seconds Rainey did six things in one smooth, continuous motion: he ejected an unfired shell from his Colt, grabbed the upright cartridge, slipped it into his gun, spun the cylinder, rolled over on the desktop to face the oncoming beast, and fired the silver bullet into its open, snarling mouth.

The thing's head snapped backward in mid-leap. It seemed to hang there a moment in the air, then crashed in a heap, half-on and half-off Rainey and the desk. Rainey felt its wiry hair, smelled its stink, waited for it to sink its giant teeth into him. But the wooly beast was dead. Its head, wide as a washtub, slid slowly backward off him and across the desktop as the weight of the rest of its body dragged it off and onto the floor. It convulsed once, the long tongue lolling from its jaws, and lay still.

Rainey and Clara stared down at it, stunned.

As they slowly looked up at each other, the door on the other side of the room opened and a frail older man with sleep-tousled hair stumbled through it. In his hand was what looked like a medieval pistol. Trembling, Clara rose from the floor, went to him, took the gun gently from his hand, and hugged him tight while Rainey climbed down off the bloody desktop.

"Pa," she said, smiling through her tears, "there's someone I'd like you to meet."

~*~

Two days later Rainey and Clara stood beside the gate in her front yard and watched a loaded mule-drawn wagon rumble in off the flats to the west. It was almost sundown; two other families had arrived in town that morning.

"Word's getting out," she said. "Some of them won't come back, but I think most will. I told you, Silverlake's a good town." She paused, thinking. "The livestock'll take time, but a woman in one of those groups earlier said she saw a dozen head of cattle grazing to the south."

"I can help round those up," Rainey said.

She turned to face him, and took his hand in hers. "It's good of you to stay awhile," she said. "Pa likes you."

Rainey smiled. "I like him too. And I like the town. You realize, don't you, that all we'd need to do now is dig a lake? The silver was here all along."

She nodded, took the empty cartridge case from the pocket of her dress, and looked at it. "Quite a surprise, that was."

"They're called miracles," he said. "And that one belongs back on your pa's desk." He took off his hat and ran a hand through his hair. "On that subject, I told your pa something yesterday, about that masked stranger and his partner who you told me came here years ago. I said they wound up saving him not once but twice."

"Guess they did, at that." She tucked the shell back into her pocket.

They fell silent then, enjoying the cool breeze and the warm sun. The driver of the wagon raised a hand, and Clara waved back. The woman on the seat beside him was smiling.

After a moment Clara said, "Think we'll ever know where that evil thing came from?"

"No. It'll just be another children's tale."

She grinned, still looking at the wagon, and squeezed his hand. "But who would I tell it to?"

Rainey turned to study her profile. The worry he'd first seen in her eyes was gone now, and her smooth, fresh face looked like he imagined it had years ago, when a former Texas Ranger and his loyal companion had arrived in town to help this little girl's father keep the peace. The afternoon sun lit her blonde hair like a halo.

He smiled too, and said, "I've been thinking about that."

The Watch
Jonah Buck

Gator Malloy adjusted his hat to keep the sun out of his eyes. He and Melody were still days from the Sierra Nevada range and California, and the desert was doing its best to turn them back east.

Gator could shoot the wings off a gnat, strum the strings of his guitar so sweetly that he'd charm jackrabbits out from their burrows, and believed that nothing tasted better than fresh grizzly meat roasted over an open fire. Gator had a lot of skills and talents that Calvin hoped he'd never need to prove.

"Calvin?" Eliza asked.

"Call me Gator. At least until we reach California. We'll be okay once we make it over the mountains."

"I didn't run away with any Gator Malloy, and you didn't run away with any Melody Brenner," Eliza said. "It's just the two of us out here. There probably isn't another person around from here to Reno."

Eliza was right. The last time he'd seen another person was when he traded the last of their cash to top off their supplies. He'd been hoping to run into a wagon train so they could blend in and maybe beg for some extra food and water. So far, no luck. He wasn't convinced they had what they needed to reach the next waystation. And if they did, how would he pay to restock their supplies again?

That wasn't his greatest fear, though.

"No idea what you're talking about, Ms. Melody. Who's this Calvin fellah you mentioned?"

Eliza sighed and tugged her bonnet lower. "You're right, Gator. All this heat must have gotten to me and turned one of our brains to mush." Her tone made it clear that she didn't think she was the one whose brain had melted to porridge.

Gator Malloy, who could spit his weight in chewing tobacco and combed his hair with a brush made from tarantula legs and cactus prickers, put his arm around her. His voice was low and soft. "Eliza, you know why we're going by fake names. Just a little bit longer." He squeezed her hand.

"No, you're right," she said in an equally low voice. "I just…I want to go back to being *us*. I wouldn't be on the run if this Gator Malloy scoundrel had tried courting me. You understand?"

"Soon, my love."

The truth was, Calvin did enjoy being Gator Malloy. The persona was a sort of security blanket.

He'd killed Eliza's father. It hadn't been his intent. He'd planned to walk up to the mansion, on the land where he had worked the fields growing up, and run off with Eliza in the dead of night. He'd been seeing Eliza in secret for months and finally worked up the courage to ask her to come away with him.

Everyone knew her father was a beast. Eliza frequently had bruises from when he'd get roaring drunk and beat her. Rumors said he'd killed Eliza's mother in a fit of rage years ago, though no one could prove it. Twice, the county doctor had been called out to set Eliza's fractures from 'falling down the stairs.' Her father was openly maneuvering to marry Eliza off to Archibald Cotts, another of the area's great land owners, but he was twice Eliza's age.

Calvin had arranged the whole thing with Eliza beforehand. They'd run off together, and never see the place again. Eliza would be giving up the lifestyle of a wealthy debutante, but that lifestyle had only been a colorful prison.

Calvin had been helping her out of a window when her father found them, a bottle of bourbon in one hand and a rifle in the other. He looked at Calvin, dropped the bottle, and took aim. There had been a struggle. The gun had gone off. Calvin had tried to apply pressure to the wound in the man's chest. Then, Eliza had pulled him away as confused shouts drew closer to the sound of the gunshot.

Calvin knew that he had only defended himself that night. He hadn't meant to hurt, let alone kill, anyone. But he didn't think the law would view it that way. Eliza's father had all the friends money could buy. There would be bounty hunters out after them. They'd throw a ball to celebrate dropping Calvin from the gallows. Archibald Cotts would probably arrive to collect Eliza as soon as Calvin's heels stopped jittering.

Calvin Frankel was a man on the run from powerful forces, hoping to disappear into the anarchy of California's gold mining territories. Gator Malloy, on the other hand, wiped his behind with men like Eliza's father. It was easier to be Gator Malloy than Calvin Frankel right now, just so long as he didn't have to live up to any of the tough guy rhetoric.

"Cal — Err, Gator? Do you see something up ahead?" Eliza pointed.

Calvin squinted. The ground shimmered as it radiated heat. For a moment, he thought it was a mirage, but no, there was something up ahead. It was another wagon.

"Hot damn," Calvin whispered. One wagon wasn't much, but they'd be less suspicious if they could travel with somebody else.

He flicked the reins, encouraging the oxen. They picked up the pace for a few steps before the heat sapped any urgency out of them.

After what felt like hours, Calvin pulled even with the other wagon. It wasn't moving. Its oxen team was dead, a scattering of disarticulated bones. The canvas covering was torn, and the wooden frame was bleached pale by the fearsome sun.

"Did they break down?" Eliza asked.

"I don't see anything that's broken. Wheels and axles look good. Probably had a sick ox and had to hitch a ride on another wagon." Calvin said. "Let's check inside. Maybe there's a few supplies left behind."

"*Calvin*," Eliza said in a sharp voice, not bothering with his nickname now. "That would be stealing."

"It's not stealing if it's abandoned," Calvin replied. In truth, he wasn't anxious to scrounge around the wagon either. But anything he could scavenge might save them a great deal of hardship. He hopped off their wagon and stepped up to the abandoned one. He pulled the canvas aside and immediately recoiled.

The body laying inside the wagon looked to have been chewed on by animals. Raw bone shone through where the desiccated, leathery flesh had been eaten away. The skeleton wore a jacket, discolored with gore, which sat oddly over the ragged bones.

"What is it?" Eliza asked.

"A, uh, err…" The great Gator Malloy stammered as he looked at the heat-mummified corpse.

Something glinted from the jacket pocket. The chain of a gold pocket watch. The sun caught the metal and it glinted like a beacon.

Eliza sidled up next to Calvin and pulled the canvas away. She made a disgusted sound but didn't turn away.

"There might be something we could use," Calvin said. He knew exactly what they could use. That pocket watch could buy them enough supplies to make it all the way to San Francisco.

She gave him a look that could tan leather. "We are not desecrating that poor man's wagon. Besides, something's been eating him." She pointed to the large number of scalloped divots in the man's flesh. Each one marked where a chunk of flesh had been scooped away. The pieces were almost surgically precise. Something with very sharp teeth must have been at him. "We're leaving before something decides we look tasty, too."

"Alright, just give me a minute." Calvin took a tentative step up onto the wagon's side rail, getting ready to hoist himself in with the corpse.

"What on earth are you doing?" Eliza asked, her voice cold enough to cut through the heat.

"I'll cover him up," Calvin said. He grabbed a rolled blanket from near the front of the wagon and unfurled it. Then, he crouched by the dead man, doing his best not to look too closely. With one swift movement, he laid the blanket over the body with one hand and snatched the watch free with the other. "Sorry, buddy," he whispered.

The gold watch was a magnificent specimen. It hung from a long chain, and it sparkled in the light. The clock face appeared to be made from mother of pearl, and the numbers stood like vigilant sentries in a tight circle.

It was a twenty-four hour watch, rather than the standard twelve-hour face. Most of the numbers were black, but a few were red. Blood red. After looking at the watch for a second, Calvin realized that the daylight hours were black, and the nighttime hours were red.

Something bothered Calvin as he hastily tucked the watch away. The watch was ticking. He didn't see a mechanism to wind it. By all rights, the watch should have died shortly after its owner if nobody was around to wind it.

He felt like a monster, stealing from a dead man. Gator Malloy wouldn't take a bauble from a dead man's pocket. But Gator Malloy wasn't real. He didn't need to eat. Calvin had to keep himself and Eliza alive through the mountains and beyond, and the pocket watch would help when he bartered it for extra supplies.

He knew Eliza didn't want her freedom from her father bought through grave robbery. It was his gift to her that she would never know his secret guilt.

~*~

"You did *what?*" Eliza hissed.

"It was the only way we could pay for enough supplies to keep going past the next waystation," Calvin said.

The ticking had given him away. He'd tried everything in his power to silence the watch. It should have died after he didn't wind it. Instead, it just kept ticking and ticking. He'd tried to cover the sound up, swathing the watch in thick cloth and bundling it deep in his pocket. He'd tried singing, which was not one of his strong suits, to cover the noise. Eliza was ready to push him out of the wagon by the time he hit a second round of *Camptown Races*.

But the next morning, as they drew closer to the foothills of the Sierra Nevada range, Eliza had woken up before Calvin, and she'd heard the ticking. It didn't take her long to find the pocket watch among his meager collection of belongings. And from there, she'd shaken him awake and given him six flavors of hell.

Calvin sat on the floor of the wagon. Eliza still wore her nightgown, and she was seething mad. And he didn't blame her. He felt lower than a snake in a wagon rut about taking the watch, but he felt worse that she knew about it.

"I thought maybe, just maybe, the watch belonged to you. But then I saw the crusted blood on it," she said.

Calvin blinked. "The…blood?"

He tried to remember seeing any blood on the watch. In his memory, it was spotless. She held up the watch by the chain, dangling it so he could see the evidence of his guilt. The gold watch was caked with red.

"That wasn't there before," Calvin said.

"The watch just appeared with your stuff? Calvin…" She looked at him with disappointment, thinking she'd caught him in a lie. That look stung Calvin's soul.

"No, the blood. The watch was clean when I took it." He stumbled up, the wagon creaking as he did so. He pulled the canvas aside, revealing the early glow of a new morning. He needed to see the watch in the light.

The oxen were dead.

Calvin stared, aghast. The animals lay where they had fallen, puddles of dark blood around their torn throats. The wounds were like perfect, semi-circular bites out of a sandwich. They weren't the ragged tears left behind by wolves or mountain lions. Calvin remembered the dead man's wounds. Exactly the same.

Calvin looked at the bloodied pocket watch again. The watch's shiny gold lid hung open like a crocodile jaw. It was almost the perfect size to…

"Well, well, well. What do we have here?" A voice Calvin didn't recognize spoke from somewhere nearby. He startled, nearly falling out of the wagon.

A man in a duster coat stepped around the side of the wagon. He pulled out a bag of tobacco and rolled a cigarette, but his eyes never left Calvin as his fingers worked. Calvin couldn't help but notice the large revolver tucked into the man's holster.

"Looks like you folks have gotten yourselves into a spot of trouble," the stranger continued.

Calvin had been so preoccupied thinking about how deep he was in with Eliza that he hadn't fully considered the implications of the dead oxen yet. If the oxen were dead, there was no way to move the wagon. And without the wagon, they had no way to haul their supplies. The two of them would be lucky to make it to the edge of the mountains on foot before heat and thirst took them.

Calvin studied the stranger, and a flash of recognition went off. A knife of cold panic stabbed toward his heart.

"Randall Overhauser is the name," the man said.

Calvin definitely knew him. He used to work for Eliza's father. He did the dirty work for the estate. When Eliza's mother died, Overhauser was the one who dug the grave and laid her in it before anyone could see for themselves how she died. Overhauser was the one who slipped a wad of money to the coroner to sign off and say it had been a natural death.

"They call me Gator Malloy. My lady and I are coming out from Louisiana." Calvin urged himself to shut up, but he kept talking. "Yup, packed up and decided to make a new life for ourselves. Having some difficulties, as you can see."

"Uh-huh." Overhauser struck a match and lit his cigarette. "You and the missus pass through a town called Lovelace on your way?"

That was where Eliza's sprawling farm estate was located and where Overhauser would no doubt have been dispatched from.

"Never heard of it. It's pretty far from the route we took. Well, I imagine it must be, since I'm not familiar with it. And I've been all over." Calvin chuckled nervously.

Overhauser gave a smile that showed too many teeth. "Well, I'd be happy to give you folks a ride to my camp. Me and some boys are set up not far from here. We could even drop you off at the next waystation, once we've completed our business."

"Oh, I couldn't possibly lean on your kindness like that." Calvin tried to wave Overhauser off. He and Eliza needed a ride out of this desert. They needed it as badly as anything, but he wasn't about to walk into that lions' den.

"Nonsense. I just have a few questions before we get going. You see, my friends and I are looking for someone. A young couple, as a matter of fact. Probably travelling alone. Their names are Calvin and Eliza, but I imagine they're using fake names. This Calvin killed a man back in Lovelace. Shot an important landowner dead and ran away with the man's daughter. And there's a reward for bringing this fugitive and his captive back home. You met anybody like that, friend?"

Overhauser took a step forward and unholstered his revolver as casually as a cook might lift a knife.

"I, uh..." Calvin swallowed hard. "Can't say I've met anyone by that description. Oh, wait. No. There was a fellah named Calvin. Met him back in Redgrave. Squirrely looking guy. He said he was going north. To Canada, I think. He had a woman with him, too. Yeah, to Canada."

Overhauser ignored Calvin. "You can come out of the wagon now, Ms. Eliza," he called.

"Eliza, run," Calvin shouted. The jig was up. He threw himself at Overhauser. In that moment, he didn't care what happened to him. He just wanted Eliza to escape.

Two fingers exploded off Calvin's hand. His brain didn't even register the sound of the gunshot right away. There was no pain, not at first. Just an odd, tingling sting, like when he clapped his hands too hard. Calvin marveled at the spot where his fingers used to be for a second, and then Overhauser punched him square in the jaw.

Calvin suddenly found himself flat on the ground. *Well that's odd*, his brain thought, still running a few seconds behind reality. He almost dipped into unconsciousness, but Overhauser none-too-gently planted a boot on Calvin's chest and pointed the revolver at his chin.

"Ms. Eliza, I'm going to give you to the count of three to get your pert self out here, or I'm going to blow Gator's jaw off. One! Two!" Overhauser said 'Gator' with the tone of voice one would use to talk about something that had come out of a sick farm animal.

Eliza hopped out of the wagon, still in her nightgown. She had the pocket watch in her hand. She dropped down next to Calvin, and the watch fell in a patch of fresh blood. The gold cover snapped shut with a surprisingly powerful *click*.

From his position on the ground, Calvin could see two more riders on the horizon, moving hard toward Overhauser. They must have followed the sound of the gunshot. Calvin's hand was starting to hurt now. He could feel blood thundering out of his fingers. The throbbing, pulsing pain grew and grew.

"Calvin, are you okay?" Eliza was on her knees above him.

"He'll be fine," Overhauser said. "The folks back home want him alive. Archibald Cotts intends to make an example of him for stealing his woman."

She lunged at him then, and he clubbed her aside with the butt of the revolver. She sprawled next to Calvin in a puff of dust.

"Don't do that again," Overhauser growled. The cigarette had never left the corner of Overhauser's mouth. He gave it a contemplative puff as his two men rode up.

"These them?" the first man asked.

"No, Pete. These are just some folks I invited over for tea. Course it's them."

"Lookee here," the second man said, pointing to the bloodied pocket watch. He had a waxed mustache. "Looks like we might get a bonus on top of the reward." He picked the watch up and stuffed it in the pocket of his dirty shirt.

Overhauser took a final look down at Calvin and smiled. Then, he pulled his boot up and smashed it down on Calvin's face. Everything went black.

~*~

Calvin awoke to the smell of campfire smoke. The sun was low on the horizon. For a second, he thought he was back at the wagon, that morning had dawned, and he'd dreamed the dead oxen and Overhauser.

Then he half-choked on the clotted blood clogging up his nostrils. He groaned and looked at his hand. It was crudely bandaged with a wadded shirt where his fingers had been. He nearly passed out again, but he heard Eliza's voice. That jolted him awake.

"Don't you touch him," she snarled.

"Easy there, spitfire. I'm just checking on him." A figure swam into Calvin's vision and resolved itself into Overhauser. "Howdy, Gator."

Overhauser wore a toothy grin. Another cigarette was clutched in his fingers. He scratched at the stubble on his cheek, and it made a raspy sound, like two snakes sharing a burrow.

"You…you've got the wrong guy," Calvin managed. The effort of speaking made him want to throw up. He'd never been knocked out before, and his senses were trying to figure out how to squirm back into his skull like drunks locked out of a house.

Overhauser laughed. "Is that so? You mind telling me how you found yourself travelling with Ms. Eliza?"

"Her name is Melody," Calvin said, managing not to vomit on himself. He took a deep breath, and the world came into sharper focus.

"I know the boss's daughter," Overhauser said, his face turning grim. "I'm no fool, boy."

Calvin looked up and saw Pete and Mustache sitting by the fire. He could see that familiar glint of gold from Mustache's shirt pocket.

He'd been close. Calvin was sure that they could have escaped their past in California, in the bustle of the gold mining districts. He'd be happy living in a little cabin with a plot of land, Eliza by his side. Seeing the watch with Overhauser's man was only a reminder of just how close they'd come.

The last rays of sunset sank below the hills, and dusk settled over the desert. The temperature was already dropping, and Calvin could feel the impending chill in his injured hand, as if someone had grafted his grave-cold fingers back on. The campfire provided a dancing circle of light, but the world beyond was bathed in shadows. Somewhere in the distance, a coyote cackled and was met with an answering chorus of yelps.

"Let me lay out the ground rules for you, Gator," Overhauser said. There was mockery in his voice as he used Calvin's alias. Gator Malloy would not end up captured. Gator Malloy would not get his fingers shot off. Gator Malloy would not get his face stomped in. Gator Malloy was a fiction, a ghost of the man Calvin secretly wanted to be on the frontier.

"Rule number one. You cause me any problem, any problem at all, I'll shoot you dead. Got it? The bounty is a lot bigger if I bring you back alive, but I'll be doing just fine if I only collect on the finder's fee for getting Ms. Eliza home. You're nothing more to me than a tick on Pete's backside, and I'll leave you for the vultures if you try anything clever. There is no rule number two. Do we understand each other?"

Calvin nodded. He knew Overhauser wasn't kidding. Eliza's father wouldn't do business with a man who was all talk, especially when it came to violence. Calvin was beaten. He'd lost everything. The watch. Eliza. His life. It was all forfeit once they got back to Lovelace.

"Good," Overhauser said. His breath smelled like cigarettes and jerked meat.

Calvin realized that the coyotes had fallen silent. The fire popped, and the sound echoed across the desert. Even the crickets had gone quiet.

The only sound Calvin could hear was the noise of the pocket watch ticking, surprisingly loud and steady. It had a peculiar rhythm to it. Almost like a heartbeat.

As if on cue, Mustache stood up from the fire and walked over to Calvin. He pulled the watch out, holding it by the thin chain.

"Meant to ask you, but you were taking a nap. How do you wind this thing? I don't see any way to keep it running."

The watch reared back and bit Mustache on the back of the hand, hinged cover snapping shut like a jaw. Mustache screamed as a length of skin and sinew peeled away in the thing's 'mouth.' The injury had a perfect, scalloped shape, like a bite mark.

The pocket watch opened its clasp wide, and Calvin could see that the clock hands had reached the red numbers on its face. Mustache tried to hurl the watch away, but the chain had wrapped around his arm. The watch hissed.

Calvin suddenly knew, even though it was insane, why there was no mechanism to wind the watch. The watch would keep going so long as it was fed. That was what happened to the poor, sun-dried corpse he first found the watch on. That was what happened to Calvin's oxen. And it was what was currently happening to Overhauser's man.

The watch struck out like a viper, clamping onto Mustache's throat and wrenching back with a bloody gobbet of flesh. The man gasped and thrashed, and the watch dropped to the ground, slithering into the darkness.

Overhauser sent two bullets whizzing into the night after it. Then he crouched next to Mustache, who gurgled and went still. "Burt? Burt, talk to me. Dammit!"

Turning to Calvin, Overhauser leveled his revolver. "What the hell was that? How did you do that? Answer me, or so help me God…"

"I don't know what that is," Calvin said, speaking in a frightened staccato that he hated to hear coming from his lips. "The watch, we found it on a dead man. I think it killed him, too. I think it killed our oxen. I'm not controlling it. I think it's alive."

"Talk some sense, damn you. It's a damn pocket watch. It's not alive."

Pete, the other member of Overhauser's posse, shouted. He flailed by the fire. The watch had its chain wrapped around his neck so tight that it dug into the skin, drawing blood. Snapping and hissing, the watch dug a crimson gouge out of Pete's face.

Overhauser yelled and swiveled his revolver toward the other man, then back to Calvin. His thumb found the hammer. Overhauser clearly thought it was some kind of trick, that Calvin was using the watch as a weapon. So, he was going to shoot him.

That's when Eliza crashed into him from behind. Overhauser went sprawling, his gun skidding under some brush. Pete screamed. Overhauser grunted. Calvin heaved himself to his feet. The tiny circle of firelight convulsed with chaotic, violent movement.

Calvin knew what he had to do. He ran past Pete's heaving body and grabbed the reins of the nearest horse. His hand exploded in pain as he tried to hold the reins with fingers that weren't there. He'd grab Eliza, throw her on the horse, and ride off as fast as they could.

"Hold it right there, lover boy," Overhauser's voice called.

Calvin turned and saw Overhauser, his arm tight around Eliza's throat, his revolver back in his hand and pointed at Eliza's head.

"Whatever damn trick you're using to puppet that watch around, you stop it right now. Stop it, or I'll plant a bullet in both your brains."

"I'm not doing it," Calvin tried to explain. "It's alive. Or cursed. I don't know."

"Have it your way," Overhauser said. He pulled the gun away from Eliza's temple and pointed it directly at Calvin. Calvin had just enough time to notice that Overhauser's other man, Pete, had gone still and silent.

Just then, the pocket watch whipped up Eliza's body, moving with furious, demonic speed, and clamped its gilded jaw onto her shoulder. She howled in pain, and the chain came up around her neck.

"No," Calvin and Overhauser shouted at the same time. Eliza was Calvin's love. He'd loved her since he was a boy in her father's fields, surreptitiously watching the young lady of the house. But she was also Overhauser's meal ticket. He needed her alive. They lunged for Eliza at the same time.

They both tried to claw the golden chain away from her neck, but they couldn't work their fingers under the metal. The watch's jaws snapped at them.

A bullet blasted past Calvin's nose, and the gunshot deafened him. Overhauser tried to shoot the watch again, but its disembodied mouth wriggled and twisted, an impossible target even from a foot away. Calvin shoved Overhauser's arm away before he could accidentally hit Eliza, and the gun went off again.

Overhauser punched Calvin in the face, and Calvin's nose exploded in a fresh gout of blood. But Calvin managed to keep his feet under him and grabbed for the watch.

The watch hissed at Calvin and snapped its jaws shut on his hand. It unwrapped its chain from Eliza's neck, apparently sensing that Calvin was the greater danger. Pain coursed up Calvin's arm, but it was manageable. The creature's bite was much less painful than he expected, actually.

Then, he saw that the watch had clamped down on the shirt covering his missing fingers. He wasn't feeling its bite sink into his flesh. The fabric of the shirt was just brushing his finger stumps as the watch tried to find his hand under the makeshift bandage.

Calvin stripped the shirt free from his hand. The watch came with it, a mouthful of fabric still in its maw.

Overhauser leveled his revolver again. Whether he was aiming for the watch or Calvin was impossible to tell. Either. Both. Calvin threw the bunched shirt in Overhauser's face. The man tried to swat the shirt out of the way. The gun went off, the bullet shooting off into the night.

Then, Overhauser screamed. And screamed. And screamed. The watch was on him, going after his eyes. Calvin didn't stop to see what happened next, though he heard the wet sound of ripping flesh.

He turned to grab Eliza, but she was already on a horse of her own. Calvin pulled himself up onto another horse and urged the animal forward. It took off with a burst of speed, leaving the campfire, the dead men, and the screaming Overhauser behind.

They rode until dawn. And when they stopped for water, they found a small supply of cash in one of the saddlebags, likely Overhauser's down payment to track them down. But it would be enough to get them to California. Enough to start a new life together.

"Cal—Err, Gator? What was that thing?"

"I don't know," he said truthfully. "But I don't think anyone else will find it. Not for a long time, anyway. Overhauser's camp was off the main path."

Despite the pain in his face and hand, he smiled. "And I don't think you need to call me Gator anymore."

Gator Malloy had been his safety blanket, a persona he put on keep his fears at bay. But now, Calvin had his own taste of untamed frontier. He'd told himself a dozen stories about Gator Malloy. But now he had a story all his own.

Trail of the Black Coach
Tim Hanlon

He dreams.

He sees the black stagecoach as it thunders through the mountain pass. Black coach, black beasts, shadowy outriders surrounding the dark vehicle, hats low and faces obscured. Ghastly hands with weapons always close. The light recedes as the coach pounds the bleak roads, drawing misery in its wake.

He sees the young woman as she stands at the train siding, alone and forsaken. She clutches a worn carpet bag to her chest but it offers scant protection. She missed the regular coach that day and it is the last mistake the woman will make.

He sees the black stagecoach shudder to a violent stop.

He hears the screams.

And wakes.

~*~

James Harden watched the bridge across the river as the sun rose and the shadows shortened. It was only a short span that the solid wooden structure traversed, but the plunge below was deep and the rocks of the dry river bed were numerous and large. A killer drop.

Harden tugged on the misshapen brim of his hat to shade his eyes. They watched the bridge unflinchingly, like two pebbles pushed into the sandy earth. There was no give in those eyes nor the worn face that carried them. No give either in the lean body that crouched above the river crossing, bent forward in anticipation.

His horse nickered behind, and Harden turned and rose from his perch. The gelding lifted its head and seemed to point at the figure hunkered down on the other side of the flat hilltop. The man, small and round and dressed like a banker, was resting on his knees, his face turned towards where Harden stood.

Harden crossed to the small man and pushed him into the dirt with his boot. The man's bound hands could not break his fall and his face smacked the earth with a thud.

"I done told you to sit tight," said Harden.

The well-dressed man squirmed so he was sitting on his rump and looked up at Harden. "You are a most disagreeable fellow," said William 'Cannibal Bill' Quincey.

"That coming from the man who eats people," Harden said. "You open that mud hole of a mouth again and I'll be putting my boot into it."

"My alleged crimes are grossly exaggerated," said Cannibal Bill. "Why, if you had not stolen me away from my jail cell, I am certain that I would have been found innocent of—"

He did not finish as Harden stepped forward. The small man's hat had been lost somewhere on the journey and his bald pate was bright and hot with sunburn. He flinched his red ball of a head away from Harden's boot.

Harden went to his horse and withdrew the blasting machine from his saddlebags. On the ground, he found the wires he had hauled up the steep incline of the hill and began to screw them into the terminals. His 1873 Springfield rifle was cradled in his left arm as he worked.

"You are like a butterfly struggling against a tornado," said Cannibal Bill, irrepressible.

Harden did not turn. "So says the fool trussed like a chicken."

"I admit that my situation is not ideal at the present moment," said Bill. "But I, at least, am on the correct side of destiny."

The lean man turned his boilerplate face to the other. "Your destiny won't be worth a runny shit in your britches when I am finished," Harden said.

Cannibal Bill swallowed but he continued. "The Vizier can trace his line back to the time of the pyramids. Can you conceive of that duration?"

Harden finished securing the second wire. "I surely can," he said. "I done seen pictures of the pyramids in a book out east. Mighty impressive structures. They will not aid you here, mister."

"The Servants of the Flame Undying will bring on the ascendancy of Kathigu-Ra. The Vizier has possession of *De Vermis Mysteriis* and now the ending will begin," Bill said. "You think you can change this but you are a foolish child."

"Well, this here child is goin' to blow that bridge and send that black coach to the rocks below. And finish any that ain't dead with a .45 to the head. Oh, and burn that damn book, too. How does that grab you as foolish?"

Cannibal Bill flashed his big white teeth in a grin, and Harden had to stop himself from kicking the man again. It had been said that when Bill was found he had been carrying a portmanteau packed with containers of human teeth and hair. Bursting-at-the-seams packed.

"And," said James Harden, "be aware that the only reason you are here is that, if'n that coach does not appear at the appointed time, we will be havin' another long chat."

"It will. I was to meet them at that bridge at this time," said Bill. "And then you will end my detention?"

Harden rose and stretched. He took his hat off and used it to block the sun and then withdrew a tarnished watch from his vest. "I'll have no use for you if'n that coach appears."

The well-dressed captive looked at him, and there was something now that could be seen behind the large smile on the round face. Harden's hand slid to the grip of the Springfield and his finger rested on the trigger guard.

"And my belongings?"

"I won't put a bullet in you," said Harden. "That's the extent of the transaction."

"Very gentlemanly of you," said Cannibal Bill. His eyes dropped to stare at the ground, but the look was still perched on his face.

The sun began to fall, and Harden examined his pocket watch again. He crossed to the lip of the hill and watched the beaten earth roadway. He watched and waited. He waited, and the sweat ran down his brow and along his spine but he did not move. He waited, and his jaw cramped from the tension. He stretched his mouth wide and, as his jaw cracked, it appeared in the distance. Dust.

The cloud grew, and now the noise ran ahead of the swirl of dust. Hooves drummed the baked earth of the roadway, and Harden heard the distinctive jangle and groan of a fast-driven stage. The stagecoach rose into view like a corpse rising from the grave. Pulled by six huge beasts as fierce as horses of war, the dark coach hurtled along the track without a care for anything in its path. Indeed, it gave the impression that all aboard would relish the opportunity to crush a living being under hoof and wheel.

The driver perched on top was hunched forward with the momentum. Monitoring the black coach were six outriders, faces hidden by hat and scarf. They ranged in front, behind, and on both sides; their mounts were mean of spirit to match the riders.

Harden took a spyglass from his saddle-bags and snapped it open. The careening stage jumped into view, and he tracked it, from the foaming mouths of the wild-eyed horses and along the paired haunches straining in their traces. He scanned the dark paneling of the coach, glossy and black like oil, his gaze lingering at the curtained windows.

He could not penetrate the heavy material, but as he watched a gloved hand appeared and drew one side back. For the first time an expression came to his face. Shock.

"Not that simple is it, my dear man," said Cannibal Bill.

"Who is she?"

"Who is she," mimicked the dapper man. "She is no one. A pawn. A tool for the Vizier's will. Someone's daughter, too. Perhaps someone's wife. Will you take her life to satisfy your petty revenge? An innocent?"

Harden lifted the glass again and saw the woman's face disappear as the curtain closed. Even distorted by the lenses, her wide eyes could be seen, her mouth drawn back in a smile that had nothing to do with joy.

"Release me now," said William Quincey, "and this may not go any further."

Harden replaced the spyglass and took the blaster in hand. He watched the black coach thunder to the bridge and heard the chuckle of the well-dressed cannibal behind him. The coach rumbled as it rolled onto the crossing as if dozens of otherworldly drums were being played.

Harden had not killed since the war between the North and South but, even though he had tried to forget, recent events had shown that he had lost nothing of that hard-won skill. Emily had calmed his spirit, and those below would regret that they had taken her from him. He turned to the smaller man but said nothing.

"No!"

Cannibal Bill came to his feet when the plunger descended. The bridge erupted as the earth threw the wooden beams into the air like an angry child. The noise rolled up the hill with the blast, flattening the grass as it went. Bill ran at Harden with a yell of sheer rage. The lean man stepped to the side and clubbed the screaming cannibal to the ground with the butt of his Springfield rifle. Blood ran from Bill's sunburnt scalp, eagerly swallowed by the dry earth.

Harden had timed the explosion perfectly. The rear two outriders were obliterated in the blast but the coach untouched. He did not have it in him to kill the innocent woman, no matter what the cost. Harden dropped to one knee and raised the Springfield to his shoulder. He settled himself and fired and saw the driver fall from the seat of the coach. The massive black vehicle began to slow but one of the outriders, in spectacular fashion, leapt from his galloping horse and onto the driver's seat. The stagecoach gained speed and rumbled onwards.

He watched the same hand emerge again from the window and point in his direction, and the three remaining outriders turned their demon mounts to the hill. Two came on, straight up the incline, and the other one disappeared from sight around the base of the knoll.

Harden ran the rifle's action and raised it to his shoulder. He fired at the first rider and saw the figure snap back under the shock of the bullet. It didn't fall. Harden opened the trapdoor in the Springfield's breech and the casing sprang out eagerly. He inserted a new round with sure hands.

He fired. The same rider whipped backwards again and the lean man saw bone and matter jump into the air, but the rider continued up the slope. Harden reloaded. The horses took the slope with vigor, and in their eyes seemed a passion for flesh that was not equine.

The second rider drew a pistol and fired at Harden. The Civil War veteran could see that it was an old Colt Walker revolver, the black powder leaving a pall of gray smoke as the huge pistol discharged. The .44 ball whipped close by but he did not flinch from his third shot.

Harden lined the first rider in his sights again, the rider close enough for the lean man to see the thing clearly. Although human in form, the rider was far from it. Harden could see the drawn skin of the thing's face, gray like putrefying flesh. The eyes above were red to match the open wounds gouged by Harden's preceding rounds. The creature, a demon on horseback, had bullet holes in its body that the sun shone through, but it was undeterred.

A ball snicked past as Harden pulled the trigger. His third bullet caught the demon on the up and punched it fully in the face. Its head exploded from the projectile's pressure and the desiccated body toppled backwards from its evil mount. The wild horse kept straining up the hill, its jaws wide and hungry.

Harden switched aim to the second rider as he reloaded. He fired directly into the charging beast, no qualms now that the demonic nature of horse and rider had been revealed. The big black horse stumbled on the slope but regained its footing. The rider shot and missed and, as the beast gained the summit, Harden slipped to the off side and fired point blank into the mount's ribs. The black monster pitched over and its demon rider was trapped underneath.

Harden moved quickly as the dark-clad thing tried to raise its big pistol, and he stamped on the demon's arm, pinning it to the ground. The demon outrider shrieked with its fetid maw as the muzzle of the Springfield touched its face and Harden pulled the trigger. The demon's head left dark, oily globs as it splattered the earth.

The first now riderless beast came at Harden from the side and the lean man tumbled backwards over the fallen mount to escape its snapping teeth. Its eyes were wide, its neck arched and taut. Harden let the rifle go as the beast danced towards him. He drew one of his Smith and Wesson Schofields and snapped a .45 off in desperation. The heavy bullet smashed the demon mount's left forelock and it crashed to the ground. Harden scrambled over the first carcass again and away from the fallen brute's snapping jaws and flailing hooves.

It was all noise and chaos and the sting of gunpowder on the hilltop. Harden's horse pulled at its tether and cried with fear, and the fallen demon mount shrieked like a totally different beast. Harden rose into a crouch as the remaining rider jumped on to the hilltop. The demon's red eyes searched and found him and it raised its hefty revolver.

Harden went low as the outrider fired. He rolled against the corpse of the first fallen horse and felt the whack of two lead balls slapping into the solid flesh of the dead beast. Harden held himself against the hard mass of the demon mount as the lead continued to smack into his barricade of flesh. He crawled forward a pace and cracked a round over the carcass, not really aiming. The stamp of the horse's hooves drummed his side through the packed earth.

The firing ceased suddenly and Harden knew it was his chance. He rose from the ground with his left hand balanced on the carcass. The outrider dropped its weapon and was reaching for another as Harden sighted down the Schofield's barrel. He had a clear shot at the demon rider.

The crippled horse drove its head over the fallen body and latched onto Harden's left hand. Its oversized teeth clamped his last two fingers and hacked them roughly from the rest of the limb. Harden yelled with pain and jerked away as his torn fingers went down the beast's gullet. He swung the Schofield and fired at the side of the mount's head. Brain and bone exploded from the other side and the equine devil fell, two human fingers heavier but considerably lighter in brain matter.

It had chewed up precious time also, the now-dead beast, and the last outrider had cleared its second revolver from its holster. Harden saw the barrel swinging towards him, and he snaked under the outrider's horse. The beast snapped at him but he was clear. Harden sent a bullet into the mount's chest as he went past and the demon horse raised its head with the shock, fouling the outrider's arm as it attempted to change aim. Harden stood firm and the Schofield thundered, and the outrider was knocked from the saddle and to the hard ground.

The lean man stepped away as the horse slumped to the earth. It lunged weakly at him but it was an evil reflex only. Harden drew his second pistol from the sash around his body and waited for the beast to be still. He circled the mound of demon horseflesh and sighted at the outrider. The fiendish stagecoach guard was dead, Harden's final .45 bullet sending the vault of its skull to who knew where.

Harden stared at the thing at his feet while blood dripped from his damaged hand. He continued to examine the demon as he returned the Schofield to his waist-sash and fished a red kerchief from a pocket. He wrapped the cloth around the stumps of his missing fingers and cinched it tight with his teeth. Harden raised his left hand and looked at the result. With a shrug he turned away.

William 'Cannibal Bill' Quincey was staring at him. Half the killer's face was painted in dark red blood, the other the shine of sunburn. Cannibal Bill shook his head. "How?" he asked. "They are not of this world."

Harden broke open his empty Smith and Wesson and began to reload. The veteran tossed a cartridge at the smaller man. Bill tried to catch it with his tied hands but missed and it bounced off his chest. He bent and retrieved the deadly combination of lead and brass from the earth. Bill looked at the bullet, and he could see the cross etched into the face of the .45.

"You think you are the only one with friends in high places?" asked Harden. "Or low places, in your case. These here bullets are blessed by the father in Rome, I'm told. Either way, they appear to be mighty effective."

Cannibal Bill tossed the round to the ground. "The Flame Eternal laughs at your god," he said.

The lean man crossed to retrieve his long gun but the solid bulk of the dead outrider's horse lay squarely on top of the rifle. Harden could not even see any part of the weapon to grab and moving the big beast was impossible. The Springfield was lost to him.

"Your everlasting fire can laugh all it wants," Harden said. "Makes no difference to me. I've still a mind for killing all its followers."

"Except for me, of course. As per our agreement," said Bill, raising his bound hands. They were a hue of red now different from the colors on his head.

The gelding tossed its head when Harden untied it, eager to be gone. He mounted and settled the horse with a calm hand on its shoulder. "I don't hold much stock in keepin' my word to a man like you," Harden said. "But I won't shoot you. Like I said. But I'll be damn'd if I'm making it easy for you. Enjoy the walk, Cannibal Bill. It's a long one."

"You will regret this," said William Quincey as Harden turned his horse to the slope. "Kathigu-Ra will see the ending of this world and I will be on his right hand! And you will be at my feet, James Harden. A dog at my feet. A slave to my…"

The lean man sent his eager horse down the hill and the shrill voice of the Servant of the Flame was lost in the stamp of solid hooves. James Harden thought no more of the dapper killer for he had a black coach to catch.

~*~

The gelding was game and pleased to be gone from the turmoil of the hillside. It lengthened its stride gloriously as they gained the level roadway and its hooves rang a martial beat. It had seemed an age but Harden knew from experience that the entire action had been over in minutes at most. The dark stagecoach of death would not be far ahead.

After Emily had disappeared and he'd started searching, a man had come to him one night in the saloon of a no-name shanty town. The fellow was well-dressed and pleasant but Harden could recognize a man weathered by experience. In the dim bar, the fellow's dog-collar peeked white beneath his coat when he leant beside Harden.

"I think," said the priest without preamble, "that we are after the same people."

"Is that so?" asked Harden. "And who might that be?"

The priest downed a shot of whiskey and held the empty glass up to the smoky lamp. "That's terrible," he said. "But there's no might be about it. It's evil and it travels in a black coach."

Harden nodded his head. "I know it."

"They search for a book that can summon the old gods. For them it is Cthugha, also known as Kathigu-Ra. A particularly evil master to be sure."

That night Harden joined an organization that had no name but a long history. It had equipped him with the information and weapons to fight a war, and he had engaged in the battle with vigor.

"I don't believe in your god no more." Harden thought he should make it clear to the priest.

The man raised his hand for another shot of liquor. "He believes in you, though," the priest said. "And he needs you to kill evil."

That Harden had done with a singular purpose.

The stage road wound higher as the sun lowered. The land seemed still, poised to run from what lay ahead. On the air, the sound of crows arguing could be heard. Unpleasant neighbors bellowing at each other over who-knew-what slights. Even from a distance and with the strike of the gelding's hooves it was a nail across the eardrums. Harden rounded a bend in the track and a town was revealed.

The settlement huddled at the base of a large hill. Or small mountain. The buildings flanked the main road and they were closed and still to match the land. The crows whirled overhead, never happy. Harden read the faded sign as he slowed the gelding. 'Brilliant Deep Mine – 3000 Souls.' Harden looked at the township and thought only one of those descriptors accurate. The buildings were run down husks displaying no luster and the population estimate grossly erroneous. It stood at three souls now, Harden estimated, and if the hunter had his way, soon to be one less than that figure.

Harden saw the black stagecoach at the far end of the street. The dark demon mounts stamped and snorted still in the traces but there was no sign of any of the passengers. The gelding jerked its head at the smell of the coach team, so the lean man turned his mount to the left and dismounted outside an abandoned barber and bone-setter. The door to the shop was open but no one lingered inside.

He hitched the horse loosely and walked along the raised walkway. His foot cracked a rotted board and then another and the veteran abandoned the shopfronts and took to the street. A crow flew down and rested on a hitching post beside him. Its feathers puffed and it dropped some shit, and Harden thought that summed up the town perfectly.

Without preamble the outrider stepped through the bat-wing doors of the one saloon down and opposite Harden's position. Harden heard the grind of the dry hinges from where he stood, and when the door swung back the left panel fell off and clattered to the floor. Harden watched the revenant stride to the center of the street. The outrider stopped in the middle and it drew its dark duster away from the Colt Walker on its right hip.

Harden walked towards the demon rider as it stood in the middle of the street. Perhaps some vestige of the life it led before its tormented soul was shackled to the Vizier's bidding remained. A long-dead shootist craving its final duel.

The sun was low and to his right, and Harden removed his hat and ran his right hand across his sweaty scalp. He held the hat at his waist with his damaged hand, and his blood stained its crown. Harden rolled his head to loosen his neck, his bones grinding like the saloon doors. He watched the outrider standing with its gaze fixed on his approach, red-coal eyes burning in its expressionless face. A fire in a desert landscape. Its hand hovered above the holstered Walker.

Harden walked still. The gap closed pace by pace. The crows flew overhead, constantly in disagreement, and the demon horses grunted and stomped the earth. His hat remained in front of his belt like a flimsy shield.

The demon went for its gun.

Harden shot through the hat and the bullet smote the revenant to the ground. He had held the drawn Schofield behind the cover of the hat, waiting to close the distance. He was not a quick-draw artist, Harden, but simply a killer.

The outrider rose to sitting like a mechanical toy, a fist-sized hole where its breast-bone had been. Bone shards tumbled loose and fell into its lap, followed by a lump of something that could have been lung. Its hand reached for its holstered gun.

Harden extended his arm and sighted down the Schofield's barrel, and this time his round shattered the outrider's head. Blood and bone and matter sprayed out like a rock had been dropped in still water and the demon fell back like a trapdoor. It did not move again.

He reloaded the Schofield as he examined the fallen outrider. A pocket watch had dislodged with the bullet's impact and lay in the thing's lap. He snapped it open, and on the inside face sat a photograph of a young woman with a child on her lap. She looked happy. Harden closed the watch and tucked it into the fob pocket of the outrider's ruined waistcoat.

"We both work for unforgivin' bosses," said Harden.

Lacking an intact skull the revenant did not reply, but a crow landed beside the dead thing and stared at Harden instead. It waddled to the outrider's head with a wary eye and took a tentative piece of the demon's face in its wicked beak. It swallowed but then jerked and spat the flesh away. Harden shook his head and holstered his pistol.

He slipped the outrider's Colt Walker from its holster. It was indeed an old model, loaded individually with powder and ball. Harden felt a momentary pang for the ruined thing before him. The veteran himself had carried one in the war and, with less luck, that could have been Harden prostrate and headless on the ground. He straightened his torn hat and adjusted his coat, and his eyes were hard as marble when he scanned the ghost town.

One to go.

Harden heard a cry and he followed the sound to a light at the base of the mountain. The road continued through the town and upwards to that point; the Brilliant Deep Mine head. The hunter returned to the gelding and pointed it along the beaten track. The horse was scared but had a big heart, and it did not shy too much when the coach beasts lunged in their traces. The crows knew better and did not follow.

The entrance to the mine glowed red. Harden saw two figures cast in the furnace light as he entered, surrounded by rock of a molten hue. They stood on the platform of the broken mine elevator, now only a rusted metal gate with the cage long since fallen to the depths. The Vizier held the young woman at his feet. Her hands were bound and his left twisted her hair in a vicious lock. In his right hand he bore a book and, in the light, the ancient tanned binding was warm like copper. His voice was loud as he read from the pages, the language foreign to Harden's ears.

The Vizier was well-dressed and handsome like the mayor of a big city. His suit was impeccably cut and of the finest cloth. His face had a strong jaw and cheek bones. And eyes that spoke of evil. When he saw Harden enter he quickly thrust the volume into an inside pocket and withdrew a knife with a curved blade.

"That is far enough, my good man," said the Vizier.

Harden paused. The mine was a giant fire pit now, the light hard red and the heat like a punch in the face. There was a noise too, rolling up from the depths, but not the crack and spark of flame. It was like the hum of a wire under tension, barely perceptible but piercing in the ancient part of the brain that remembered what it heralded.

"Your pistols. Toss them in the pit, please."

Harden's hands moved slowly to his Schofields. The Vizier pressed the knife to the young woman's neck and she cried out. The veteran looked at her; her hair was wild and tangled under the Vizier's hand and her dress torn in places. Her eyes, however, were alert and watchful. She reached for the knife but the Vizier twisted her hair viciously and she relented. Harden held his pistols with grips reversed and tossed them over the rusty barrier. He did not hear them strike bottom.

"Weak," said the Vizier as he drew the knife away from the woman's throat. "Your so-called morals simply mean that you are easily manipulated by your superiors. Like an angry puppet you twist and turn on your strings, to no avail."

Harden stepped a pace forward. He took his hat off and ran his hand across his scalp. His hat came to rest in front of his belt buckle. "Lordy, you do bang on like a shit-house door in the wind," he said.

The Vizier bristled and the woman winced as his hand tightened. She gripped the handsome man's wrist with her own hands, and Harden could see red spring on her captor's skin from her nails.

"Kill him!" she called.

"I will, Miss," said Harden. "Just be patient a moment." He took another step towards the Vizier. "The book?"

The Vizier shook his head at the temerity of the peasant before him. His knife dropped towards the young woman's throat again. "It is as the legends foretold," the Vizier said. "I have summoned the old god Kathigu-Ra, and his power will soon be manifest. The Servants of the Flame Undying shall sit at his right hand to oversee his dominion of this broken world. And you and your ilk will be nothing but slaves."

The hum continued to grow from the fiery mine pit. A tentacle of flame licked up from the depths and lay on the pit's edge like something was crawling tentatively from a grave. Feeling around before committing to the climb. The heat was thick as if they were insects caught in molasses. The Vizier saw the tendril and his eyes widened with joy at what he had wrought.

"I once fought a war over people wantin' to keep other people as chattel," said Harden as he stepped closer, his hat still poised at his waist. "Didn't end well for 'em."

The Vizier laughed at such nonsense. "I will finish the summoning and then all that is needed is a sacrifice," he said. "Or in this case, two!" He began to speak in that forgotten language as he raised the curved knife high, the woman's head tilted back to expose her throat.

Harden threw his hat at the Vizier's face and the man, used to others fighting for him, flinched back and away. Harden's hand snaked under his coat at the rear and he drew the outrider's Colt Walker, the big pistol ripping material as it went. The veteran raised the Walker and fired and the big lead ball jumped across the short space. It caught the Vizier in his right shoulder and the man's arm collapsed with the destruction of muscle and bone, the curved knife spinning away into the mine pit. The Vizier cried out like an iron roof tearing in a storm and he let go of the young woman and clutched at what remained of his shoulder. The spell of Summoning died in his throat as the pain surged.

The young woman rose as The Vizier stepped back and she slammed her palms into the well-dressed man's chest. The Vizier fell against the rusted railing but it held. He reached for her with his remaining hand and it clutched her hair again. The woman pushed once more and the railing groaned and snapped. The Vizier toppled back into space as the woman jerked her head away, strands of hair clenched in his fingers. His screams went on for a long time as he fell into the fiery abyss.

Harden joined the woman at the edge of the broken platform and they both looked down. The light from the fire below pulsed. It swelled so that the humans raised their hands in front of their faces, but then it subsided abruptly. The mine pit was dark. It was quiet.

It was empty.

Harden cut the bindings from the woman's wrist and she shook her hands as the circulation returned. She nodded her thanks and looked at Harden with clear eyes. The West was not a place that bred the weak of heart.

"What now?" she asked.

"Now," said Harden as they turned from the dark pit, the world for the moment safe. "Now I need a new hat."

Entrails West

Gregory Nicoll

"Whatever the hell that thing was," said Big Link, "two slugs from my Spencer hardly slowed it." The trooper shivered and clutched his carbine tightly. "What do we do now, Captain?"

Captain Amos Washington slowly exhaled. He had faced challenging situations in his long years with the Army, leading expeditions of his fellow Buffalo Soldiers across hostile territories all along the expanding frontier, but he had never faced a situation as peculiar as this, and never one in nearly total darkness.

The spring night was cool and the air crisp, but its pleasantness was undone by the horrid odors of burnt hair and flesh from the corpse at his feet. The moon was just a thin crescent overhead amid the canopy of stars, but the white rocks of the creek bed reflected enough of its light that Washington could discern the shapes of his troopers encircling the smoldering remains.

"You're certain Major Fowler's death was an accident?" he asked, paying close attention for any response. He knew that the death of the commanding officer — the only white member of their patrol — would become the subject of a military inquest, quite possibly a career-ending one. He needed all the facts.

The assembled troopers murmured quietly, but Big Link spoke up.

"Yes, sir, Captain, sir. He was climbin' down from the first wagon when the oil lantern fell off the seat, an' it broke across his shoulder. The oil spilled an' started burnin' him awful bad, all over his head. He come running down here to save hisself — I reckon he was gonna jump in the deep water over yonder — but he stumbled here in these loose rocks. Broke his neck."

Washington nodded. He had heard Fowler's screams abruptly cut short. Big Link's explanation made sense. "And you were right behind him?"

Big Link nodded. "Yes, sir, Captain, sir. I was tryin' help him."

"So, what exactly did you *shoot* at?"

It was quiet for a moment. The only sounds were water trickling in the creek and a soft wind stirring the limbs of the trees along the embankment.

"I called out for help…and I was waitin' here, here with Major Fowler, when…something came out from the trees."

Washington frowned. "Something?"

Big Link spoke quietly. "It was big — maybe a man, maybe a grizzly — so hard to see…I yelled at it to stop but it kept comin' at me. Then Miller an' Wee Link got here, a-callin' out my name real loud, and the thing stopped."

"That's what happened," agreed Miller. "It was the biggest Comanche I ever done seen. Well, either a Comanche or a bear. It turned towards me an' Weevil, and then it looked back to Big Link and kinda *jumped* at him."

"That's when I fired on it," Big Link asserted. "I hit it — no way could I miss, 'cause it was so close — but my shot—"

Miller interrupted. "His round hit that thing dead center. I saw the shape o' something burst outa its back, maybe a big clot o' blood an' maybe some fur. Then it turned around."

"That's when I fired again," said Big Link. "But it just walked real fast across the creek an' went back into them trees."

Washington turned to Trooper Weevil Lincoln, the one they called Wee Link because he stood two feet shorter than Big Link. "Weevil, what did *you* see?"

Wee Link shrugged. "Didn't see nothing, Captain, sir. I don't see good in this dark. I was just following Miller."

Miller turned toward Big Link. "What you reckon that thing wanted? Why you think it was comin' at ya?"

"The thing wanted to kill me."

Washington shook his head. "I don't think so." He reached down and unbuckled the heavy leather belt from the dead officer's waist. "Major Fowler was carrying our orders and the mission map." He displayed the bulging pouch fastened to the belt, only dimly visible in the darkness.

The belt's excessive weight strained Washington's arm. In addition to the map pouch, Fowler had also carried a flap holster with a Remington .44 revolver secured inside it. Washington unsnapped the holster and eased the Model 1858 out. It was longer and heavier than his own Colt, and because Fowler had paid extra to have a bright nickel-silver finish applied to it, the weapon was easy to make out in the dim light.

"Whoever that intruder was, he likely wanted the papers, or this revolver, or both."

"I dunno," said Big Link, "you didn't see it comin' at me like I did."

"Pshaw!" said Wee Link. "Ain't nobody able to see *anything* in this dark."

Washington held up his gloved right hand. "Silence please, troopers. Miller and Weevil, carry the major back up to the wagons. Cut some fresh pine boughs and lay them over him to cover the smell, and find an extra canvas tarp we can wrap around him. Big Link, reload that carbine and guard them while they work."

He tucked the Remington into own belt and slung Fowler's belt over his shoulder. "Now, where's Isaiah?"

~*~

Isaiah Dorman had been gone for a couple of hours, but was waiting by the wagons when Captain Washington returned from the creek bed. The scout was a big, powerful man, his skin tone even darker than Washington's own. He was clad entirely in fringed brown buckskin, and as usual his non-regulation Winchester repeater was cradled in his arms.

Dorman had taken the liberty of starting a small fire and was cooking a skinned jackrabbit on the end of a long stick. The aroma of roasting rabbit provided a pleasant contrast to the stink of Fowler's charred corpse, which the others had dragged through the campsite a few moments before.

Washington squatted down beside the fire. "Good to see you back, Isaiah. You heard about Major Fowler?"

Dorman nodded. "Weevil showed me the body. Awful way to go, suh."

Washington nodded. "I have his map," he said, unslinging the dead man's belt from his shoulder and opening the dispatch pouch. "It'll be up to you and me now to nurse-maid these wagons home to the fort."

"You'd best know, Cap'n Washington, that Major Fowler was takin' a awful chance leadin' us this way. Even the Indians — apart from a few rogue Comanches, that is — are downright scared of this land we're rolling through. They say it's an evil place — accursed ground. That's why Yellow Dog refused to come along on the mission with us this time."

Washington sighed. "I have always counted on Yellow Dog, fine scout that he is, but you're skilled with different Indian languages and I'm very grateful you're here, Isaiah. Now, I had wondered why—"

"It was all a military secret," said Dorman, interrupting. "Only me and Major Fowler knew the particulars."

"I should have been told."

"The Army didn't want it to get back to the troopers. Didn't want 'em rattled about travelin' through these parts."

Washington nodded. He eased the papers out of Fowler's pouch and examined them in the flickering firelight, grateful that Dorman had set some sticks burning despite the injunction against cook-fires. They had started out with two lanterns — one for each wagon — but broke the first one almost immediately and had now lost the second one to Fowler's hideous accident. Only the light from Dorman's small fire allowed him to see the paperwork.

"I don't know what the Army was so afraid of," Washington commented. "Seems to me we're facing more danger from lantern accidents and slippery riverside rocks than from evil spirits." He paused. "Oh, unless you mean that hairy phantom Big Link says was charging at him."

Dorman's eyes widened. "What?"

Washington shrugged. "A few troopers say there was something, a man or an animal, down by the creek where Fowler died. Didn't get a good look, but it apparently caught at least one slug from Big Link's Spencer before it ran off."

The scout quickly lifted the stick from the fire. "Let's share this rabbit, Cap'n, right now, and eat it up quick."

"Is it cooked?"

"Cooked enough," answered Dorman as he got up on his feet and promptly stomped out the fire.

~*~

It was Wee Link who found the footprint.

The air was chilly in the first gray light of dawn, and even colder down at the creek bed. A low fog covered the water and drifted along the loose rocks of the embankment, making it especially treacherous to walk there. The troopers used extreme caution as they refilled the canteens and water barrels. Isaiah Dorman had found a thin, intermittent blood trail and tracked it across the creek, following it onto the other side. Wee Link, with an empty canteen awaiting his attention in each hand, had watched Dorman for a few minutes until the scout disappeared at the distant tree line. The little man then knelt down at the water's edge to begin his work, only to raise his voice in cold inarticulate terror at what he saw in the mud.

His scream brought the troopers running.

Captain Washington's boots crunched loudly in the loose rocks as he caught up to the group, who had formed a tight circle around Wee Link's position. In the distance he saw Dorman returning from the far tree line and scrambling to reach the others. Washington edged Trooper Bell and Trooper Miller aside.

The footprint was enormous, at least half again the size of the bootprint of the biggest men in Washington's patrol. But whatever made that print wore no shoeleather. It was barefoot, with five toes each the size of a railroad spike.

Doorman pushed through the circle and knelt down beside Washington.

"How did you miss this?" Washington asked his scout.

Dorman shrugged. "This track's from last night when it was *coming*. Me, I was following the blood trail it left when it was *going*."

Washington nodded. "You find anything?"

Dorman pointed at the footprint. "Just more of those — a *lot* more."

"Well," the captain said grimly, "whatever it is, let's hope it can't run."

Dorman shook his head. "Ain't no *it*, Cap'n. More like *they*." He glanced over his own shoulder and then over Washington's. "There's more than one of 'em."

~*~

The wagons were making good time.

Pulled by strong, well-rested mule teams, they moved steadily along the rough, irregular trail despite the excessive weight of their cargo, oak beams creaking and groaning as they rolled. Although the patrol's mission was supposedly secret, each vehicle was loaded down with wooden crates marked 45-70 GOV'T in large stenciled characters. Even troopers who never had a single day of schooling could recognize this designation. They were carrying an enormous supply of ammunition for the military's new Springfield rifles.

A driver and guard occupied the seats of both wagons, the guard with a Spencer carbine and the driver with a bullwhip. A second guard was positioned at the rear of each wagon, and cavalrymen on fast horses flanked them on both sides. Some rode at a regular pace, matching the wagons' speed, while others swiftly galloped far ahead and then circled back at regular intervals, constantly monitoring the trail conditions.

Following behind at a considerable distance was a lone trooper whose horse dragged a litter, hastily assembled from pine poles and spare canvas, on which Major Fowler's corpse was transported. A thick cloud of flies buzzed noisily around it.

The sun was high overhead and the afternoon air had briefly turned warm when Isaiah Dorman rode up beside the captain. "What is it?" asked Washington.

"You seen those two Comanches tracking us?"

Washington shook his head. "Comanches? Where?"

They had been crossing an open plain for more than an hour, but now the column was moving into hilly country. Following the mapped route, they would soon pass through a narrow valley.

"Don't want to point right to 'em," said Dorman, "but up yonder on the left hilltop, you see those three trees?"

"Yes."

"Well, keep your head pointed that way, like you're admirin' the trees, but move your eyes to the right and look at the long flat rock on the other side. There's two Comanches behind it."

Washington resisted the strong urge to turn his head. After a moment he noticed something flutter from behind the rock. It could have been long feathers or loose rags. Then came a brief glint of sunlight reflecting off a rifle barrel. Then nothing.

"Right now it's just those two. They're most likely part of a bigger group, because I can't figure two lone Indians going through *this* country on their own."

"Should we be concerned?"

Dorman smiled. "They're carrying captured Army rifles — the new Springfields, not these old Spencers our colored troops get issued — so it's a fair bet the Comanches will be wantin' our cargo. Question is, are those two braves bold enough to try something by their lonesome, or will they wait for the rest of their party to catch up and join in?"

"How could they possibly know what we're carrying?"

"Oh, they seen the crates, suh, an' the crates is marked. Same marks painted there — '45-70' — is stamped in the metal on them Springfields they're carryin.'"

Washington nodded grimly. "Isaiah, get the word to all the troopers. From now on, no-one goes unarmed — not even the wagon drivers."

~*~

The sun had dipped close to the horizon and the air had grown noticeably cooler when they all heard, from somewhere in the distance up the trail, the sound of a man's scream. This was followed immediately by the crack of rifle fire, and then another scream which was cut short.

The patrol had just passed uneventfully through the valley and reached an open area surrounded by low hills, like the bottom of a gigantic bowl. Captain Washington gave the order to make camp for the night, so they drew the wagons up in the center of the open space and established pickets for their horses and mules. Dorman reported the two Comanches shadowing them were now just one, the second brave having mysteriously slipped off.

The captain and Dorman were discussing whether or not to allow cooking fires — Washington wanted another cold camp overnight, but the scout protested that their position was already known so it didn't matter any longer — when the rifle shot and screams cut short their debate. The troopers were on immediate alert. Men scrambled to their feet, eagerly retrieving carbines from saddle scabbards and fumbling with ammo boxes. Others pulled out the long, well-honed knives from their belt sheaths and stared grimly in the direction of the awful sounds.

"Isaiah, while there's still light—"

"I'm on my way, Cap'n," said the scout, swinging himself up into the saddle. He levered a round into the chamber of his Winchester and then set off.

A few minutes later the troopers heard three shots, then four more.

There was still a faint glow of daylight beyond the hilltops, and the first stars were now visible in the darkening sky overhead, when Dorman returned. He rode solemnly into camp, leading a Comanche pony with a body draped over it and secured by a rope. Washington had given in and allowed the men to start campfires, one of which was burning unexpectedly bright. Dorman led the second horse up close to the biggest fire so the men could see the body.

"It's a Indian," exclaimed Wee Link.

"Well, no, it's *part* of a Indian," said Miller.

The captain stepped closer. "*Part* of?"

Dorman reached down from his position in the saddle of the first horse. He used his belt knife to cut the rope, sending the Comanche's remains tumbling to the ground beside the fire. The body had been roughly, brutally gutted, and huge strips of flesh had been torn from the arms and legs.

"Somethin' tried to *eat* him!" Big Link yelled. "I told y'all! It's gotta be that same bear-man thing that was comin' for me by the creek!"

"Easy there, troopers!" Washington called out. Once the men had fallen silent again, he turned to Dorman. "What did you see?"

"Horse tracks showed me the two braves split up, this one going ahead and the other circling back behind us. Never did find any more sign of that second fellow, but this one... Well, before I found him, I followed a long an' bloody trail of his innards."

"Innards?"

"Yes, suh — his *guts*, tore right outta his belly. Strung along over quite some ways."

The troopers began murmuring but Washington silenced them by raising his hand. "And where was his body?"

Dorman shook his head. "It was like Big Link said. There was a thing, a *big* thing, and it was holdin' the body...an' *eatin'* on it..."

"A thing? Was the thing a man...or?"

"Bigger than a bear, bigger than a man. I fired a volley into it. It dropped the Comanche, but it didn't run off till after I fired another four."

"Them little pebble rounds outta that Winchester cain't do better than my Spencer did last night, Isaiah," declared Big Link. "What we need to fight that thing is a .45-70, which we ain't got."

Dorman fumbled in his saddle scabbard and then held up the dead Comanche's Springfield, which the brave had decorated with beads and feathers. Its long barrel gleamed in the firelight. "We got *one*."

Washington was about to order Big Link and Miller to fetch a crate of ammo from the first wagon, but he was distracted by a rapid pounding of hoofbeats from behind. He turned to see Trooper Bell reining up near the fire. This alarmed him slightly since Bell had been assigned to guard Major Fowler's corpse.

"Cap'n Washington," said Bell breathlessly, looking down from the saddle, "there's Indians comin' our way — a lot of 'em, suh."

~*~

Light from the fading western sunset illuminated the faces of the Comanches approaching from the east. The evening air was cool now, with more stars visible overhead, but Washington estimated that full night was still a half hour away. Enough time, he hoped, to sort out the intentions of these visitors.

Washington counted about twenty of them. They were all dismounted, with a few at the rear of the group holding the leads of Indian ponies. Over one of these horses was draped a dead body and, even at this distance, the captain could see it had suffered mutilations comparable to the corpse back by their campfire.

These were seasoned warriors, armed with captured Army-issue Springfields, and many had scalps dangling from their rawhide clothing. Most were bare-headed except for a single feather, but one brave — the apparent leader of the group — wore a headpiece made from a buffalo with upright horns. Holding his rifle aloft with one hand, he gestured with the other.

"*Tunaki,*" he said. "*Tusu'naa.*"

Washington glanced at Dorman, who had a reputation as the Army's best interpreter. "What's he saying?"

Dorman answered quietly. "Comanches don't exactly have any words for 'peace,' but those are the closest they got."

"Tell them we don't want to fight them."

Dorman wetted his lips and began communicating, partly with strange words the captain could not understand and partly with gestures. The Comanche responded in kind, and rapid conversation ensued.

By the time the sun had completely faded, the group was ready. Small fires encircled the encampment at regular intervals, guarded by teams of troopers and braves whose weapons pointed out into the surrounding darkness. Thanks to Dorman's remarkable skills as both translator and negotiator, Washington and the Comanche leader — now known to them as Standing Buffalo — determined by mutual agreement that their dead companions should be burned in a massive central fire, rather than risk those corpses falling into the hands of the man-eaters. It was as this great bonfire crackled and raged, spewing sparks up into the night sky, that the monsters appeared.

The canopy of stars stretched from horizon to horizon, but then, incredibly, dozens of similar stars also gleamed *below* the horizon line. It was a few moments before Washington realized that the 'stars' he saw at ground-level were actually reflections in the eyes of the man-eaters.

"They's comin'!" cried Big Link, clutching the big Springfield which Dorman had recovered.

The invaders charged the encampment, their immense hairy bodies framed against the light of the little campfires, their eyes eerily silver.

The first fiery volley of shots rippled around the camp's protective ring like a circular bolt of lightning. Immediately the stink of burnt gunpowder dominated the night air and thick, cottony clouds of smoke added to the confusion and mayhem. Men began firing at will. The Spencer repeaters cracked more rapidly, but the single-shot Springfields compensated with tremendous force. Ejected copper casings jingled on the hard ground.

Several of the man-beasts overran the defenses. One of them loped toward Washington and Standing Buffalo, both positioned by the central bonfire. The Comanche pointed his rifle, but the captain drew his revolver and turned back the monster with five shots at its chest. When another creature overpowered a Comanche brave, Trooper Miller pounded it with his carbine's buttstock and forced it back into the darkness with two close-range rounds.

Big Link took the worst of it. A man-beast overran his position just as he was fumbling to reload the unfamiliar Springfield. Taking advantage of his distraction, the monster sunk its claws into his chest and ripped him open down to his beltline. He fell back screaming as the thing bit deeply into his neck. After two Comanches forced the monster away, the trooper lay dying by the firelight. With blood gurgling in his throat, he begged for someone to finish him off.

The captain used Major Fowler's Remington to do it.

~*~

It was over by dawn.

At first light Washington sent men out to gather firewood for the funeral pyre. In addition to Big Link they had lost Trooper Bell and three of the Comanche braves. He would have preferred to bury their dead, but feared the corpses would be excavated and eaten, so once again the great fire was called upon. Black troopers and red Indians passed over to the next life together.

In gratitude for their assistance, Washington gave Standing Buffalo's men an entire case of .45-70 rounds, which he would report lost on the trail. His own troops gladly pledged their silence about this, something the Army would deem a punishable indiscretion if not a hanging offense.

After the funeral, the two factions traveled together to the trailhead. They parted company at the crossroads, the Comanches taking a longer route back to avoid re-crossing unholy ground. With Isaiah Dorman's help, Washington had practiced the pronunciation of their 'peace' words and was thus able to send Standing Buffalo off with a heartfelt, "*Tunaki. Tusu'naa.*"

Dorman had been away scouting when the braves departed, but he rejoined the troop at their trailhead camp. "Cap'n, suh," he said, "I must tell you something, something important."

Washington gestured for him to speak.

"Suh, I rode a full mile back from the battleground. I circled in the hills. I criss-crossed the game trails."

"And what did you find?"

Dorman shook his head. "Nothing, suh. Not one single hide of any one of them things we were all fightin'. We drove 'em off, suh — an' those bigger rifles was a mighty help — but I can't say we *killed* any of 'em. No, suh. Not a single one. Near as I can figure it, they're all still out there. Still out there *waitin'* for us."

Washington nodded grimly. He took a fresh-sharpened pencil from Major Fowler's leather belt pouch and placed its tip against the paper of the map they had been using. Carefully and deliberately, he drew a large letter X completely covering the territory they had crossed.

~*~ ~*~

Historical Footnote:

The United States' Eighth and Ninth Cavalry were made up of Negro troopers, nicknamed "Buffalo Soldiers" by the Native Americans, who believed these men's hair resembled the hides of bison. They served from the 19th Century up into the 20th, many of them eventually teaching horsemanship to the cadets at the West Point Military Academy until the U.S. Army discontinued the use of mounted troops in the 1940s.

The characters in this story are fictional, with one exception. Isaiah Dorman (1832-1876) was a real-life scout and interpreter who had a distinguished career on the western frontier. By numerous accounts he was loved, respected, and trusted by most of the white military officials for whom he worked. While assigned as an interpreter to Lt. Col. George Armstrong Custer, Dorman was killed in action at the Battle of the Little Bighorn. On the official roster of the dead from that conflict, his is the only name with the designation "(Colored)" written beside it.

The Cost of Gold
Henry Herz

Covered in trail dust, 3rd Cavalry Corporal Michael Gibbs and Private Bryan Schmidt limped to the polished oak bar.

"Welcome to the Gem Variety Theater, the finest saloon in all Deadwood," said the keen-eyed barkeep with a theatrical sweep of his arm. "I'm Al. What can I getcha?"

Nearly out of money, the pair ordered beers.

Gibbs took a long pull on his mug. "Ah." He withdrew a wrinkled envelope from his jacket and stared.

"That from yer sweetheart?" asked Schmidt. "How is Jenny?"

"Fine," Gibbs replied, furrowing his brow. "Maybe too fine. She keeps mentioning how helpful Don's been. That wealthy loiter-sack's never worked a day in his life." He slapped the envelope onto the bar top.

Schmidt belched. "What's eatin' you? Oh, you think he fancies Jenny? Well, our enlistments expire tomorrow. You should get yerself home to Laramie, run off that dandy Don, and marry the girl."

"When I've got barely two bits to my name?" replied Gibbs, shaking his head. "No. Not until I've saved enough to buy a homestead and offer Jenny a decent life."

"So, reenlist in the Army, then," said Schmidt, tapping his unit insignia.

Gibbs shook his head. "Not that either. Much as I enjoy eating horse meat, being shot at, and risking having my scalp taken, Army wages are too thin. Women like to be cared for."

"That may be. But what you know about women couldn't fill a thimble," replied Schmidt, giving Gibbs's arm a friendly punch. "Women care about a man's character. You treat her kindly. Yer brave, you survived the Battle of Little Bighorn, didn't ya? Yer tough, you saved my life at the Battle of Slim Buttes despite bein' half starved to death. And yer a handsome fella' to boot."

"Then maybe *you* should marry him, Schmidt," said a grinning Lieutenant Charles Varnum, clapping the men's shoulders. "I prefer the ladies, myself."

The troopers stood and saluted, even though Varnum wore civilian clothing.

"None of that, now," said Varnum. "I resigned. I came in here to wet my whistle, but I may also have a solution to your predicament. Next round's on me."

"You resigned, sir?" asked Gibbs, his eyes widening.

"Last week." Varnum's smile faded. "Much as I'd rather seek vengeance on the filthy bastards who butchered Colonel Custer, I can't ride all day like I used to. I'll never fully recover from the wound I got at Little Bighorn. My Sioux-hunting days are over, damnit. And I found a job I couldn't ignore."

"And what might that be, sir?" asked Schmidt, leaning in.

Varnum pulled up a stool. "George Hearst owns a nearby gold mine. He fired his foreman for incompetence."

"Incompetence, sir?" asked Gibbs.

"Yes. The kind that gets people killed," replied Varnum, scowling. "Same as in the cavalry. A number of miners have died. Now all kinds of dark rumors are floating 'round about how the mine is haunted by 'malign spirits.' Injun nonsense. The deaths are probably from unsafe practices. So Hearst hired me to get his operation running smoothly, and I am *empowered* to do so."

"Empowered?" asked Schmidt.

"Yes. First off, by hiring miners unafraid of superstitions. How does *triple* your Army pay sound?"

Gibbs's and Schmidt's jaws fell open.

"I thought that might get your attention," said Varnum, grinning. "Come see me at the Homestake mine tomorrow." He left.

"I still think you should head home and marry your woman," Schmidt offered.

Gibbs nodded. "It would be nice to see Jenny's sweet smile. And I wouldn't mind warm food and taking a bath more than once a month."

"None of us would mind you bathing more often," joked Schmidt, brushing some dust off Gibbs's jacket.

"Still," continued Gibbs, "triple wages. That settles it for me. I'm gonna stay in Deadwood to earn the price of a homestead."

Schmidt sighed. "Well, if yer gonna stay, I reckon I will too. Someone's gotta keep you outta trouble."

Gibbs glanced over Schmidt's shoulder as a Native American in a 3rd Cavalry uniform entered the saloon. He waved. "Goes Ahead!"

The Crow joined the other cavalrymen.

"Goes Ahead was a scout with me and Varnum when we were in the 7th Cavalry," said Gibbs.

Schmidt's eyebrows raised. "Nice to meet ya. Nothing personal, but I've gotta get rid of the two beers in my belly." He rose and left.

Gibbs switched from English to Apsáalooke Nation language. "Good to see you."

Goes Ahead nodded. "And you, Michael. How is 3rd?"

"Same job, different men," Gibbs replied. "Now Varnum's managing a gold mine and looking to hire. Good pay. Want to try mining?"

Goes Ahead scowled and leaned back. "You speak our language, but you do not know our ways. I will not dig under the mountains." He thrust out his arm in a gesture of negation.

"Why's that?" asked Gibbs, eyebrows raised at the emphatic reaction.

"The Crow Nation mountains are sacred," replied Goes Ahead. "That is where the First Maker travels, watching his creation. Fierce underground spirits, Awakkule, guard the mountains. They punish anyone who trespasses on holy ground. Do not go into the earth, my friend." Goes Ahead turned and left before Gibbs could reply.

~*~

Schmidt returned. "Where's yer friend? Did he think you need a bath, too?" he asked, pinching his nose.

Gibbs stared into space, unseeing. He relayed Goes Ahead's concern.

"Well, that's just superstitious hogwash," replied Schmidt, shrugging his shoulders. "That must be the rumor Lieutenant Varnum mentioned."

"Yeah." Gibbs tossed some coins on the bar. "Well, I reckon we should let the captain know we won't be re-enlisting."

~*~

Gibbs and Schmidt woke as a dreary day dawned. They ate a modest breakfast and hiked to the wooden shack just outside the mine.

Varnum offered them a warm welcome and signed them up. "If we meet our weekly quota, there's a bonus for everyone. Go on into the mine. I'll be joining the crew shortly."

Gibbs and Schmidt grabbed pickaxes and trudged into the bowels of the mountainside. Despite the oil wick lamps hung along the tunnel walls, the mine's darkness loomed, a palpable oppressive thing.

"Does it seem colder than it oughta?" Schmidt asked, his voice echoing longer than it should have. "I have this weird feeling. I'm starting to understand why Goes Ahead wanted nothing to do with this mine."

Gibbs nodded, unwilling to disturb their environment unnecessarily as they strode deeper into the mountain. *Shouldn't we be hearing the sounds of digging by now? I hope we're going the right way.*

Even the sound of their own footsteps somehow became ominous. They rounded a bend to find a dozen miners conversing in frantic whispers, axes and shovels slung over their shoulders.

The miners started at the arrival of the two troopers.

"I'm Gibbs. This is Schmidt. We're new. Where are we supposed to dig?" His breath fogged slightly. Again, the words echoed unnaturally.

"Keep yer voice down," urged a miner with a leathery face and wiry gray beard. "Tate's gone missing. We're gonna do a search. Once we find him, we'll get back to work." He divided the men into two groups. "Gibbs and Schmidt, go with those fellas down tunnel twelve. I'll take these lads down tunnel thirteen. Meet back here in an hour."

The miners nodded and split up.

~*~

"Is it always this cool in here?" Schmidt asked the miner walking next to him.

"Yeah," the miner replied, rubbing his hands together. "I've dug many a tunnel in my day, but none so cold as this one."

Gibbs frowned. "So, how many miners have been lost?" The rough-hewn tunnel walls felt like they were gradually constricting. His breathing became labored even though they walked at a normal pace.

"Tate makes eleven," the miner replied.

Eleven! Lordy, thought Gibbs. *No wonder they're behind quota and look like they're staring down the wrong end of a Springfield.* "Is it normal to lose so many men tunneling?"

The miner shook his head. "Ain't nothing normal about this mine. If I didn't need the money so bad, I'd be miles from here."

Schmidt tasted bile and cleared his throat. "Did the men desert?"

"No. We find 'em...cut to pieces."

Maybe I should reconsider, thought Gibbs. He caught Schmidt's attention. Their eyes widened further at faint but nerve-grating high-pitched shrieks. "What the hell is that? Bats?"

"Fresh-cut tunnels don't have bats," the miner replied, fear written on his face. "The shrieking gets louder the deeper we go. Varnum's told us to ignore it and keep diggin'."

The group reached the end of tunnel twelve. "Tate ain't here," said one. "Let's head on back."

"Belay that," replied Varnum striding up wearing his Army pistol belt, carrying a lantern in one hand and a bulky sack in his other. "We're bein' paid to pull gold from the mountain, so let's get to it. Here's dynamite and blasting gear."

Gibbs and Schmidt made way for the others with mining experience, who prepared a charge under Varnum's stern gaze.

"Everyone back up a safe distance," Varnum ordered. He nodded to a miner, who lit the fuse. "Fire in the hole!"

The dynamite *boomed* and tore chunks out of the tunnel wall. The miners pulled bandanas up over their mouths and noses against the acrid dust, twinkling in the dim light of Varnum's lantern. Once the debris settled, they tossed rubble into the empty mine cart. Gibbs and Schmidt pitched in, rolling the cart away from the end of the tunnel when the miners finished.

Varnum stepped through the swirling dust and pointed. "There!"

A thick gold vein meandered up the wall.

The miners smiled until faint echoes of high-pitched shrieking wiped the grins off their faces.

Gibbs grasped the hilt of his Bowie knife. Sweat beaded on his brow. *I should have gone home to Jenny.*

The miners mumbled among themselves.

"Pay that racket no mind," ordered Varnum. "Hit it again."

Under Varnum's glare, the miners repeated the process followed by another loud boom. Chunks of ore-laden stone rattled in the narrow passageway.

A rush of stale, ancient air roiled the dust, raising goosebumps on Schmidt's bare forearms. His eyes widened, for the tunnel now connected to a dark void.

Varnum pushed past his stunned men, climbing over the rubble. He raised the lantern to illuminate a fifty by fifty foot smooth-walled room. In the middle of the floor, forty-nine stone tombs formed a seven by seven grid. For once, the experienced soldier was at a loss for words.

Gibbs and Schmidt stepped in behind Varnum, noting the diminutive size of the sepulchers, perhaps two feet long, a foot wide, and a foot high.

The hairs on their necks rose when it became apparent that about half of the rectangular stone lids rested askew.

The shadows cast by the tombs feel odd somehow, thought Gibbs. *Wrong angles? Too dark?* He stepped toward an open one and peered inside. Empty. *Were these tombs robbed, or did something climb out?* The low ceiling added to his feeling of claustrophobia.

The shrieking sounds grew louder. A sudden gust of chill, fetid air rushed through the narrow tunnel into the cavern, extinguishing the wall lamps. The miners dropped their tools and scrambled toward the light of Varnum's lantern in the room, but the darkness, tight quarters, and piles of debris hindered them.

Gibbs and Schmidt positioned themselves on either side of the opening, encouraging the men to hurry; all held their pickaxes at the ready.

The men winced, covering their ears as the volume of shrieking intensified.

The last miner in line screamed. Warm liquid splattered across the back of the man in front of him. "Something got Jonesy!" he cried, panicking.

The shrieking receded as the miners gathered in the room.

Gibbs spun the gore-stained man by the shoulders to check for wounds. "This isn't your blood. What happened?"

The wild-eyed man could not muster a response before the distant shrieking resumed.

"Quick," cried Gibbs, his military discipline forcing down the fear. "We need to block the passageway. Whatever's out there is worse than an empty room, no matter how creepy."

Schmidt followed Gibbs back into the cramped tunnel. Working by feel and using their axe handles for leverage, they rocked the mine cart back and forth until it tipped over, then hurried back into the room.

"Everyone, pile the debris on top of the cart," ordered Gibbs. "Lieutenant, they'll need light."

Shaking with terror but understanding the urgent need to act, the miners scrambled back into the tunnel. Varnum stepped up behind them and raised his lantern.

The miners quickly sealed the tunnel with a pile of rocks.

"That was fast thinking, Gibbs," whispered Varnum. "But now we're trapped with a limited air supply and only one lantern."

"You're right, sir," replied Gibbs, nodding. "But we needed more time to figure out our next move."

Schmidt's head swiveled at scrabbling sounds from the far side of the rubble pile. "Something's pawing at the barricade. Don't stop piling on the rocks," he told the miners. "Keep the tunnel blocked."

Gibbs glanced at the floor. *Damn. Damn. Damn.* Not only was their air supply limited, but so, too, their supply of rocks. "Sir, we're gonna need more rubble."

Varnum nodded. "I can't blast right here. That'd kill my men." He scanned the room and handed the lantern to Gibbs. "Schmidt, come with me." Varnum led Schmidt to the far side of the room and began setting a charge of dynamite.

The air grew colder.

"Fire in the hole!"

The explosion set everyone's ears to ringing. Immediately, Schmidt swung his pickaxe to break the larger pieces of new rubble into chunks light enough to be carried to the tunnel.

"You four," cried Gibbs, turning and pointing, "go grab rubble from where Schmidt's standing and bring it here for the barricade."

The shrieking intensified. Still shining the lantern into the tunnel, Gibbs shivered.

A slight movement in the center of the room caught Schmidt's eye, halting him mid-swing. The lid from one of the crypts grated open, and a blurry, human-shape creature, wreathed in viscous shadow, emerged from the tomb like ink vomiting tar. Its right arm elongated into the shape of a saber. Its black eyes, wells into madness, turned toward Gibbs's lantern, the only light source in the room.

A chill raised the hairs on the nape of Schmidt's neck. His eyes mutinied, refusing to focus. Or perhaps the creature lacked a distinct outline. He charged, raising the pickaxe above his head. "Gibbs!"

The creature spun and leaped.

Schmidt's powerful pickaxe blow shattered the crypt lid. The creature slashed at his neck as it sprang away with freakish speed, landing silently behind him. Schmidt's pickaxe slipped from his grasp, his severed head toppling to the ground.

"No!" screamed Gibbs.

Varnum's Colt single-action revolver barked twice. The shadow dissolved, its corpse stench mixing with the smell of gunpowder. The howling assault on the barricade escalated.

Varnum reloaded.

"Schmidt!" Gibbs set down the lantern at the tunnel entrance, rushed over, and fell to his knees. *What have I done? He wouldn't even have been here except for me. I should've listened to Goes Ahead.* His shoulders shuddered. *If I make it out of here, I'm heading straight home to Jenny, gold be damned.* He gathered himself and snatched up Schmidt's pickaxe.

"Schmidt was a good man, but he's gone," said Varnum. "Focus. We needed a wall to keep them out. But now we know there may be more monsters locked in here with us," he continued, pointing at the unopened crypts. "We've gotta get outta here and fast."

Gibbs counted only ten rounds on Varnum's gun belt. He counted the open tombs. *We're good and truly screwed. Now I'll never see her again.* Gibbs stared back at Varnum with fire in his eyes, though it wasn't clear if his ire was intended for Schmidt's murderer or for Varnum. He took a long, deep breath to regain his composure. "Do you have a diagram of the tunnels, sir?"

Varnum nodded and pulled a folded map from his pants pocket.

"Can you show me where we are on the map," asked Gibbs.

"Mr. Varnum," called a miner, "whatever these things are, they're murmuring to each other. And they're still digging. The barricade ain't gonna hold much longer."

Varnum's eyes never left Gibbs. "Keep reinforcing it."

A barricade won't save us if more of those monsters climb out of their crypts in here, thought Gibbs.

A miner lugging a rock caught sight of Schmidt's decapitated body. He stumbled, dropped the rock, and vomited on the cold stone floor.

Gibbs considered the map. "Sir, we're close to the southeast edge of the mountain. Can we dynamite our way to daylight?"

Varnum smiled grimly. "Yup. Or die trying."

"I don't know anything about blasting. But I know my way around a Colt, sir," said Gibbs.

Varnum paused. "You're right. Keep your eyes on the unopened crypts." Varnum unstrapped his gun belt and handed it to Gibbs.

"Yes, sir," replied Gibbs, putting on the belt, picking up a rock, and lugging it to the tunnel.

The rubble barricade vibrated ominously from the efforts of their unseen assailants, accompanied by blood-chilling murmurs. Another explosion. Gibbs started from the blast, but kept watch on the crypts.

Varnum set another charge. Miners shuttled rubble from Varnum to the barricade with heads down, averting their gazes from Schmidt's body.

Gibbs coughed from the dust and lingering stench from the crypts. *Don't worry about that. We're gonna run out of bullets before we run out of air.*

The shrieking rose, like a hoe dragging across Gibbs's skull.

A crypt lid slid open. The room temperature dropped. Another hideously ugly creature emerged, baring jagged black fangs. Gibbs fired twice and missed.

The creature leaped at a miner. It slashed once, severing a leg at mid-thigh. The miner screamed and toppled, writhing.

Gibbs fired four times, hitting the fast-moving creature with his last round. The gun shots echoed briefly before dying. *God, I'll give up all the gold in the world to be with Jenny.* He reloaded. *Only four bullets in my belt now.*

Spurting blood from the miner's thigh pooled on the ground.

The prospect of more creatures trapped inside the room with them shattered the fragile remnants of the miners' discipline. They panicked and ran to tear down the blockade in an attempt to escape.

Varnum retreated from the far wall. "Fire in the hole!" Another boom and fresh air wafted into the room along with a shaft of daylight.

"We've got an exit," yelled Varnum. "Go, go, go!"

The miners raced for the hole blown through the hillside. Gibbs turned to face the open tunnel to provide covering fire. Rocks at the top of the barricade tumbled to the ground. The shrieking doubled in volume. More of the barricade gave way as if dislodged by the spiteful cacophony.

Gibbs shuddered, muttered a brief prayer, and stepped toward the tunnel. Varnum caught him by the arm and pointed at the crypts. Two lids grated open.

Damn. Gibbs emptied his revolver, destroying the shadow-wreathed creatures.

"Save yourself, Gibbs," ordered Varnum. "I'll stop them."

Gibbs ran toward the breach before halting. *I can't leave Varnum to face them alone.* He reloaded, one shell slipping from his shaking fingers.

Varnum strode to the center of the room and stepped atop a closed crypt. He faced the tunnel, a bundle in one hand, a lit match in the other. "Get out, Gibbs," he called sharply over his shoulder, a captain going down with his ship.

The shadowed creatures surged over the broken barricade into the room like a storm tide, smothering the lantern. The faint illumination from

Varnum's match looked like a waterlogged rowboat, bobbing in a dark turbulent sea. Gibbs dashed for the exit.

"Fire in the hole," said Varnum, barely above a whisper. He lit the six remaining sticks of dynamite. They fell on him like a crashing wave of death.

BOOM!

~*~ ~*~

Author's Note:

While obviously a work of fiction, this short story includes some historical facts:
- A Crow (Apsáalooke Nation) warrior called Goes Ahead served as a scout for Custer's 7th Cavalry and survived the Battle of Little Bighorn.
- 2nd Lieutenant Charles Varnum served as leader of scouts for Custer's 7th Cavalry and although wounded, also survived the Battle of Little Bighorn.
- Awakkule are trickster spirits in Crow mythology, though I've taken liberties with the legend.
- As depicted in the acclaimed HBO TV series of the same name, Deadwood was an illegally founded, lawless gold rush town in the Black Hills of the South Dakota Territory. It did feature a saloon called the Gem Variety Theater, operated by Al Swearengen. The nearby Homestake mine was owned by George Hearst.
- After the Battle of Little Bighorn, General George Crook led a punitive pursuit of the Sioux Indians that included the Battle of Slim Buttes and ended near Deadwood. The campaign became known as the Horsemeat March because the troopers ran out of rations and had to eat some of their horses.
- Custer's 7th Cavalry were equipped with Springfield trapdoor rifles and Colt single-action revolvers.

By the way, the last phrase of the story, "They fell on him," is an homage to Stephen King's *Salem's Lot*. That line terrified me when I first read it.

A Day's Ride from Tarabuco
Gustavo Bondoni

"We ain't in Peru, Henry," Butch Cassidy told the Sundance Kid.

"We don't need to be in Peru. The Incas were all over the place. Here in Bolivia, and even farther south in Argentina," Sundance replied. "And if these injuns know what they're talking about, there's a burial chamber just up the trail."

Cassidy shrugged. "If they know about it, there won't be anything left to take. Old bones won't pay Gómez's monthly bribe."

"Tulu says the injuns won't go in there because they're too scared. They say the Incas left magic behind to keep anyone from trying anything." He grinned. "And you know what else the Incas left everywhere? Gold, that's what."

Cassidy leaned back on his chair and, lifting his hat out of his eyes, peered at his companion. "You shouldn't take those injuns seriously. Have you ever seen any gold in Bolivia?" He gestured at the dusty landscape around them and the mountains in the distance. They'd ridden through most of the country, and they'd found two kinds of places: poor and poorer. It had come to the point where they didn't even bother holding up travelers anymore. No one had any money.

"It can't hurt to look, can it?" Sundance replied. His mustache, which he liked to keep neatly trimmed, was lost in the beard he'd grown out over the past few weeks. "Besides, we've either got to get something for Gómez or we've gotta get out of here. He knows where to find the Pinkertons, and if he ever finds out how much the reward is, he'll sell us in a minute flat."

Gómez was the local law, a retired army lieutenant who'd been made a *Juez de Paz* and given a pension and a miniscule budget which, in the tiny outpost of Tarabuco, gave him the capacity to raise a posse big enough to respect.

"He'll take our money until we run out," Cassidy replied. "He doesn't trust gringos he can't control."

"Well, we're out of money, and he's a day's ride away. If we don't pay him, he'll come for us. Or he'll send the Pinkertons."

Cassidy spat. The detectives were implacable, capable, well-paid and well-fed, and as long as the reward was as big as it was, they wouldn't give up.

The Kid stood. "Well, I'm off to have a look. If I'm not back in a couple of days, it's because I found El Dorado and bought myself a pardon."

Cassidy grunted, acquiesced, and followed him across the dirt yard beside the yellow adobe house they'd holed up in. It belonged to Gómez, too, which might have seemed ironic if it weren't always the same story: the local law in South America went both ways. If you kept them happy, they were the ones who would protect you. But only until a better offer came along. It was much better than up north, where lawmen would hunt you for the honor of it, or where the reputation of an agency depended on them finding you…like the blasted Pinkertons.

They saddled up their horses, loaded the pack mule with water, and started out into the hills. It wasn't worth the trouble to lock up the little house. They'd left nothing inside worth stealing, and the *peones*, the natives who kept the property for Gómez in exchange for a place to live, would come at you with sticks if you tried, not defending the gringos' stuff, but Gómez's property.

The land they rode through had once been a sheep farm, suited for the hardy arid-land sheep brought in from Patagonia, but the farm had long since gone under and the house was the only thing left.

A trail led to the east. Up.

The hills looked just like the lands below: yellowish-gray dirt dotted with short green scrubs. Not quite desert, not quite farmland, but that lonely kind of land that could support a few hardy souls and a few rugged animals.

"Did the *peones* say which of the hills is supposed to be the haunted treasure place?" Cassidy asked.

"Of course. Half a day that way. Over and between four little hills and across a dry creek. A mountain shaped like a bird."

Cassidy snorted. "Like a bird? They're always saying things look like one animal or another, and it's always impossible to see it."

"I guess we'll need to look for the dry creek then," Sundance replied.

They rode in silence for four hours. When two men had been partners for so long, there wasn't much they wanted to talk about.

Cassidy broke the silence: "Creek," he said, pointing to the right.

A slight depression filled with rounded stones and slightly grayer dirt wound between two hills.

"Reckon you're right." Sundance spurred his horse up a rise and looked around. "And that's the bird mountain over there."

Cassidy didn't need to see for himself, and since he was leading the mule, he simply headed in the direction Sundance was pointing.

The wind picked up as they crested the last rise to find a single triangular peak in front of them, the last lonely mount before the hills beyond became even higher and rockier.

A gust nearly pulled Cassidy's hat from his head. He looked up. "I think we'll get some rain soon."

"Just our luck," Sundance replied.

It rained occasionally in the dry hills. Clouds full of water coming up from the Pacific would hit the hills and get pushed up or something. Since it was cold up high, they lost their water.

A fat raindrop landed on his shoulder, but Cassidy ignored it. They'd been wet before, and it was best not to hurry when climbing narrow paths in the mountains. That was a good way to lose a horse.

An overhang let them watch the worst of the shower without getting too soaked. Cassidy inhaled deeply, breathing in the smell of wet dirt.

After ten minutes, the rain hadn't stopped, and the wind, if anything, appeared to be picking up. It hissed between stones and made a sound like a train.

"The injuns say the cave's just on the path that leads up the mountain," Sundance said. "I think we should leave the horses here."

Cassidy studied the rocky climb. It looked like it had been worn into the stones by hundreds of feet, but it was covered in dust now, with weeds growing through the cracks.

He dismounted and hobbled his horse. These horses had come all the way from the Argentine, and he didn't want to have to replace them with local stock.

Then they began the climb.

The first few steps were easy enough. The path wound around the hill in a wide arc on a stone base. The important thing was to avoid slipping on the dust that covered everything, which the rain had turned into a slick of slippery mud.

The path, rising slowly, wound almost all the way around the mountain, which had the benefit of interrupting the rain. At the far eastern side of the rocky outcropping, ancient hands had cut stone steps into the hill.

"See," Sundance said, "I told you this was Inca."

"All I see so far," Cassidy replied, "is a long staircase I'm gonna have to climb." As they put one foot in front of the other, he reflected that this was an obvious choice for an Inca site. It was the first of the gray stone mountains that rose above the tree line and the dun-colored hills, but it stood far enough from the bigger mountains behind it to seem like a sentinel. The perfect place to bury your dead: honored but apart.

He shuddered. Cemeteries had always scared him, ever since he shot his first man. Since then, he'd come close to death so many times that he always felt that stepping into a cemetery would be to tempt fate. A lot of men never left.

The steps ended at another path, flat and carved out of the rock, which circled the mountain in both directions, more like a platform than a path.

"It must have been hell to build this without explosives," Sundance said. "You ever wonder how the savages did it?"

"I reckon they didn't have much else to do," Cassidy replied.

Following the platform around the mountain took them back into the rain. Cassidy felt his boots slipping on the polished rock as the wind tried to drop him into the valley down below.

He looked out into the rain. You could see for miles from here. The sea was out there somewhere. All this water had come from the ocean.

"Will you look at that," Sundance said.

Cassidy walked up to where the Kid was standing. A cave entrance opened up off of the platform and dove into the mountain at a slight angle. It was almost impossible to tell how deep the shaft went, however: a lush forest had grown up at the mouth of the cavern.

"I wasn't expecting a jungle up here," Cassidy said.

"Must be all this damned water," Sundance replied, plucking a flower the size of his fist. "These sure don't look like the same plants that live on the plains. The Incas must have brought them in from wherever they came from."

Cassidy wondered about that. Generally, you needed insects for plants to grow this well, but he couldn't detect the telltale buzzing in the cavern.

He pushed past the plants until they thinned out, then turned back. "We're gonna need light in here."

"I've got some flint in my pack," Sundance said. "But I'm not going down to the horses for a lantern."

"No need," Cassidy replied. He dug under the plants and pulled out some thick branches. They lit a branch inside, out of the rain. It burned slowly. "That should work."

They each took a few extra small branches for tender and placed them in their belts. Thus armed, they pushed further into the cavern.

"No one has been in here in ages," Cassidy said, pushing aside a wall of cobwebs.

"Good," Sundance replied. "More for us."

The foliage around the cave mouth appeared to serve as a filter that kept the outside humidity from the inside of the cave. The air against Cassidy's cheeks felt completely dry. Then he stopped, staring at the flame. "You know what?"

"What?"

"The wind is blowing the wrong way."

"How would you know which way the wind should blow in a cave?" the Kid asked.

"It was blowing inward, from the sea, remember? And now, it's blowing from the inside."

"As long as it's blowing from a big pile of gold, I don't care."

Like the path, the cave floor was well-worn, but unlike the path, this one wound its way downward.

Finally, the tunnel opened into a wider cavern too big for their guttering, makeshift lanterns to illuminate. They saw only large shapes and the impression of a roof high overhead.

"No stalactites," Sundance noted.

"I think this is a different kind of cave," Cassidy replied. "More like a crack in the stone than something made by water."

They advanced a few steps deeper into the cave. Something crunched under Cassidy's foot. He brought the torch down for a closer look and saw that he had crushed a skull.

"We're in the right place, at least," he said. "I've already found some of the dead people."

"Good. Now let's find all that gold."

Bones skittered as they kicked them out of the way. A large slab of stone with a flat top blocked their advance. When Cassidy shone his light on it, he saw that the white rock was discolored by dark stains. He shuddered and walked around the stone.

Beyond the altar the cavern continued, still strewn with remains. Sundance stepped up to one of the walls. "Look at this."

Cassidy walked over. "What?"

"This wall isn't solid." He moved his torch closer until Cassidy saw long, ruler-straight cracks that ran along the walls, with stone wedges jamming a portion of rock into place. "Help me pull this out. They probably put the gold back there."

They gripped the nearest wedge and, by dint of pushing it one way and the other, managed to pull it out. The stone didn't budge, so they went after the next one.

Four wedges later, the slab crashed to the ground, barely missing their toes as they jumped out of the way.

"Nice," Sundance said as he peered inside the niche in the wall exposed by the missing stone. "Looks like we won't be having any more money trouble with Gómez."

The torchlight reflected off yellow gold: jewelry, tiny figurines, even little discs that looked like coins. There was perhaps a double handful of treasure in the niche, piled neatly at the feet of a desiccated corpse.

Cassidy studied its features. "I've heard of this," he said. "The dry air inside these mountains dries out the bodies and mummifies them. This one looks like it just got really old and never died."

"Who cares?" Sundance said. He scooped the gold into a leather sack and moved to the next set of wedges.

Over a backbreaking few hours, with occasional breaks to get more kindling for their makeshift torches, they pulled down a dozen stone slabs and harvested the treasure within.

"I think we've got enough," Cassidy said, hefting his sack. "We can always come back for more."

"Look." The Kid pointed. "Let's just open that one. It looks bigger than the rest, and someone drew a bunch of things on it. It's got to be special."

"I guess," Cassidy replied.

This one wasn't wedged shut but actually mortared, and they spent an hour chipping away the cement with chunks of stone until, with a monumental crash, the big slab, too, fell to the floor.

A cloud of dust obscured the interior of the larger niche and they waited impatiently for the treasure to be revealed. If the smaller ones had held a fortune, what might be in here?

"Now that's a sight you don't see every day," Sundance said.

"Not unless you're a guard at some museum back East," Cassidy replied.

There were no necklaces or bracelets at the corpse's feet, no shiny discs, but just a filigreed gold base with an enormous blood-red ruby at the very top.

As Sundance reached out to take it, Cassidy's eyes were drawn to the stone slab that had covered the larger niche. This one hadn't broken when it fell, and he saw lines, parallel lines, gouged into it.

Four lines, worn through the rock as if by the action, during centuries, of...

"Don't touch that!" Cassidy said.

Sundance turned towards him. "Don't worry, Butch, You know we always share and share alike. I'm not planning on taking it for myself."

With that, his fist closed around the gold base and he lifted it from the dusty shelf that was the niche.

A keening sound filled the cave, a noise like the screams of a dying horse, except magnified...loud enough to fill the whole colossal cavern.

Cassidy dropped the bag and put his hands over his ears. Sundance did the same but removed one hand to point at the niche.

The mummified body was sitting up, pushing itself upright with hands that, Cassidy saw, had fingers that were worn down to the knuckles, where white bone could be seen.

That was what had made the marks on the rock slab. That thing trying to get out.

And now they'd liberated it.

The screaming — Cassidy realized it came from the dead man climbing down from the niche — died down. He and Sundance stepped back slowly, keeping their eyes on the monster.

As they moved away, the Sundance Kid bent over to pick up the ruby.

"You know it's probably that stone it's coming for," Cassidy said, as he risked a quick glance back to avoid tripping on anything behind them.

"Yeah, well it ain't getting it," the Kid shot back. "Not unless it finds a six shooter and gets the draw on me."

The cave was suddenly alive with rustling noises. Cassidy tensed involuntarily, because the sound reminded him of bats. Or maybe the other bodies were coming awake. "I don't think a dead thing needs a six shooter," he replied.

"We'll see about that." Sundance lowered his hand to his hip, pulled his gun out of its holster, aimed carefully at the creature shambling towards them and shot it in the forehead.

A look of utter confusion crossed the mummy's face.

Then it fell into a heap on the ground and, once again, the partners were covered with dust as it disintegrated.

"I wouldn't breathe that stuff if I was you," Sundance said.

Cassidy was already moving. He grabbed his bag and the burning stick from the ground and said, "I'm not staying here another minute. I don't know what that thing was, but I'm not looking to find another one."

"I reckon you're right," Sundance said.

They started for the exit, but stopped in their tracks. Gigantic red ants poured down the ramp in a living river.

Cassidy tried to stomp through them, but his boot disappeared to the ankle and the ants swarmed up. He jumped away and removed the ants by passing the burning stick along the leather. When it was clear, he realized the boot was gouged and thinned.

"The other way!" he yelled. "They can eat through leather."

They ran back into the large chamber, followed by the ants, but the insects didn't follow them. Instead, they flowed into the open niches.

Still, more of them poured in.

"Those dead guys aren't going to hold them very long," Cassidy said. "We need to find another way out."

"I'm right behind you," Sundance said.

They ran into the depths of the cave and burst through an old cloth curtain which dissolved with their passage. Cassidy tried to stop, but his boot slipped on the polished stone and he plunged headlong into a black abyss.

For about two feet.

A strong hand grabbed his upper arm and, using his own momentum, swung him back along the ledge and onto the rock.

"Thanks," Cassidy said.

"Now we're even," the Kid replied.

"Even?"

"Yeah, for that time you pulled me onto your horse back in Mercedes."

"What about the time—"

The old argument stopped dead as a roar filled the chamber.

"The hell..." Cassidy said when the echo died down.

"How should I know? But we can't go back."

"We'd better. Look."

Deep in the darkness below, where their light barely reached, shadows folded upon themselves, blackness on deeper black.

"What's that?"

"It's big, that's what it is," Cassidy replied. "And I think it's getting closer."

No sooner had the words left his mouth than a deep whoosh sounded as a cylinder ten feet across shot upward in front of them, occupying most of the shaft.

Then it bent and Cassidy found himself looking into the twin of the ruby the Sundance Kid had pulled from the largest of the tombs.

He stepped away and realized the stone was an eye, set into an elongated head of golden scales. The line of a mouth, with two protruding fangs suddenly gaped open, and an enormous bifurcated tongue lashed out at him.

A giant snake with a ruby for an eye...*and very much alive.*

Cassidy stumbled back out of the way and kept going in reverse as fast as he could. He half turned onto his hands and knees and stood...then shouted: "Run!"

"I'm way ahead of you, partner." Sundance showed Cassidy a pair of heels as they made their escape. "Did you see the snake's wings?" he yelled.

"I was too busy avoiding the mouth!" came the reply.

They ran back the way they'd come, through the original enormous cavern.

Suddenly, several bright lanterns illuminated them.

"Hold it right there," a voice said. "Cassidy and Sundance, you'd better put your hands in the air. There's eight of us and we've all got the draw on you."

"Who are you?" Cassidy said, holding his hands above his head and dropping the sack he'd been holding.

"I work for the Pinkerton Detective Agency," the man replied. "And I've been trying to track you boys down for almost a year."

"Gómez sold us out," Cassidy swore.

Sundance, his hands also over his head, spat. "What happened to the ants?" he said.

"What ants?"

"This place was covered with red ants. Big mean things," Cassidy explained.

"They're not here. What are those noises?"

The sound of the colossal snake working its way through the thin choke point was getting louder.

"We don't know," Sundance lied.

"And what's that in your hand?" the agent said.

Sundance shrugged. "Some kind of stone. I don't think it's worth much."

"Yeah, right. Toss it over here, real slow," the Pinkerton said.

Cassidy saw Sundance tense. He whispered, "Do it. Trust me on this, and do it now."

"They're gonna shoot us," Sundance replied.

Sundance was probably right. Those posters always said 'Dead or Alive' and they meant it. It was much easier to shoot two fugitives than to drag them along alive. It was bad enough when you only had to go as far as the next town, but when you were stuck way down in the wilds of Bolivia, that made it infinitely worse.

Suddenly, a second group of figures appeared behind the Pinkerton and his assistants. In the dim light, these seemed to be animated lumps of clay with skin whose exterior moved around.

No, not skin. They were covered with ants…and Cassidy suspected he knew exactly who they were.

One of the assistants yelled when he realized what was behind them. At the same time, Cassidy heard a crash and the flutter of enormous wings.

"Throw the rock now!" he yelled at Sundance.

Sundance obeyed, letting the enormous ruby roll toward the Pinkerton. "Thank you," the man said, bending down to pick it up.

That was the signal they needed. Without even having to discuss it, Cassidy dove to his right while Sundance jumped to the left.

Only one of the Pinkerton's helpers let fly with his gun; but it was just as well that they'd gotten out of the way, because countless tons of winged snake drove through the space they'd just vacated and bowled over men and ant-men indiscriminately. Unlike the tight confines of the passageway behind them, here in the cavern, the serpent had room to maneuver.

It coiled back on itself and struck at one of the Pinkerton's helpers. Huge jaws opened and closed like a bear trap — operating so quickly that only the bottom half of the man remained after they snapped shut. The lantern the man had been holding rolled away, miraculously unbroken.

Cassidy stayed behind a solid rock, possibly another altar. The size of the serpent meant that it wouldn't take only the mouth to kill you — if the tail happened to slam into you, you would be crushed.

Everyone else, both the ant-covered mummies and the detective's posse forgot about everything except the snake. Shots rang out in the cavern, and one of the mummy men managed to climb onto the snake's neck, attempting to make its way to the head. The winged reptile thrashed and roared.

"You all right?" he shouted to the Kid.

The Kid laughed. He always laughed when things got really exciting. "Yeah, I'm good. Watch this."

He stepped into the open and took a bead on one of the Pinkerton's men. The shot flew true and the guy dropped.

"Stop that. They're fighting our war for us! Let them distract the snake. We need to make a run for it."

"I want to take down that Pinkerton," Sundance retorted. "He's not going to stop."

"You're going to get us killed," Cassidy said. "There's another way out of the cavern back there. We should go while the going's good."

Screams made it impossible to hear Sundance's reply, but the Kid moved towards the Pinkerton and the serpent as opposed to the exit.

Cassidy sighed and followed.

Suddenly, Sundance cursed and dropped to the ground, holding his right arm. Cassidy ran over.

"What happened?"

"Someone must have shot a chunk out of a rock and it flew into my arm. Look." He handed Cassidy a shard of stone with a dark edge where it had cut into his skin.

"Don't whine," Cassidy said. "You should have followed me. Besides, I've seen you take a bullet to the leg and not even blink."

"Yeah…well this one surprised me." He stood, tucking his shirt into his pants, and stared at the fight. "You know…that dragon is going to kill them pretty quick. How about we slow it down?"

"You want to help the Pinkerton?" Cassidy asked.

"Not really. I just want the fight to last long enough to cover our retreat."

Cassidy shrugged and they both emptied their six-shooters into the serpent's back, right where the wings met the scales. The snake, which had been fighting in an upright position, held up by its wings, collapsed onto the ground and attacked from below. The mummy on its head, however, was thrown off and, when it hit the floor, collapsed into a million ants.

They ran back to the rear of the cavern and along the ramp that circumnavigated the huge hole in the ground. The bottom smelled like the vilest sewer they could imagine but, by dint of following the breeze, they found a small crack they could slip though, which opened up into a cave and deposited them at the base of the mountain, on the eastern side.

Daybreak was already turning the morning pink when they finally arrived at their horses, which had been joined by those of the posse. The Indian guard the Pinkerton had left behind was asleep at his post, so they tied and gagged him and took all the horses and supplies back the way they'd come.

The two friends rode into the sunset and Cassidy said softly, "I reckon we should ride south for a bit. Somewhere the Incas didn't go. Did you manage to bring the bag along?"

"No, I dropped it when that cursed Pinkerton appeared."

Cassidy grunted. "Me, too. But these horses should help us defray some of the cost. So you won't need that ruby."

Sundance rode for a few moments in silence. "You saw that?"

"Of course. That little stone chip didn't drop you. You dove to grab the rock. Then you hid it in your pants."

"It's worth more than all that gold put together," Sundance replied petulantly.

"Yes. But that big snake wants its other eye back. It will chase you all over the world for it, and I reckon now that we broke whatever Inca magic was keeping it controlled, it won't take long to get out of that cave and come after us."

"You're saying I have to give the stone up?"

Cassidy shook his head. "I'd never tell you what to do. I'm just saying that, while you've got that rock, I'm not riding with you. So we'll divvy up these here horses and go our separate ways until you cash in that rock. I don't fancy my chances against that flying serpent thing."

Sundance rode in silence for some steps. "You know we'd have a better chance if it was two of us."

"It won't be two of us."

This time, the silence was much longer, and at the end of it, Sundance reached into his pocket and pulled out the stone. He looked at the way the sun glistened redly in its facets, then sighed and threw it out into the scrub, as far as he could.

Cassidy smiled and they rode on.

The Hills Had a Heartbeat
Trevor Denning

"What did they tell you about me?"

I reached into my vest pocket and unfolded a paper. "Cole Remus: Wanted for murder," I read. "Dead or alive. Reward $500." I turned it so he could see the drawing. "That's you," I said. "In my line of work, that's about all I need to know."

I'd been on Remus's trail for three weeks before cornering him near Cheyanne. He was a big, ugly hombre, but didn't put up much of a fight.

Across the fire my prisoner laughed and rattled his chains. "Looks just like me, don't it? If you was wondering, I tore a man's throat out with my teeth." He chuckled, low, more like a growl. "You ever taste human blood?"

I shrugged and averted my eyes. He laughed again, this time at me.

"Nope," I said. "Had horsemeat once. Too sweet for my taste." If he wanted to rattle me like his chains, well, it worked. I tried not to let it show. "We'll just have pork and beans tonight."

I pushed the tins closer to the flames, being careful not to look directly at the fire. Beyond the trees of our encampment there were things that I might need to see.

Remus took a deep breath in through his nose and let it out again with a loud, "Hoo-eeh! Gonna be a full moon tonight." I ignored him. "You know what that means, bounty man?"

"Name's Chris Pryce, and I reckon it means it'll be a little brighter this night than most. Now shut up and eat." I'd collected bounties on all kinds of men and never cared for conversating with them. They were the means to my personal payroll, not new friends. "We move at sunup." I turned so that I could keep an eye on the snake without looking over the fire, and ate.

My prisoner slurped noisily, letting bean juice dribble down his beard. "Why're you taking in me alive, anyway?"

"Dead isn't my way," I said. "You get a reputation for always bringing in your man across the saddle instead of on it, and things get harder in the long run. Next fella might put up more of a fight." It wasn't purely practical, of course. For some men, killing is as easy as breathing. To my mind, life and death had too much value for me to weigh out. "Could make an exception for you, though. Don't think I won't if you give me trouble."

The manacles clanked as Remus stood.

I raised my revolver. "Remus, what do you think you're doing?"

"You want me to piss in the fire?"

"Fine, go over there. Just know I'll have this gun on you." He turned away from the circle of firelight toward the brush. "That's far enough." The moon cut a silver light through the trees and he deliberately stepped into a patch of the eerie glow. His shoulders jerked with a loud snap of muscle and bone, his head went down.

And he started to swell.

I scrambled to my feet. "Hey, what're you doing?"

He continued to twist and grow, making ungodly noises. Looking up to the sky, he let loose with a howl, his face was gone and in its place was the muzzle of a wolf. I didn't think. I shot. My bullets tore into the tattered clothes that still hung from his oversized body. All it did was get his attention, and that's when I realized I'd made a grave mistake.

I didn't want his attention.

Remus turned to face me, half man and half wolf. The part of him that was man smiled as he snapped his chains. Before I knew it, he lunged and hit me like a runaway train. I dropped my gun as I instinctively reached to hold him at arm's length. All I could think about was what he'd said about ripping out the other man's throat, so I made sure to protect mine.

People have said that I fight like a wildcat, and that night I scrapped like never before or since. His fingers, now claws, raked my sides and I felt the blood flow. The horses screamed and stamped as we rolled into them and back towards the fire. Remus snarled. I swore. I kicked and thrashed, trying to get on top so I could smash his skull against a rock or log. There was grit in my eyes. He was on top of me, pushing my head toward the glowing coals.

With a twist and a shove, a wrestling trick I'd picked up, I flipped Remus into the flames. The smell of burning hair hit my nose as he howled in pain. I got up as best I could in case he came at me again, only making it to one knee. But Remus jumped up from the fire, clothes and pelt still aflame, and ran like a torch into the woods. I tried to take a step after him, fell, and everything went black.

~*~

I heard later I was out for three days. When I finally came to, my head and torso were wrapped, and my whole everything hurt. "Ugh," I groaned.

"Look who's back from the dead." It was an old man's voice. "How do you feel?"

Prying a swollen eye open, I looked at him. White stubble covered a fleshy face under a bowler hat. The man looked tired, but gave an impish grin. I tried to speak but my tongue was too dry. After the old man held a canteen to my mouth and the cobwebs cleared out, I tried again. "Feels like I was on the wrong side of a horse in a stampede."

The old guy chuckled. "I'll bet. Not everyone who tangles with a loup garou is so lucky." He pulled a kettle from the fire. "It ain't coffee, but it'll take the chill off."

I nodded, realizing I was cold. It was morning. "What did you say?" I asked, pulling myself upright.

"Loup garou," he said, handing me a mug. I recognized the smell of chicory and sipped. "They go by all kinds of names, but that's what I call 'em. Good move throwing him into the fire like you did. It's the only thing they can't tolerate, and his trail is how I found you." He chuckled again. "Sorry, I'm forgetting my manners. Name's Louis."

"Mighty obliged." The hot drink seemed to loosen my stiff joints. "I'm Chris Pryce, and this chicory almost has me feeling human again."

"I see you're a man of taste." He got up with a groan and ambled over to a buckboard. A book lay where he'd been sitting. "I'll whip up some bacon and biscuits that'll have us back on our feet in no time."

I nodded. "What'cha reading there?" Unless it was a family Bible, in this part of the country you still didn't see many books. It was hard to tell from where I lay, but it didn't look like any Bible. Back home we'd had readers in school, which I'd always enjoyed, and whatever Louis had wasn't one of those either.

"Oh, that?" Louis said, squatting next to the smoky fire. He chuckled. "I won it from a riverboat gambler before coming out this way. He must not have thought much of it, because I'm no hand at cards." He was quiet for a moment while bacon sizzled. "You know much about ancient Egypt, Mr. Pryce?"

"Only what I heard in Sunday school," I admitted.

"That's about all I knew myself, to be honest." Louis cleared his throat. "According to that book, the Egyptians were pretty busy folk. They sailed ships across the ocean and traded with the friendly tribes 'round here. They wrapped their dead in cloth and buried them with treasure to have in their afterlife." He stopped to flip the bacon, wincing as the hot grease bit at his arm. "That book there is the journal of a fellow who claims to have found one of them pha-raohs with all his treasure buried in a cave out this way."

"You reckon it's still there?" I asked, not really interested. It sounded like a fool's errand to me. People had been searching these hills for gold for years, though this was the first time I'd heard of buried treasure.

Louis chuckled. "I aim to find out. From what he wrote, the fella left it intending to come back later with wagons and a crew, but he took sick and didn't make it. Thought mebbe it was a curse. Can you believe that? At any rate, I found a map stitched in the back cover." He squinted at me. "Could use a hand if you're game. I'll give you a percentage of whatever we find."

I just shook my head. "The offer is appreciated," I said. "But I hunt bounties, not treasure."

"Uh-huh." Louis passed me a tin plate of food. "I see how that's working out. After tangling with a loup garou you still gonna say that anything ain't impossible?" He chewed thoughtfully. "It'll be a while 'fore you're ready to hit the trail again and catch anyone. In the meantime, why not go after something that won't fight back?"

Well, he had me there.

"What do you say?" Louis asked. "Partner?"

~*~

When I was ready we found the river and followed it northeast. Louis consulted his book and map, sometimes letting me look at them. It was the journal of someone named Goodnight, and he must have been one of the first white men to explore the area over a hundred years ago. On the one hand, it seemed like any treasure would have been found by now. But on the other, if a tomb filled with gold and jewels had been dug up, I figured I'd have heard something about it.

The journal was written after old Goodnight took ill, and before he died he must have done some research back east. Between what he learned from the locals and whatever history books he read, Goodnight believed that he'd come across the final resting place of some Egyptian name of Hor Ko-Tep, who sailed here after the death of his sweetheart. By the time he got here he must have felt better, because he fell in love with the chief's daughter. But before he could take her as his wife another tribe attacked.

In the scuffle, his Indian princess was killed, Hor Ko-Tep died of a twice-broken heart, and his kinsmen buried them together with all the treasure he carried, which Goodnight claimed was considerable. Before the other Egyptians sailed home they told the Indians that if anyone entered the tomb he'd die of a wasting disease. Goodnight was warned, didn't listen, and believed he'd suffered the consequences. Not that Louis was too concerned.

Louis didn't seem like the sort of man who concerned himself with much. From what I gathered as we rode, he'd been raised in the swamps of the deep south. "I've seen and heard things out there that would turn your hair white," he said. During the war he'd run guns, but lost all his money betting on the wrong side. "Except for winning that journal, if I didn't have bad luck I wouldn't have any luck at all." So, like many others, he'd packed up and moved west to start over.

"I reckon we must be getting close," Louis said one night. "Mebbe tomorrow."

Before I could agree, something went crashing through the woods and I jumped. Ever since I'd tangled with Remus I'd been a little edgy after dark. Without realizing it, I was on my feet, gun drawn, searching the darkness for the cause of the sound. When nothing happened, I forced myself to sit down again.

Louis chuckled. "You're not wrong."

"About what?"

"That fella Remus has been following right along," he said. "I've seen him a couple times, when he thought I wasn't looking."

I tried to keep my hand from shaking around my mug and took a slow sip. "Is he still a wolf?" Once I'd caught him as a man. If I could keep my nerve — and if there were limits on when he could turn into a wolf — I might stand a chance.

"Mebbe, mebbe not." Louis shrugged. "They say the longer he's a loup garou the easier he can switch between man and wolf. At first it just happens when there's a full moon, but it tends to only come on folks that are already bad all the way through. They like being the monster and learn to control it. Really, it's the monster controlling them."

~*~

"Halt." Two of the craziest dressed men I ever saw blocked our path. They had dark suits and matching neckties, which wasn't too odd for city folk. Only we were days from civilization. More odd, both men had white sashes with gold embroidery like girls who'd just won a pageant. "Turn back now, or we will exercise violence," the tall one said. His accent was difficult to understand, but the meaning was clear.

We'd been traveling hard all day, thinking we were closer than we were, and I was beat. Violence isn't my way, but this guy was just about asking for some. Before I could say anything I'd regret, Louis leaned forward from his seat on the buckboard. "Sorry, we didn't mean to intrude. But I reckon you all found something interesting in a cave down there. Mind if we take a look?" He pushed his bowler up and squinted at them. "Can't be no harm in that."

The spokesman lifted his rifle. "Turn back right now."

But Louis wasn't ready to give up just yet. "Now you boys don't get too excited. I'm just gonna reach down and show you something." He pulled out his trump card. "I got some information here that might interest you. This here is the Goodnight journal. Mebbe you've heard of it?" I watched carefully, in case they had any ideas of taking it by force.

I needn't have worried. The tall guard, obviously the leader, looked at the other man. "You stay here. I'll take them to see Lord Kensington." They stepped aside and he motioned for us to follow him. "Lord Kensington is the authority on Egyptology and leader of this expedition. You'll share your information with him."

"Happy to help," Louis said placidly. I didn't believe him. I doubt the guard did either.

We followed a trail down into a canyon. From the looks of it, plenty of heavy wagons had passed through recently. Their camp was about the strangest thing I ever saw, though I had to admire their tents and banners with designs at sharp angles. There were unlit torches ready for nightfall. Unusual, but not unwarranted if they wanted them. I wondered why they'd bothered hauling so much frilly nonsense up into the mountains. The cave mouth had another pair of guards posted next to more torches. I didn't see anyone coming in or out, and counted fifteen men.

Lord Kensington met us like he'd expected our intrusion. "Hello gentlemen, always nice to meet the locals." His sash was green, with a white shirt to match his hair and mustache. Little spectacles glinted in the waning sunlight. "I expect you have justification for being here. Let's go inside and talk."

He led us to a big canvas tent with the flaps pinned back, where we took seats and introduced ourselves. That settled, Louis lifted the book and Kensington's eyes lit up. He quickly related Goodnight's story and what he'd learned about Hor Ko-Tep. "Rumor is you're headed into a world of trouble. Now, I don't know that I believe in curses, but I thought you should know."

"Psh!" Kensington waved away the comment. "I'm a man of science. We don't believe in curses. Still," he paused and smoothed his mustache with barely concealed excitement, "that is quite interesting."

I leaned back in my chair and studied the Englishman, trying to decide how far I trusted or could throw him. I'd never met a world traveler before, so I figured he wouldn't be like you and me. Anyone who'd bother bringing all those banners and torches along either had to be a little crazy or have a darn good reason, and I couldn't quite pin down which.

"Aside from the aforementioned curse," Louis was saying, "Goodnight mentioned two sections to the cave. The first was the treasure room, so's to speak. He went in there. The other half was sealed off, but he figured it's the tomb of Hor Ko-Tep and his Indian bride. I take it you boys are just getting started?"

"Yes, we just arrived yesterday from the north."

Coming from the other direction was why our paths hadn't crossed. So far nothing seemed off, except why the guards? I figured I might as well just come out and ask. "You expecting trouble, Kensington?"

"Hm?" he mumbled, lost in thought. "Would you like to see the cave?"

There was a sudden shriek followed by a volley of gunshots. We rushed outside to see what all the commotion was about. Some of the guards were waving their rifles around, not seeing a target. The shorter guard, the one left to watch the trail we'd come in on, lay in the dirt. Dead. His throat was torn out so his head was only just hanging on.

"What happened?" Kensington barked.

One of the men ran off to vomit. Another took a deep breath and spoke. "Something—" he choked. "Something threw Fitzroy into the camp from up there." He pointed toward the trees that hung over the canyon. "I don't...I just don't know."

"Remus," I said. Louis nodded.

"An associate of yours?" Kensington asked.

I shook my head. "Not exactly, no."

A long howl echoed off the hills and sent a tremor through my limbs.

"What was that?" Could be Kensington had been around enough to know that wasn't a regular wolf. "And what does it want?"

"Well, Mr. Kensington," I said, pushing back my hat. "I reckon he wants me. Remus has been following our back trail ever since we had a tussle that ended in a draw." I figured the man of science wouldn't take any stock in what Louis had told me, but I believed it now more than ever. "I do apologize for involving you."

Kensington glared at me. "Nothing to be done for it now." Turning to the tall guard, he said, "Shefford, we need to get started. Tonight." The other man started to object and was cut off. "The stars are fine. Light the torches and make things ready. We will do what we came for and, should we survive the night, vacate in the morning."

"Yes, sir." The guard called Shefford walked away and started giving orders.

~*~

While the men worked, Kensington took us up to the cave. "Before we go in, I'm afraid I have some unfortunate news. All the treasure, as you might expect, is long gone. I wouldn't be surprised if one of Goodnight's party came back after he took ill."

Louis sighed. "Probably so."

Pausing, Kensington gave me a long look. "Why are you here, Mr. Pryce? I'm here for research, and your friend for treasure. Before I show you the tomb, I need to know. What do you want?"

I considered. "When Louis found me I was half dead and in no condition to go after Remus. But Louis got me back on my feet and invited me along, and I agreed. I'm just here to see things through."

"Very good, then." He lifted a lit torch and led us to what could only be the entrance to the burial chamber. It was sealed by a slab of rock, with something that looked like wax or pitch holding it in place. There were drawings painted on the stone of men with animal heads and what I assumed was writing. "I was working on translation when you arrived, but now that you've told me what Goodnight said it's perfectly clear. These inscriptions tell the same story, along with the curse.

"Furthermore," Kensington went on, "I need to clarify something. Though I am a man of science, I believe there are things that are as of yet unknown and thus only perceptible as, well, magic." I had no idea where he was going with this speech. But as someone who had just survived an attack by a man-wolf, I couldn't disagree. Louis gave me a look and he shrugged, clueless as I was.

"You aren't the only one with a book," Kensington said, lifting something as big as a Bible from a table. "This is the translation of a very ancient text written by Egyptian priests. It contains the secret of eternal life, a ritual to bring back Hor Ko-Tep from the dead. Tonight I shall take their role and perform the experiment. This will be a great moment of scientific discovery, and you shall be my witnesses."

My innards gathered up in a cold knot. "Kensington, seems I recall the good book saying that man is appointed to die once and face his judgment. Seems to me tampering with that is a bit misguided."

Kensington waved away my thoughts like so many gnats. "There's nothing misguided about my work. Unlocking the secrets of life and overcoming death is the purpose of science."

"Either way," Louis said, "I don't imagine he'll be too happy to wake up and find his supplies gone. Happened to me a time or two, so I would know."

Before he could respond, Shefford came in carrying a white robe. "Everything is prepared, your lordship," he said, helping Kensington into his outfit. "Whenever you're ready."

Kensington nodded. "If you will all excuse me, I need a moment alone."

Outside it was dark, but all the torches were lit and the flickering light cast weird shadows on the canyon walls and trees far above us. Most of the men had put on robes and stood at attention in two rows either side of the cave. Somewhere a drum beat a low, steady tattoo as if the hills had a heartbeat. *Dum, dum dum!* Out in the darkness Remus howled, causing a momentary hitch in the rhythm. Silently, I cursed the torches that blinded me to everything beyond their light.

Louis and I drifted off to the side where we figured we'd be out of the way. "This is some bad juju," he whispered. I agreed. But neither of us tried to leave. Something about the ceremony kept us there, and would have even without Remus stalking the darkness. "What do you reckon will happen?" he asked.

"Nothing good." A tremendous crash echoed from the cave and sent out a cloud of dust, which showed golden in the firelight. Maybe it was a trick of the flickering flames, but I could have sworn it looked for a moment like a face. A strong gust of air pushed the cloud up into the sky with a loud rush that blew my hat off my head. "Nope," I muttered. "Nothing good at all."

"You thinking what I'm thinking?" Louis said.

"What's that?"

Louis mopped his face with a handkerchief. "In order for that dust cloud to come out, the slab blocking off the burial chamber must've fallen this a'way."

"You mean...?" I trailed off, not wanting to say it.

"It got pushed from *his* side."

I put a hand on my gun.

The moment I touched iron two things happened at once. Remus in wolf form crashed into a line of guards, slashing and snarling, and Kensington shrieked and ran from the cave. Blood running down his face, he stumbled and fell to his knees. Everything was chaos, and I admit I didn't know which way to run myself. And that's when Remus turned my direction. I knew bullets couldn't hurt him, but I emptied all six rounds in him anyway as he came at me.

For as long as I'd dreaded and feared that moment, now that it was here I was calm. Like I said, never show fear. Whatever he was, the men he'd killed deserved justice and if I couldn't take him in, well, maybe I could still set things right. I held my ground and let Remus come. Everything else faded into the back. I focused on his eyes. I waited for that moment you can't see so much as sense before an attack.

I was so focused on Remus I didn't see Kensington until he ran into my side. "I can't see," he shouted to no one in particular. All the blood on his face, I noticed, came from his eyes.

The second I took my attention off him Remus lunged. I pushed Kensington back and braced myself for another fight with the loup garou. But just before he reached me Louis swung one of the torches like an ax. It exploded in a shower of sparks, and Remus fell back on his haunches.

"Don't just stand there," Louis said, "get going!"

Maybe we could get our backs to the cave and take our stand. I grabbed Kensington and moved that way and froze. A second monster stood before us, better than seven feet tall and wrapped in bandages from head to toe, even over its face. One of the panicked men ran too close and got swatted away by a massive arm. I heard his bones shatter as he flew from sight.

"Not that way," I said through gritted teeth. I spun back and saw Remus back on his feet. I cursed. Louis stepped up beside me, now holding a fresh torch that he pointed at Remus like a spear. Kensington crumpled as I tried to hold him upright, though it was no use. "Now what?"

Hor Ko-Tep — because who else could it be? — let loose with a hollow roar. "UGH!" Everyone froze and it even drew Remus's attention. His lips curled back with a fresh snarl. You might think I lost my senses but I swear it's true, I heard Hor Ko-Tep's voice in my head and understood the meaning of his words. "*ANUBIS,*" he said. "*YOU WILL NOT RETURN ME TO THE UNDERWORLD.*"

Throwing his head back, Remus howled and charged. Hor Ko-Tep tried to bat him away as he had the first man, but Remus's jaws clamped down on the arm and held fast. His opponent tried to wrap his free hand around the loup garou's neck. Remus let go and raked his claws down Hor Ko-Tep's face. The bandages shredded, revealing gray skin that seemed molded from clay and eyes blacker than the pits of hell.

I reloaded my gun, not sure what use it would be but knowing it was useless empty. Hell itself had broken loose, as men screamed and the creatures clashed. Over the din I heard someone shout, "It's their fault!" It was Shefford, pointing in our direction. "They brought the wolf. They ruined the ceremony."

To my mind there were bigger problems, like what happened after either Remus or Hor Ko-Tep bested the other. But it seemed the growing circle of men was most upset with us. To our backs the combatants raged, while an angry human mob stood before us. "Well, ain't that something," I said.

I heard the loud snap of breaking bone and Remus scream in agony. I turned just in time to see Hor Ko-Tep holding the broken body over his head before casting it aside. "That won't take," Louis said. "But it might buy us some time."

"Kill the outsiders," Kensington ordered from where he lay at my feet.

Louis waved another torch. I lifted my pistol and the men raised their guns. We were hopelessly outnumbered, but you can't win a surrender. Most of them didn't look like real fighting men and I prayed a drawn gun would give them pause. Besides, they couldn't let loose on us without hitting their leader.

"Kill them!" Kensington shrieked.

Hor Ko-Tep started to chant aloud in a gravely whisper that unnerved us all. He stood, gray and terrible at the mouth of his black tomb, arms uplifted to the starry night. Balls of red hot fire appeared between the stars, growing larger as they drew near. The first one stuck Kensington's tent, sending it up in a torrent of flame. Soon there were more, striking the ground with earth-shattering explosions.

The mob scattered and tried to take cover. But where do you run when the sky is your enemy?

Remus came bounding from the shadows, recovered and oblivious in his rage. He slammed into Hor Ko-Tep's midsection and they both fell back into the tomb. Either by accident or fate, the wolf-man sent the dead back where he belonged. My feet were rooted where I stood, and it was a moment before I noticed Louis shaking me. "This way," he said, pointing at the canyon wall. I took no pity on Kensington and left him to his fate.

Before I took two steps someone grabbed my arm, nearly jerking me off my feet. "Hold it," he said. My fist was in motion before I knew who it was. I only realized when it struck that the man was Shefford. Not that it would have mattered. Even in the moment, I recall feeling a strong sense of satisfaction.

From the safety of the rock wall, Louis and I watched. Hor Ko-Tep must have thrown Remus again, because he came sailing out of the cave. One of the fireballs fell on him, and in a second he was nothing but ashes. I saw it happen. Another ball of flame hit just above the mouth of the cave, causing a landslide and once again sealing Hor Ko-Tep in his tomb.

Whether he's dead or alive, or something else altogether, I'll never know.

Louis and I ran to the buckboard, tied my horse on behind, and didn't stop moving until the encampment was nothing more than an orange stain at our backs. Once we were sure no one was following us, he reined in the horses. "Louis," I said, "if you didn't have bad luck…"

"I wouldn't have any at all." He laughed and pulled a whiskey bottle from under the seat. "But we've still got the skins on our teeth. That's something."

"Something is about right. You hear about any more treasure, though, keep me out of it. I'm going back to bringing in bounties." I accepted the bottle and took a long pull. "What's next for you?"

Everything we'd just seen hadn't dulled the impish glint in his eyes as he patted Goodnight's journal. "I intend to lose a hand of poker."

"Louis, with your luck you'll win the pot and be stuck with that thing forever. I'll collect a percentage the next time I see you."

The old man roared with laughter. "Fair enough, partner. Fair enough."

Birds of Prey
Stoney M. Setzer

Thunder boomed, shattering the quiet and shaking the ground. All of the ranch hands looked upward, only to see that the azure sky was perfectly clear.

Dan Harbin, the owner of the ranch, emerged from the house. He used to be the first one out to work in the morning, his work ethic setting the example for everyone else. Nowadays he was usually the last one out. "What was that?"

"Sounded like thunder, but not a cloud in the sky," remarked Clem, his brother and foreman. Dan might have been the boss in name, but Clem was the one the hands looked to for leadership. Everybody knew it except Dan himself.

"What was it, then?" Dan asked, his tone disinterested. His mind was somewhere else, just as it always was nowadays.

Another thunderclap boomed. Dan and Clem immediately turned and looked at each other. "The mines!" Dan exclaimed.

Clem nodded. "Dynamite! They're blasting!"

Dan shook his head. For just a moment, he was back to his old self, his old fire back in him. "Beats everything I've ever seen. Some fool says something about gold, and next thing you know…"

"Well, at least we get to be away from it for a few days when we have our next cattle drive," Clem remarked. "All right, men, back to work!"

"Uh, yeah, about that." Dan fidgeted noticeably as the other hands dispersed. "I think I'm gonna let you head up the cattle drive this time around. You're good enough to handle it, and I trust you."

Clem's jaw dropped. "Why am I not surprised?"

Whatever fire had flashed in Dan's countenance a moment ago was gone now, down to the last ember. "You can handle it," he repeated.

"How long are you gonna do this to yourself?"

"I don't know what you mean."

"Yeah, you do. Sylvia's gone, Dan. You've got every right to miss her, but sooner or later you've got to…"

"Hush your mouth, Clem. You don't know what it's like, you never having had…" Dan trailed off.

"Well," Clem said after a moment, "I think I need to run into town for a little bit." Not exactly a lie. He did need to go to town at some point in the day, but he hadn't originally planned on going right then — until just then.

"All right, I'll be out there with the men before too long," Dan said without looking at him. He was back in the house in the blink of an eye.

Heading out from the ranch, Clem could have sworn that he heard a loud noise — way off in the distance — one that sounded like an animal. The cry of a hawk, maybe. Seeing nothing in the sky, he thought nothing more of it.

~*~

The town was a bustling hive of people, as usual. Clem was usually one for doing his business and getting out as quickly as possible, but he didn't want to be in as much of a hurry today. If he came back too quickly, Dan might find some excuse to retreat back to the house. Staying away a little longer might force the big wheel to do some actual work for a change.

Unfortunately, he couldn't convince himself that it would really work out that way. Dan had loved Sylvia more than life itself, and it showed now that she was gone. Clem kept hoping that sooner or later he would recover, but it was as if Sylvia had taken part of Dan into the grave with her. Clem feared what he might return to if he stayed gone too long. Duty won out, and he hurried through his tasks as quickly as he could manage. Before long, he was back on his steed, riding back the way he came.

As he rode past the outer limits of the town, he saw a peddler's wagon approaching. In the driver's seat was a burly man with silver hair and a thick mustache. Curious, Clem slowed down as he approached and noticed the peddler doing the same. *Great, now he's going to try to sell me something*, he thought. Nevertheless, he decided to stop for a minute and hear the man out.

"Greetings!" the older man called. "Professor Obadiah Riddle, at your service!"

"Hey," Clem replied noncommittally. He wanted to ride away, but somehow he couldn't bring himself to. It was as if some unseen force was keeping him there. Not a force from without, but rather one from within.

"Funny thing," Riddle said. "I wasn't planning on coming out this way at all today, but I felt the Lord telling me that I needed to. Then I seldom stop for single riders outside of a town, and yet here I am. Somehow I suspect that this isn't exactly normal for you either."

"You're right about that, sir," Clem replied, feeling more unnerved than he could ever recall feeling.

Riddle nodded. "I suspect that this is a divine appointment, and now I think I might know why. How good of a shot are you, young man?"

"Pretty fair, I reckon."

Riddle descended from his wagon with surprising agility for a man of his girth. He reached into his wagon and produced a small wooden box. "I'm feeling led to give these to you, free of charge." He thrust the box into Clem's hands.

Slowly, Clem opened the box. It contained a Colt .45 and six bullets, but something looked different. These bullets seemed to shine even though the sun was not hitting them directly at this angle. It was almost as if they glowed from some inner luminescence. "Free?" he asked incredulously. "You can't mean it!"

"I do," the older man said. "Those are not just ordinary bullets. I can't say why, but somehow I suspect that you are going to need them, and very soon at that."

"Then why are you giving them away for free then? If these shopkeepers in town operated like that, they'd be out of business."

"I'm not one of those shopkeepers," Riddle replied with a hint of indignation. "I sell things, sure. I have to make a living, as you say. But this is different. I can't accept your money for those. They were given to me, and I am giving them to you. Now, go your way with them. I have other business elsewhere, please."

Clem tried to look casual despite his apprehension. "In other words, I have nothing to lose."

"Not if you accept those, no."

"All right, thank you."

Riddle raised an eyebrow at him. "Maybe you want to go ahead and load that? You never know."

"Huh? Oh, yeah. Thanks." Clem inserted six bullets in spite of his trepidation. Even as they went their separate ways, the strangeness of the encounter made Clem's hair stand up on end.

~*~

As the ranch came back into sight, Clem heard a sound that he could scarcely believe. "Whoa!" he commanded the horse as he strained to hear it again. It came again a moment later — the mooing of a cow, sounding much closer than the ranch itself. One must have gotten out somehow, perhaps unnoticed as of yet. Clem squinted, trying to spot it. A shadow passed on the ground — a bird of some sort, he supposed.

Two gunshots rang out, giving him pause. *Cattle rustlers,* he thought immediately. He reached for his Colt and was about to spur his horse forward when the cow let out another moo, urgent and frightened. This time the sound froze him with disbelief.

A cow mooing from ground level wasn't too peculiar. When it came from directly overhead, it was impossible to ignore. Clem looked up into the azure blue sky and immediately wished that he hadn't.

One of their cows had been stolen, but not by any human rustler. Flying overhead was a winged creature, carrying a cow like a hawk holds its prey. It must have been huge, for it seemed to dwarf the cow that it held. Another cry pierced the air, the same one that he heard just before he left the ranch. This time there could be no mistake that it came from the flying creature.

More shots rang out, with no effect on the bird. The cow let out one last moo, one that sounded horrifically painful, and then nothing. Either a bullet had struck it instead of its intended target, or else the bird had killed it.

That gunfire could have only come from one place, and the same was true for the cow. Shock gave way to terror, and Clem spurred his horse on, racing to the ranch.

All of the ranch hands were gathered outside, most of them brandishing rifles. Dan was in the midst of them. Looking beyond them, Clem tried to see if any more cattle were missing. From his vantage point, it was difficult to tell. He slowed as he approached, and everyone turned as one to look at him.

Dan pointed heavenward. "Clem! Did you see that…thing up in the sky?"

Clem nodded grimly. "Yeah. What happened?"

Dan looked out across the ranch hands for help, and Simmons, one of the older wranglers, spoke up.

"Started out with this crazy sound like a hawk, off in the distance. That's exactly what we thought it was at first, a hawk. Didn't think too much of it, really. It went on like that for a little while, and then we saw this big shadow moving across the ground, like some kind of a bird flying in front of the sun, only it was way too big for that.

"We all look up and see this big creature like nothing anybody's ever seen, just circling overhead like some overgrown buzzard. Saw right off that it must have been huge, because it's so high up and its shadow was covering the ground—"

"That's when they came and got me out here," Dan interjected. "I don't even know how to describe it. Them big old wings, more like a bat than a bird, but that body, I swear it looked more like an alligator than anything else. It hollered again, this loud, blood-curdling scream. I didn't like it one bit, and I told Bob and Marcus they'd better grab their shooting irons just in case."

Bob and Marcus? The two best marksmen on this ranch, and they still couldn't hit it? Clem thought. *Or what if they did hit it, and their bullets just didn't kill it?* He thought about the old man, Obadiah Riddle, and his gift but he held his tongue.

"Then it hollered again," Dan continued, "and then it attacked. Swooped right down and scooped up a cow like it was nothin'. Then another."

"It got more than one?" Clem exclaimed. Seeing one cow getting carried off was shocking enough, but knowing that wasn't the first one was alarming.

"Three so far. Quick as lightning, so quick you can't hardly…" Dan stopped as a gigantic shadow swept past, followed by a loud cry from overhead. "There it goes again! It's back! Somebody shoot that thing!"

Bedlam erupted as the men ran around in a panic, shouting at each other. Their voices were quickly drowned out by the screeches of the winged creature as it swooped in. Its passing generated a powerful wind that knocked down Clem and most of the other men. He spit out a mouthful of dirt as he watched the thing climb back high into the air.

"It'll be back!" Dan yelled. "That's just to stymie us!"

True to his prediction, the creature turned back around and swooped in once more. Marcus struggled back upright enough to take a shot at it and squeezed off a couple of rounds as Clem watched intently. There was no way Marcus could have missed, not given his skill and the size of the target. However, the bullets did nothing to stop it.

The bullets.

Clem fumbled for the revolver that Riddle had given him. By the time he was ready, the creature had already grabbed another cow and was flying off with it, slowed down by the weight of its prey. Hurriedly, he took aim and squeezed the trigger.

The creature screeched in pain as the bullet split one of its wings, almost severing half of it. Feverishly, it flapped its other wing, but the bullet had hampered its flying ability enough that it could not overcome the weight of the cow in its talons. Slowly, the creature descended back to the earth despite its best efforts. Once the cow's hooves touched the ground again, the talons opened releasing the cow, and the thing started to rise, slowly and erratically.

"Good shot! Hit it again!" somebody shouted. Bob aimed for its head. It was a perfectly placed shot, but it simply bounced off of its huge skull, as ineffective as throwing a pebble.

These bullets are the only ones that do any good against that thing! Clem realized.

Stepping forward, he took aim at the creature's head. There was a spurt of blood dark enough to pass for ink, and then the creature hit the ground with a thud powerful enough to shake the earth. Everyone waited a few minutes to make sure the creature was absolutely still before approaching it.

The monster's head was similar to that of an alligator — protruding eyes, long snout, and thick jaws. Its teeth were longer and sharper-looking than anything Clem had ever seen. He kept a respectful distance from its mouth, just in case it might have one last spark of life in it. A bite from that thing would almost certainly be a one way ticket to meet one's Maker.

Many of the ranch hands walked around the carcass to examine it from all sides, and Clem followed suit. The massive wings were shaped like those of a bat and were translucent, tinting everything under them a light green. It only had two legs, making it more like a bird or a bat, but it had a long tail like an alligator. All told, Clem estimated that it was well over a hundred feet long, maybe half that again.

"What is it?" somebody asked.

"Don't know, but it don't matter," Dan said. "Only thing that matters is that Clem killed it, so now we ain't gotta worry about…"

His words were drowned out by another blood curdling screech. Everyone jumped back from the monster's carcass. Another screech, and Clem realized that it came from overhead…

Another powerful wind knocked him down. He looked up and saw a second winged creature rising into the sky. Terrifying, but not nearly so much as the other two swooping down. "More than one?" he croaked, thinking about how three cows had already been taken.

One dove down toward the ground. It snatched one of the men up into the air, its screech drowning out any noise he might have made. In the blink of an eye, a similar fate befell a second man. Clem scrambled for his weapon.

The third creature was swooping back down for its own attack. Clem didn't really aim, just pointed and shot. Instead of taking a man, the creature hit the ground like a boulder, its momentum digging a trench behind it.

Clem spun around to see the two other creatures flying away with their prey, well out of range. They soared toward the hills, toward—

"The mines!" Dan exclaimed. "Could they have come from there?"

"Possible," Clem answered. "We never saw them before the miners started blasting this morning. Don't make much sense, but they could be connected…"

"You think they'll be back?"

"Could be. I'd hate to rest too easy." Clem turned to face the other hands. "Who are we missing? Who did those monsters get?"

"Got Hank and Pete," somebody replied from the back of the group.

Dan nodded. "All right, then. Clem, you take a group of men up to the mines with some rifles, and…"

"No." Clem looked his brother straight in the eye.

Dan's jaw dropped. "What do you mean, no?"

Clem felt the weight of everyone's stares. "I'll go, of course, but this is your ranch. Your livelihood, and the lives of your men are your responsibility. You need to take part in it, lead us all. Time was, you would have, and wild horses couldn't have stopped you." Murmurs of agreement rose from the men behind him.

"But…"

"Look, we all know why. But these men need a leader, and you're supposed to be it. You haven't been doing it lately."

"You don't know what I've been through these past couple of weeks!" Dan snapped.

"It's been over a month, Dan," Clem answered, doing his best to stay calm. "We know you loved Sylvia. You've got every right to mourn, but she wouldn't want you to stop living on account of it. What do you think she'd tell you if she was here right now?"

Dan pondered the question for a moment. "She'd tell me to get out there with y'all and fight to protect this ranch. She'd tell me to quit acting a fool. Then she'd tell me that if I took care of it and got back alive, she'd reward me by…" He cleared his throat, and the slightest hint of a smile appeared. Faint, but there. "Well, you don't have to know *everything* she would have said, do you?"

"So what's the verdict, Dan?"

He nodded grimly. "We ride together. Let me get myself a rifle."

~*~

Three bullets left, Clem kept reminding himself. He hadn't told anyone else about Obadiah Riddle yet, but it wasn't lost on him that his shots had been the only effective ones so far. Clem reckoned that couldn't be coincidental. *What if running across that old peddler wasn't a coincidence, either?* It was a hard question to ponder, but it was even more difficult to ignore.

Dan led the way in stoic silence. He still didn't seem quite himself, but at least he was out here, doing something. The rest of the men followed his example, not saying a word as they approached the mine.

The mine itself was surprisingly quiet. At a certain distance, they should have been able to hear voices, picks hitting rock, something. They should have seen somebody moving around by now. Instead, there was no activity to be seen. Clem thought he heard strange noises that could have been attributable to the creatures, but he wasn't sure if they were real or if his mind was playing tricks on him.

The wind shifted, carrying a powerful stench. Everyone gagged, and Clem heard at least one man behind him vomit. No one could mistake the distinctive smell of carrion. Dan rode on, barely flinching, and everyone else followed, trying to hold down their last meal as best they could.

The opening to the mine shaft was far bigger than it should have been, plenty big enough to accommodate the creatures. Huge chunks of rock were scattered all around, as if something from within had burst through it. One of the creatures screeched from within, its voice echoing through the shaft. Whether it was aware of their presence or not, the meaning was unmistakable. They had arrived at the monsters' nest.

Clem thought about the dynamite earlier in the day, how it had stopped after a while and how they didn't hear the screeches until later. *That ain't a coincidence, either. Somehow, all that blasting must have stirred these beasts up, and now…*

Something burst out of the mine shaft like a shot out of a cannon. The blast of wind that it left in its wake knocked over horses and riders alike. Thrown off his steed, Clem landed on his back and rolled over several times. When he righted himself, he was staring down into the mine. The expanded entrance allowed enough daylight for him to see the other creature.

A pair of circles opened toward the head of the silhouette — two luminous, protruding eyes. Clem reached for his pistol...

Suddenly the earth fell away from him with lightning speed. It took him a second to realize that wasn't right, that he had been snatched up into the air. "—got Clem!" somebody shouted from below. Dan, he thought.

The creature made a big loop in the air, turning Clem's stomach. Gunshots rang out as the creature flew straight into the mine's opening. It suddenly dropped him, even though the drop was less than a foot. He landed near something that he thought looked suspiciously like a piece of bone.

Both of the creatures cried out, their echoes thundering up and down the shaft. Terror pierced Clem's soul. He tried to crawl away but accidentally put his knee in something squishy. Instinctively he recoiled. One pair of eyes drew closer, but Clem was frozen in place.

Running footsteps echoed down the shaft. "Clem!" Dan yelled. "Can you hear me? Speak to me!"

The sound of his brother's voice snapped Clem's mind back into clarity. *Three bullets left!* He reached for the pistol, relieved to find that he hadn't lost it in the ruckus that brought him down here. As he raised it, he saw that the luminosity of the bullets glowed even inside the pistol, producing a dim light around the cylinder. Dim, but enough to make it easier to aim.

He pointed it toward the pair of eyes and fired. The shot was deafening, as was the thud of the creature's body collapsing. The eyes gleamed no more.

"Clem, is that you?"

"Yeah! Look out! There's still one more—"

The remaining creature grabbed Dan in its jaws and lifted him off the ground. Reacting quickly, Clem fired again, hitting one of its eyes dead-center. It died instantly, dropping Dan as it slumped over.

Dan trembled violently. "That...that thing...it almost..."

"Yeah, I know. I saw." Clem helped his brother to his feet. "But it didn't. That's what counts."

"I've been living like a dead man for a long time now, haven't I, Clem?"

"Can't deny it."

Dan shook his head. "That just then, that opened my eyes. I miss Sylvia, but I ain't quite ready to go join her yet, you know?"

Clem clasped his brother's shoulder. "Yeah, I know."

They had walked about halfway out of the shaft when they heard a crackling sound behind them. Only then did they notice the eggs — half a dozen of them, all in various stages of hatching. Dan cursed, the expletive echoing off the walls of the shaft.

Only one bullet left! Clem thought. No way he could kill all of them. Desperately he looked around. This was a mine shaft. Miners used dynamite. Surely there had to be…

There! One stick of dynamite, maybe about eight feet from the eggs. "Dan! Run!" he shouted as he raised the Colt toward the dynamite.

Without looking to see if his brother complied, Clem pulled the trigger. There was a thunderous boom as the dynamite exploded, plunging Clem into darkness….

~*~

"Clem! Clem! Can you hear me? Clem!"

"Quit yelling already," Clem groaned. His head felt as if it was about to split open. The bright sunlight overhead did nothing to help.

"He's alive, fellas!" Dan exclaimed. "He made it!"

"Yeah, because you pulled him out of there," Marcus said. "Otherwise…"

Slowly the memories started coming back to Clem. "The creatures…the eggs…did it work? Did we…?"

"That was quick thinking, shooting at the dynamite like that," Dan said. "Those varmints are buried under a ton of rock right now. We ain't likely to hear from them again."

"Good. Let's get out of here."

As they made their way back to the ranch, they saw a peddler's wagon moving in the opposite direction. They passed about fifty yards apart, but Clem was able to see the heavy-set man sitting in the driver's seat, tipping his hat as they passed.

The Price of Gold
Su Haddrell

Callie replaced the bolt and ejector on her rifle and slid the receiver back into place. Smooth as churned butter. Quinn and Eli had been gone longer than expected, but that usually meant they'd picked up the scent of something and there'd be work afoot. She glanced up at the sound of thundering hooves. A grin crept onto the corners of her mouth. Callie slung her rifle over her shoulder and joined the rest of the camp in greeting their return.

"We got ourselves a goodun!" Quinn called out to them. He swung down from the saddle and handed the reins to one of the lads.

"There's some stew over the fire," Callie told him, "Bird managed to score a barrel of hooch as well."

Quinn clapped her on the back. "Callie Jane Jackson, as I live and breathe! Damn it's good to be home!"

~*~

It was a few hours before Callie finally heard the tale of it. Camp their size meant that everyone wanted the ear of Quinn and his brother Eli, and there was plenty of housekeeping to catch up on. Once the horses were groomed and settled and the quartermaster had said his piece on the state of their stores, the camp finally came to gather around the fire.

"We've taken respite within half a day's ride of a town called Patience — a small and sturdy congregation of God-fearing folk as we ever saw." Quinn spread his arms wide; a storyteller weaving his tale. His grin was wolfish beneath a long dark moustache, and the heat of the fire set his ruddy cheeks aglow. His brother, Eli, sat faithfully by his side, stoic as ever, his gaze drawn to the flames but his ears open to all.

"In a few months, maybe less, this dusty desert hamlet is goin' to be another Boomtown, full of all manner of folk ready to set up shop as well as a fair few of the likes of us."

"A Boomtown, boss? There's a mine there?" a young voice called out.

"Aye, Noah, my sharp lad, there is!" Quinn rose to his feet. Callie cocked her head up to him with interest. A mine was a new venture. They tended towards bounties or scoring the odd stagecoach route. Next thing you know, they'd be going after the railroads. What in hell's name were they going to do with a mine? She cast a glance over to Eli, trying to catch his eye, but the younger brother was still staring into nothingness.

"This is going to take a little time to set up, but believe me, the payoff will be enough to keep us going all winter and beyond!"

The gathered audience murmured with excitement. Callie watched the orange flames flickering in Quinn's eyes. The gold fever had finally got to him. For a second she thought she could actually see it in the flush on his brow, the heave of his chest. Maybe such a thing was a fever — a sickness that man succumbed to.

"What's the set up?" she asked. If he didn't get to the point soon, half the camp would be drunk on their fantasies of riches before they'd even put a plan into place. The camp settled again. Quinn turned his grin down to her, and for a second her stomach flipped as their eyes met. She disguised her reaction with a raised eyebrow. Damn the man and his charm. Quinn resumed his seat and leaned forward, elbows on his knees.

"Young prospector by the name of Emerson Waller has staked a claim on a section of river just south of Patience and set to mining the area. Mine's still fairly recent, and the fellah has taken the locals into his employ. They're grateful for it — work in these parts is scarce enough, and they're all able enough to swing a pick-axe. Me and Eli got to sharing a few drinks with the local Sheriff, who let it slip that Mr. Waller was a might bit concerned about bandits and suchlike attacking his new establishment." This last generated a burst of raucous laughter from his audience.

"Don't know of no bandits round here, do we Quinn?" shouted one. Quinn grinned and raised his hands for quiet.

"'Well,' I says to the Sheriff, 'my brother and I ain't no good with a pick-axe, but we've a fair bit of experience in providing a bit of security to the odd stagecoach and the like.'" The camp sniggered again. "'We could use the coin, if you think Mr. Waller would be acceptin'?'"

Callie frowned. Seemed a lot of set up and trouble.

"Why don't we just ride in and raid the place?" she spoke up. She felt the camp hush once more. There weren't many that would stand up to Quinn and Eli, but Callie knew she was one of the few. It wasn't that she was questioning their ideas, although previous arguments had certainly suggested that; she just wanted to make sure she understood their reasoning. That way, when they eventually got themselves shot to hell in one fight or another, she could run the place just as well.

"'Cause we ain't the Dennison gang, just racing in and shootin' everythin'. This way we can get a good feel for the layout and the rota and a decent sized payload at just the right moment. We'll re-con the place for a span and then send for everyone. We do it right, we'll take the whole place in the dead of night and be long gone before they even realized what's happened!"

The camp cheered; Callie with them. It was a good plan — methodical, careful and underhanded. Just the way they liked to work.

~*~

It wasn't long before Callie and Bird got themselves on Emerson Waller's detail as well. They each made the prospectors acquaintance and offered their services. The illusion of not knowing one another wasn't difficult to uphold. Callie enjoyed the game of it — passing sly winks onto Eli who, in turn, liked to nudge and trip Bird at every hidden opportunity. Quinn was focused on the job. Emerson Waller was a man with a great deal on his mind. Tall and lean, he propped spectacles on his hooked nose to read. He didn't seem to have all that much experience in getting his hands dirty but certainly had the willing.

The mine was set into a dusty gulch not far up from the riverbed. Waller had it in mind to set up a kind of hydro system, but for the moment they worked with explosives. He employed an assortment of workers, many of them wearing tattoos that indicated previous incarcerations. The parched days were filled with dust and the smell of cordite. They set up camp at the mine itself to ensure there was security during the night hours, but there was ample opportunity for a hot bath and meal back at the town.

Some weeks later, Callie took patrol at an hour past midnight. Quinn sat at the campfire with Eli and Bird, eagerly discussing how they were going to fence the processed ore. The fever really was getting to Quinn. He was more interested in the workings of the mine than in talking to her right now, but she was damned if she was going to let him know how much it bothered her.

The night was clear and the stars in the heavens seemed to gather into infinity. The breeze whipped up the cooling sand dunes to sting at her cheeks. Callie usually preferred the early dawn watch, when the dew was fragrant and the birds were stirring, but there was something peaceful about idly pacing the encampment in the dead of night. The land up top was scattered with brittlebrush and silverleaf. The town of Patience twinkled in the distance.

She turned and headed back down into the gulch, sure-footed on the steep sandy track and moving onward towards the mouth of the mine. Up close, the pitch-dark maw was deep and imposing. Callie was suddenly very aware of its stillness, as though the mine was fathomless and to step into the black was to pass into nothingness. She wondered if anyone had lost themselves in the labyrinth of shafts. If she were to step over the threshold into the shadow, would she return? Or would the blackened gullet swallow her whole?

Something in the darkness glittered, catching the starlight.

Callie drew a sharp breath.

Black.

Whatever it was had disappeared.

What the...?

Footsteps shifted behind her. Callie spun on her heel, her rifle raised before she even realized she was aiming.

"Easy girl, only me." Quinn's voice was soft with amusement. Callie let the barrel drop. "What's got you so spooked?" he asked.

"I thought there was something...? She shook her head. "Nothin'. Just spookin' myself." She grinned and Quinn returned the smile, his eyes full of mischief.

"It certainly looks a lot less foreboding during the daylight hours. Although, there's a lot to be said for hiding in the shadows." He slipped an arm around her waist and Callie couldn't resist the tingle of pleasure it gave her.

"Thought you had all eyes on the job," she said, wriggling free.

"Always got half an eye on you though." He followed her movement and she stepped back out of reach.

"Half an eye on my behind you mean," she teased.

"Well, you do wiggle it so!" Quinn lunged forward and grabbed her belt. Callie let herself be drawn to him like a horse on a lasso.

Something thumped in the darkness of the mine.

The pair leapt apart, twisting to search the black. Something shuffled in the dust. Callie took a pace forward, sensing Quinn sidestepping around beside her, his hands hovering over his holsters. The shuffling came again, and Callie saw that same sparkle, a curious sickly gray-gold that caught the moonlight and vanished. She pumped the lever on her repeater. The crack of it bounced and echoed off of the rocks.

A shadow leapt from the gloom.

It shot across the sand.

Callie cried out in surprise and fired.

The muzzle flashed. The shadow leapt, a shrieking, shimmering mass moving too quickly. The thing was on top of her, pinning her shoulders, screaming like a banshee into her face. All Callie could see was the glitter of its eyes and crystalline structures where its face should be. The creature's teeth were jagged metallic lumps, its breath a stench of sulphur.

A loud bang thundered through the cavern.

The creature collapsed.

Callie gasped, winded.

The thing was as heavy as a wagon wheel. She pushed, trying to lever it off. Suddenly, Quinn and the others appeared. Together, they heaved and rolled the creature over onto the ground.

Callie leapt to her feet and then bent over double, wheezing and coughing.

"What in God's name...?" Bird cried, staring at the corpse.

"Damned if I know. Don't think God had much to do with it. Came out the damn mine." She choked. Eli leaned over and held his lantern over the thing's face. He nudged it with his toe. A black goo escaped from the mess on the side of its head. In the golden lamplight, it began to crystallize, forming gray-gold shards and miniature towers on the sand. The crystals edged towards Eli's foot and he shuffled out of reach.

"Don't get any of its shit on you," he said slowly.

"You know what it is?" Callie asked. She felt unclean.

"No, I do not. But it looks to be catchin'." Eli held her gaze until she glanced away, uncomfortable with the way he looked at her.

"We need to get rid of it," Quinn said suddenly.

"We gonna tell Mr. Waller?" Bird asked.

"Not if we want this job to go through. We're not leaving without that gold." There was a fixation in Quinn's tone that Callie did not like.

She'd been attacked, but he was more interested in the gold. She moved away from the corpse. Eli backed away from her.

"I ain't caught anything, don't you look at me like that!" She glared at the brother. "You don't know where that thing came from."

Eli gave a lazy shrug. "Tattoo on its arm. It's one of the miners." Callie gripped her rifle a little tighter. The thing looked almost human. *What if Eli was right*, she thought. *What had happened to the miners?*

"What if there are more?" Bird twitched from one foot to the other, a habit that had borne his namesake.

"We get rid of this tonight. It's about time we stopped waitin' around anyway. Tomorrow's loadin' day and then it'll go for shippin'. Bird, you'll go tell the others. Once the load is ready and shift is finished, they can drop in and we'll haul out with the lot."

~*~

The following day passed with the low level tension of an incoming tornado. Emerson Waller was of a fierce temper and prowled the site barking orders and wiping his brow with a dirtied handkerchief. A number of the miners had disappeared overnight and the remaining workers were lethargic and argumentative. One or two determined that some of the shafts were unsafe — there was rubble piling along the track and the dust was as thick as a sandstorm deeper in. Waller was struggling to get his workforce under control and so it went unnoticed that Bird had disappeared and there were only three wards left to monitor the grounds.

For her part, Callie was looking forward to getting out and moving on. She'd already doused herself thoroughly in the freezing waters of the river but she kept catching herself checking her skin, waiting to see the tell-tale gray-gold crystal. The sight of the creature attacking her kept flitting into her thoughts, the lumpy metallic formations and creeping gold scouring its face. Callie closed her eyes and shook her head. When she opened them again, Eli was watching her with concern. She gave a shrug, slung her rifle over her shoulder and set out on patrol again.

A thunderous boom stopped her. The sound resonated from around the rocky gulch followed by a huge belch of dust. Screams rang through the air and suddenly everyone was running to the entrance. Callie stood her ground, casting her eyes about for Quinn and Eli.

The dust blew thick across the gulch, a gritty sandstorm that made her eyes prickle. She pulled her scarf over her nose and mouth. The brothers were nowhere in sight. She couldn't see more than a few feet ahead. Shouts and screams echoed around her. The air stank of sulphur and the fog shimmered unnaturally. Another sound joined the shrieks, a low rumble that thudded through the ground beneath her feet. Horse hooves. For a split second, Callie felt relief. The rest of the camp had arrived.

But it was too soon...

Rifles cracked. Shots rang out.

Callie dashed through the dust into cover. Whoops and cries filled the air. They were under attack. She wished she knew where the brothers had vanished to. In the cavern behind her, she could hear Emerson Waller calling out orders and his voice fading away. They were all dealing with the crisis inside, oblivious to the one developing outside. Callie cocked her rifle. *Might as well earn that payday.* Swinging the repeater into position, she leaned over the crate. The sound of hooves pummeled the sand, drawing closer. The dust churned the air, a sparkling mist. Callie heard the gang circling, firing their rifles into the air. Celebrating before they'd even taken the place.

A shot rang out from above her. Quinn's Winchester. She'd recognize the sound anywhere. A second shot, and the sound of the hooves changed. She still couldn't see shit. Should have found elevation like Quinn had done. Still, they'd come for her eventually. Callie breathed slowly into her scarf.

Waited.

Shadows began to form, silhouettes in the silvery gloom. Four, seven, ten...many. Quinn fired again. One of the shadows fell, and the others began to spin their horses around, rifles raised. Callie leaned into the crate, aimed and fired. Another down. She pumped the lever, fired again. The group scattered, glittering hazes that danced in the dust. She caught one in her sights, pushed the tip of her barrel a fraction ahead of its path and fired. The bandit went down. Gunfire burst around her. They knew her position. Wood erupted into splinters. Callie dropped to the ground, her chin scuffing the dirt, her rifle pulled to her side. The bullets whistled overhead and then fell silent. She breathed sand, panting heavily beneath her scarf.

"We kill y'all?" A calm sardonic drawl called out of the dust. A nasally voice that should have belonged to a tax man or goods inspector. It belonged to Claude Dennison. They'd been rivals with the double-dealing leader and his gang for as long as Callie could remember.

"Get lost Dennison!" Quinn shouted from the top of the gulch.

Deep within the blackened depths of the cavern, Callie could hear the monsters stirring. She realized that she had been aware of it for some time, a nagging pulse that flexed and sparked behind her eyes. Faintly, she could hear them screeching at one another through the shadows. The screams of miners suddenly cut off. An awareness of blood, hot and thick and satisfying and...

Callie wrenched herself out from the reverie and rolled over onto her back. The sky was blue once more, clean as a new shirt. She listened to Quinn and Dennison taunting one another. Bandits to the front and monsters at their rear. She pulled her scarf away from her face and breathed hot dry air. Raised her hands before her eyes. Dropped them to her sides again.

Well...

"You want the gold, Dennison?" she called to the sky, loud and clear. "I'll take you to it." The silence that fell across the canyon was as heavy as the gold they thirsted for.

"What makes you think we couldn't just go in and take it ourselves?" their enemy called.

"Part of the tunnel section's collapsed so you'll be wandering a while before you find a way to it. By which point the rest of Quinn's crew will have caught up." She felt very calm, given the circumstances.

"You *bitch*!" Quinn screamed down from the ledge.

"Ain't personal, Quinn," she called back, keeping her tone neutral.

"Yeah, Quinn, you'd better listen to your lady there," Dennison chimed in.

Callie rose to her feet. The dust had finally settled and she got a good look at the lot of them. There were only seven left, pulling their horses to a standstill. Dennison swung his leg over the saddle and dismounted. Quinn and Eli had been picking the gang off more successfully than she'd realized, there weren't as many left as she'd thought. Still, best give 'em what they wanted while she still could. Callie could sense patterns shifting behind her eyes, like a migraine aura splintering across her skull.

She stared out across the dirt, glaring at Claude Dennison. He was as scrawny as his voice, with a thin beard that patched his sunken cheekbones. His eyes were wary. His crew looked like they hadn't eaten in over a week, and they hunched over their saddle pommels as though they'd drunk a bellyful of gut-rot. Dennison let his hand hover over his holster. Callie held her ground. After a moment, Dennison gave a slight nod and the rest of his crew dismounted.

"Dammit Callie, I'll see you riddled with holes and hanging by your neck when I'm done with you!" Quinn shouted.

"You better keep your distance, Quinn," she called back. "Let this be and you'll come out the other end with your guts still intact."

Callie turned her back on Dennison and his gang and walked into the mouth of the mine.

~*~

She'd never explored the mine before, preferring to patrol the gulch and tend the fire in the evenings. The fractal patterns across her sight sharpened in the darkness, almost dizzying in their intensity. Dennison and four of his crew approached from behind, pulling a small wagon with them.

"This way," she ordered, forestalling any discussion.

They found the tunnel collapse a short way in. They had been digging another shaft, a further offshoot from the main route. The heavy wooden beams had given way to a mountain of loose earth and ruined stone. The rubble piled up across the width of the pit, and the grime hung thick in the air. There was no sign of the crew, no sound from Waller. The tunnel was empty. They carefully navigated over the rubble, three of Dennison's men having to help lift the little wagon across.

Callie led them deeper down the track where the air grew foul with the stink of rotten eggs. The lanterns along the walls were dim and low on oil. Torches were struck and dark shadows flickered across the tight space. She could hear the monsters further in, sense their strange communications, pulses and sparks like lightning strikes across her skin. Amid the sulphuric smell was the scent of blood, and she was suddenly acutely aware of the men behind her, their hearts pumping healthy warm fluid that would taste of copper and minerals and...

"Hey, enough with the merry dance, where's the damn gold?" Dennison snapped. Callie stopped. The mine shaft was narrow and hot. Callie pressed her hands to her temples, trying to calm the kaleidoscope of patterns. Dennison grabbed her shoulder, spinning her around to face him. "Y'hear me? Where's the gold?"

It took all her willpower not to rip his throat out.

"Nearly there," she said softly, both to him and herself. "Nearly there." She turned away, realizing her vision had changed. She could *see* the gold — a bright glowing vein of it coursing through the bedrock. The creatures ahead called to her, their oscillations thrumming over her. "Nearly there..."

"Lord Almighty, I don't like this boss," one of the men at the rear said. There were murmurs of agreement.

"We ain't leavin' until we got what we came for!" said Dennison.

The oil lamps spluttered and died. Callie led them on, following the call, drawn to it as though to a flame. One of the wheels on the wagon clicked as it turned and the sound echoed around. She came to a halt near the entrance of a cavern and pointed the way. She could see the gleam of crystal shimmer across her blackened skin.

"Gold's in the cavern. They was waitin' to load it out when the tunnel collapsed," she said.

Her tongue felt thick in her mouth. Dennison looked at her for a long moment and she wondered what he saw. Had her eyes hardened into rocks? Did her face appear metallic? She held his gaze, daring him to question her. His gaunt face burst into a grin, revealing blackened teeth.

"Let's load up boys!" The crew cheered.

Callie stepped aside. They rushed into the chamber, a curved blast area carved into the bedrock. The gold ore had been dug out and was piled into heaps. To Callie's vision, it shone like a summer's dawn. Tools and pick-axes scattered the ground. Still there was no sign of the miners. Callie watched the silhouettes of Dennison's crew lug the heavy rock into the wagon. Listened to them crowing their luck, their voices loud and obnoxious. She gazed further into the cavern, beyond the jubilant gang, following the seams of rich amber deeper into darkened shafts that the gang had yet to notice.

She sensed the spark of their connection. Could feel it prickling across her skin like static. The creatures crept out of the shaft, rippling across the rock's surface, unnoticed by the thieves. Callie's head thrummed with tension. The creatures waited, expectant, hungry. How she longed to join them! The scent of blood was almost too much to bear. She bit down hard on her tongue, focused on the pain. It was enough. She felt the vibrations from the creatures, their quivering communication. If she concentrated she could communicate back. She clenched her fists and sent a pulsing signal.

The creatures screeched. They launched themselves from the walls. In the flickering torchlight they were spindly crystalline things, their skin a shimmering diseased gray of jagged crusts, their teeth a mass of metallic blades set into a sickly rust colored maw. Dennison and his men didn't even get a chance to fire off a shot. The first had his feet pulled from beneath him and was wrenched onto his back with a thud. Two others were thrown to the wall by the pouncing, ravenous beasts. The wet red tear of skin and sinew mingled with the banshee screech of the monsters and the agonized howl of their prey. Another creature leapt onto the broad shoulders of the last of the gang members. The man spun around, panicked and caught off balance. A fountain of dark wine sprayed across the gold ore as the thing adeptly wrenched the man's head from his shoulders.

Dennison stood at their center, his mouth agape. Callie watched him from the cavern entrance, feeling a kind of sly satisfaction at his horror. He locked his gaze onto her and dropped to his knees, incapable of thought or action. Callie had no sympathy. Her new kin were devoid of heart or understanding. They knew only hunger. The cavern was a riot of blood splatter, severed limbs and candy colored organs. Her mouth watered. She bit her tongue again, tasting her own blood in her mouth. It would satisfy for now. She couldn't succumb to the craving. Not yet. She had to see Quinn. Just one last time.

The creatures circled around the whimpering gang leader. Dennison hung his head. A pool of dark liquid trickled from between his thighs onto the dust. The creatures squawked, a strange kind of laughter. They attacked, swooping in together, sinking bladed teeth into his skin, pinning him beneath needle claws. Dennison didn't make a sound.

The moment unnerved Callie briefly. Had he wanted to die or had he just given up? She squeezed her eyes shut, taking comfort from the silver that patterned her eyelids. When she opened them, the creatures had slunk back to the darkness of the shafts. The ground was a chaotic wreckage of burst body parts, glistening crimson. The cavern was silent and still. The little cart sat at its center, the craggy lumps of gold ore mired by lumps of tissue and grayish hunks of matter. She just wanted to feed...

"God Almighty!" Quinn said behind her. Callie spun on her heel, whipped her hands up.

"Stay back!" she cried. Quinn and Eli took a pace back. Behind them were the rest of the gang, a group of torch lit shadows in the darkened tunnel.

"Stay back," Callie whispered again. Her love stared at her, his dark eyes mirroring what she had become — eyes crystalline, skin rippled with grayish gold. Quinn's expression sank from horror into sadness. He absently reached beside him, pushed on his brother's arm, forcing Eli to lower his pistol.

"You lured them here," Quinn said. Callie nodded. Her hunger burned. If she took him now, he would be with her. They would be together forever. Would it be so bad?

"The gold is yours, you just got to get it out," she told him.

"What about...?"

"They'll stay away. For now. You ain't got much time." Callie stepped to the side. The gang clamored in protest. It was Eli who calmed them.

"Those who wish to leave are free to do so. Ain't no harm or bad feelin'. But that cart there has more gold than any of us'll see in a lifetime. Enough for us each to build a home. We just gotta go take it."

"But the monsters...!" came a voice.

"Callie says we're safe for now. I trust her wit," Eli said gently. Quinn glanced over to him and nodded his gratitude.

~*~

They had enough manpower to lug the cart in the end. Some folk left and Quinn let them go in peace. Callie knew they'd receive a cut of the loot anyway. Quinn had always been a fair man. It was a grim job and no one spoke. They finally got the thing rolling up the tunnel, alternately pulling and pushing. The cart trundled away into the darkness, its wheels rattling beneath the heavy weight of fortune.

Callie felt calm, as though some strange force were allowing her a moment's peace before she finally relinquished control to the monster inside her. Quinn and Eli remained as the cart and crowd disappeared. Eli, a man given to many observations but very few words, looked at her for a long moment. Then he nodded, tipped his hat and walked away without a look back. Quinn kept his distance from her.

"Callie, I'm..."

"You gotta blow the mine Quinn. You gotta seal it," Callie whispered urgently. Time was slipping away now. As much as she wanted the moment to last, she was impatient for him to be gone. It would all be worthless if he didn't get out.

"I know. I will." Quinn's eyes gleamed wet. The fever behind them had dissipated. The gold no longer held its sway as it once had.

"Be at peace my love. Enjoy your gains and live a long life," she told him.

Quinn wiped his eyes with the back of his hand.

"Always a price," he whispered.

Callie saw him pull himself together. The leader who dragged his crew through a dozen scrapes, who could talk his way out of anything, who never got caught.

"You'll be the tale of a thousand campfires." He grinned and she felt her stomach flip with the heat of it.

"Get out of here you stupid bastard."

Quinn turned and jogged up the tunnel. Behind her, Callie could feel the stirring of the creatures, her new kin, in the shaft. She couldn't join them yet. She had to hold on.

Her vision sparkled.

After an eternity, the fire finally came. The boom shook the cavern and rubble fell from above.

The creature dropped onto all fours and loped into the darkness.

Light in the Mine

Marc Sorondo

"Martin…Martin…"

Dimly aware of the sound of his own name and of a gentle pressure on his shoulder that rocked him side to side, Martin struggled to open his eyes.

"Martin…The lights are back."

His eyes opened. He was immediately awake and alert, and his gaze went straight to the window. Ana had said lights, but he saw only one, a curved sliver of yellow brilliance, like a stone polished by a river until reflectively smooth and worn almost completely away.

He grunted as he got out of bed. He grabbed the Spencer repeating rifle that he'd leaned against the corner as he walked out the bedroom door. That was the gun that had kept him alive at Gettysburg, but it hadn't proven to be very effective against the things that came in the night.

"You know what to do," he said.

She nodded and waddled over to get his revolver, her nightshirt straining to cover the growing curve of her belly.

"Be careful," she called after him as he headed through the front door.

~*~

Martin looked from the corner of his eye and saw that Ana was watching him from the bedroom window. She had the Confederate revolver he'd won off of Edward Creed in a poker game shortly after he and Ana had arrived in Nevada resting against the sill and aimed in the vague direction of the light in the sky.

The light hovered over the sheep's enclosure. They bleated and clumped together against one interior angle of the fence.

He strode through tall grass, checking to be sure his rifle was loaded although he already knew it was.

Then a beam of light shot from the center of the bright disk. It was the same yellow hue but even more intense than the glow that had woken Ana.

"Not another one," Martin muttered. He lifted the rifle, jamming the butt against his shoulder and sighting along the barrel.

A single ewe had risen from the ground, pulled away by the beam of light, a long shaft of brilliance that gradually receded with the sheep at the end of its grasp. It bleated — a high, terrified sound — again and again as it rode the angle of the light towards the underside of the flying disk.

Martin fired and then quickly looked away, his eyes watering from the strain of staring into that luminescence. The bullet struck the light with a sound like a note from a singing saw: a wobbly, metallic sound that Martin understood only to mean that his weapon had been as ineffective as ever.

The sheep was engulfed by the brightness.

"Damn it," Martin growled. He debated firing off another shot.

Then the light rose into the sky. It moved slowly at first, like a balloon rising on a current of warm air. Then, once it had reached a height that dwarfed its size with distance, it shot off like a bullet towards the west.

"Damn it." Saying it again, Martin had lost his growl. He sounded tired, defeated.

That had been the third sheep in just over a week, and he knew he'd never see it alive again.

~*~

Martin examined it by the light of dawn. It lay on one side. The eye was gone, as was the tissue over the mouth on half of its face. There was a small wound in the neck, perfectly round and the size of a small coin. A perfect square on the sheep's belly had been shaved; within that square another perfect square of skin had been removed.

Martin took a step back and looked down at it. With its teeth exposed that way, it was as if the sheep grinned up at him maniacally. Martin could imagine it winking at him, its eyelid snapping shut over its empty socket.

There was no blood — not a drop of it, not a fleck of rusty red on the sheep's white wool.

None of it surprised him. Of the several prior animals that had been taken, none of the others had been returned in better shape. From one, a rectangular panel of meat had been excised, from which the organs had been taken. Another animal's anus had been removed, the whole thing cut as if with an apple corer. The wounds varied, but the fact that pieces had been taken, without any blood spilled, was consistent.

Martin sucked his teeth, then growled a curse. Now he'd have to get rid of the body. The last thing he needed was to attract predators…of the normal variety.

~*~

That night, at supper, Ana was quiet.

"What are you thinking?" Martin asked.

Light in the Mine

"What are we going to do?"

He sighed. "I don't know. This keeps up…maybe head back east?"

"East?"

He shrugged. "Further west."

"The lights come from the west," Ana said.

Martin nodded. "Jude Baker says he knows where. Said he got fed up after watching his sheep disappear like ours only to come back dead. He rode west a ways and came to an old silver mine." He cleared his throat. "Said it glowed."

Ana's brow furrowed but she said nothing.

Martin cleared his throat again. "Said there was light pouring out of the mouth of the mine, same sort of light we've all been seeing in the sky."

"What was in there?"

Martin shook his head. "Jude said he lost his nerve before he got too close."

"Guns don't work," Ana said. "Can't say I blame him for being scared."

"No one could. It's not as if a posse ran out there."

"Maybe you're right. Maybe we should leave," Ana said.

Martin sighed. "Maybe."

~*~

The lights woke him. They were so bright he was half blind before he'd even opened his eyes. Squinting against the sheer brilliance, he found the entire room was full of radiance. He reached to his side but just felt empty space over the bed where Ana should have been.

He got up and stumbled to the window. There was a figure lying prone at the end of the beam of yellow shining down from the sky: it was Ana, sleeping or paralyzed, still as flat as if the bed were beneath her.

Martin grabbed his useless rifle and jumped through the window.

"Ana!"

Sleeping or paralyzed, she floated overhead, her body motionless aside from its sliding at an upward angle toward the yellow disk in the sky.

Martin aimed and fired off a shot. The bullet struck with that wobbly note, useless as always.

"Ana!"

She met the circle of luminescence in the sky and was engulfed.

The craft rose into the sky.

Martin stood there, his rifle in one hand. He watched it ascend. Then it shot off towards the west. He knew where it was headed. Jude had been there and seen it; he'd said the light glowed from within.

Rubbing his eyes, he decided. He was going to that silver mine, and he wouldn't lose his nerve. The sheep were always taken and returned later, dead and mutilated, missing organs and patches of skin, drained of blood. Every moment of delay hurt his chances for reaching her in time.

~*~

He got more ammunition for his rifle. He strapped on a wide leather belt that held the holstered Confederate revolver. He slid a Bowie knife into a sheath in his boot.

He saddled Zaldi. Her coat — chestnut brown in the day — was black and lustrous in the moonlight. Martin toyed with the idea of going for help. This was his wife, pregnant no less. How could anyone refuse to help him save her?

He could see her, lips cut away into a permanent smile, eye socket empty, a rectangle cut out of her belly, exposing a bloodless cavern where their baby had been. He held that thought in his mind. Against his own revulsion, he dwelt on the image, knowing it would steel him for the task at hand.

She would, likely as not, be that way by first light. He didn't have the time to beg for aid, especially aid that might not come. His neighbors were good people, but he had no trouble imagining them sheepishly avoiding his gaze as they mumbled their excuses for not riding out west to the glowing silver mine with him.

He had no time to waste on a foolish errand like asking for help. He mounted Zaldi, clicked his tongue and poked at her rump with his spurs.

He rode westward.

~*~

Martin had no trouble finding the place. It was due west and an even shorter ride than Jude Baker had described. There was no room to doubt he'd found the right mine: this one was lit from within, not by a fiery flickering source of light, but by something as bright and constant as the sun.

Zaldi slowed as they neared and flat out refused to approach any closer when they were still far outside the reach of the glow issuing forth from the mouth of the silver mine.

Martin hopped down and led Zaldi over to a half dead shrub clinging to an otherwise grassy hillside. If she got really spooked, she'd be able to uproot the entire plant and carry it away. There was nothing else though, so Martin tied her to it, took his rifle, and strode toward the mine.

~*~

He stood before the mouth of the mine, bathed in the yellow glow. It made his head ache, that light. He squinted against it and stepped inside. There were illuminated panels running along the ceiling. No lanterns, these were rectangular and flat, and the light they gave off didn't dance the way a flame would.

Lights aside, the mine appeared normal for the first stretch. The walls were rough stone and the floor was packed dirt. Then he hit a fork, and the walls of either tine were smooth and white and the floors were clean and polished. These halls were distinctly rectangular, their angles perfectly square, their lines painfully straight.

Each hall was labeled with a sign Martin couldn't read. The letters were all wrong, more like hieroglyphics or elaborate runes than any letters he understood.

Both halls were deserted, but he could hear faint sounds come echoing down the length of the hall to his left. He checked his rifle, ensuring it was loaded though he already knew it was, and entered it.

As he walked, he saw glass tanks on the walls filled with translucent, green liquid; each held a living creature hooked up to tubes that bubbled where they met the animal's faces. Martin could not recognize most of these: one looked like a hairless raccoon, another like a cross between a cat and a squirrel, and a third like a fish with legs. Between their odd shapes and the tubing obscuring their faces, he couldn't be sure as to the identity of a single one.

This tank-lined length of hall moved in a gradual curve as it led deeper into the ground. The sounds that had echoed to its end were louder and clearer now: a man hummed as he worked, his equipment made of some metal that resonated if he banged it too hard.

Martin kept his rifle up as he made his way around the bend in the hall, noticing the inhabitants of more tanks as he passed: what seemed a huge frog with a wide body and flat tail, a snake with innumerable legs like a reptilian millipede, a bulbous creature with eight tentacles splayed out from its central mass.

The hall widened, and Martin came into a sort of laboratory area. The humming man stood at the far end of the lab, near another opening where it narrowed back into a hallway that led deeper into what he still thought of as a mine.

Busied with his work constructing a new tank and distracted by his own humming, the man remained with his back turned as Martin crept closer. The man had a mess of wavy brown hair and wore a long, red coat. Martin thought its cut militaristic, the coat an officer in an army might wear.

Martin cleared his throat and the man turned, smiling, to face him.

"Hello," the man said pleasantly enough. He spoke like an Englishman. "And who might you be?"

"I've come for my wife," Martin said.

The man's smiled widened. "Did you now?"

His eyes were opened so wide Martin could make out the whites all around the edges. "Very courageous of you. We did not really consider the possibility that anyone would be brave enough to follow us here. I am both impressed and a bit embarrassed."

"Where's my wife?"

"She is quite safe, let me assure you. We are merely—"

"Seen what you do to sheep," Martin growled. "You harm a hair on her head…"

The man nodded but continued smiling. "Those are animals. My employers would never treat a human being with such disregard."

"Your employers?"

"People from a star a billion miles away," he said, his smile rapturous. "Scientists. They've come here to study."

Martin's eyes narrowed.

"They have already learned much. They have quite a lot to offer those inclined to assist them."

"Where's my wife?"

"Would you believe that I am over a hundred years old?" When Martin did not react, he added, "I fought in your war of rebellion before coming to their attention."

Martin took another step forward, his aim unwavering.

"I would think a man of your clear bravery could be very useful to them. If you would lower your weapon and listen."

"I want no part in what you do here. I just want my wife."

"You must understand, the work we do is important, for us as well as them. Here we plumb the depths of natural philosophy; we map the very heart of the planet; we speak the language of the infinite and the infinitesimal."

His smile grew even wider, as did his unblinking eyes.

"They've unlocked the secret language of life, the code that makes us all what we are. I no longer age. I no longer get sick."

"Did they make you bulletproof?"

The man's smile fell away. "What?"

Martin fired, just once. He put a bullet into the man's forehead, just above and between his over-wide eyes.

The man's employers, his scientists from a billion miles away, had apparently not made him bulletproof.

~*~

Martin was still careful to be as quiet as possible as he moved deeper into the mine; he knew the gunshot had revealed his presence, but thought its incredible volume echoing along the halls wouldn't have given away his position.

His head ached worse and worse as he spent time under that light. It seemed to burn his squinted eyes, burn right back to his brain.

The next length of hall was empty of life but full of drawings and diagrams, all in that language he couldn't read. One particularly large diagram seemed to compare two similar shapes: one was like a ladder, its rungs all straight but its side planks twisted so that it made a long, ribbed spiral; the second had a similar helical shape but had three side planks all twisted around each other and connected by y-shaped spokes rather than simple rungs.

Martin walked past these and onto the next area full of diagrams. These were more decipherable to him: maps of the stars, though not ones he recognized from the night sky anywhere he'd ever lived.

After that he passed what seemed to be a huge map of the world cut into puzzle pieces. They were pulled apart, but Martin could have fit them together to reproduce the continents and oceans that he'd seen on the large, framed map at the courthouse back east.

He continued on, passing all manner of information that had ceased to be interesting and had become — viewed through squinted eyes and a raging, throbbing headache — increasingly unnerving.

Then he heard voices. At least two people were talking, their voices loud and agitated; it was the sound of an argument, though Martin could not quite make out the specific words at first. Then, he got closer.

"They told us to wait," one said.

"What's taking them so long?"

"Have they ever failed to take care of us?"

Martin's lip curled back into a sneer. The way these men talked about the star people, as if they were saviors, as if they were gods rather than kidnappers and mutilators; it disgusted him.

He stepped around the curve, rifle up and ready, and the two men farther down the hall turned to face him and fell silent. Martin examined them in an instant: one wore the tanned leather garments of a frontiersman; the other wore the crudely stitched pelts of a fur trapper from fifty years earlier.

"They can't protect you from everything," Martin said.

The two men looked at each other, then back at Martin.

"Where is she?" Martin's voice was calm, quiet. His head hurt too badly to speak any louder.

Neither man answered.

"Tell me or I'll shoot you dead. No one can save you from that."

The man in the furs pointed past Martin. His eyes had that same, wide mania in them that the Redcoat's had. "They can."

Martin turned. There were three standing behind him. Each was a head taller than Martin but of such slender build that he was almost certainly heavier. They wore no clothing. Their skin was gray and leathery; their emaciated bodies were featureless.

They had no nose, no mouth nor ears, but much of their faces were taken up by two enormous eyes, black as spilled ink, black as crude oil and pure evil.

The one in the middle lifted its left hand, a single long finger pointed up at the ceiling. The brightness of the lights gained intensity.

Martin squinted harder, looking through slits that burned, his head pounding like cannon fire.

The lights seemed oddly warm, and he felt sluggish as a snake lying on a sun-heated stone. His muscles felt weak and tired, and he lowered his arms. His eyes — squinting so hard he could barely see through them — had grown so heavy. He fought to keep them open, eyes locked on the two pools of midnight that were the central creature's eyes.

He fought so hard, but that light was irresistible, and finally his eyes closed.

In his mind a single image existed. It was all he could see, all he could imagine, and it was all that mattered: Ana, eyes and lips cut away, wide curve of belly split open and hollowed out, a red maw where there should have been smooth skin and new life.

Screaming filled Martin's throbbing head. Only when his eyes snapped open did he recognize the scream as his own.

He stood there, arms down at his sides, holding his repeating rifle by the barrel. Every beat of his heart felt like a pickaxe to his forehead, magnified by the background agony of his own screaming. His muscles seemed to wake, first with a twitch and then fully in his command again.

He lifted his rifle, gripping it by the barrel with both hands, and — screaming, always screaming — bashed it down like a club onto those glossy black eyes.

The central figure fell with one hit, but Martin smashed down once more before swinging hard to the right — that creature's face crushing in where the stock met it — and then down and to the left, snapping through the third creature's spindly gray leg.

Martin smashed downward again and again. He went from one prone body to the next and then back again. It didn't matter that they weren't moving anymore; it didn't matter that their eyes had popped and oozed out and their faces were mushed and their appendages bent at jagged angles.

He couldn't stop screaming and he couldn't stop pounding.

Then he remembered.

He turned to face the frontiersman and the fur trapper. He was panting as he lifted his rifle to his shoulder, wiping viscous, black gore onto his shirt.

The two men had backed themselves to the wall. Their eyes were wide still, but it was terror in them now.

"Where is my wife?"

The fur trapper, hands and voice trembling, said, "There are others. You cannot..."

Martin fired. He'd been aiming for the trapper's forehead, but his heavy breathing affected his aim; the bullet struck the bridge of the man's nose and destroyed his whole face.

The body dropped hard to the mine floor.

Martin brought his aim to the frontiersman.

"The other spur," he said, pointing over Martin's shoulder. "When you first came in, you went left. They took her to the right."

"Show me."

~*~

Partway down the other hall, several other creatures waited for him. They tried their trick with the lights again, but this time Martin fired a shot into the ceiling as soon as he spotted them. There was no ricochet, no sound like a musical saw. The lights shattered and rained little bits of brilliance down around them; these glowing slivers dimmed gradually.

The creatures backed up, heading for a section of tunnel that remained lit. A few turned to run, but their bodies weren't built for action and their retreat was slow.

Martin fired off several shots, felling three of the creatures before his rifle ran out of ammunition. Holding his rifle in his left hand, he drew his revolver. He spent a bullet each on the last two.

He turned to the frontiersman. "I'm going to reload. You try anything, and I'll kill you and find Ana myself."

The frontiersman nodded.

"How many more are there?"

The frontiersman shrugged. "Can't say for sure. They all look the same. They don't speak, not with a voice the way we do. They can sort of put pictures in your mind..."

"And you like that?"

He shrugged again. "I'm seventy-four years old. Haven't aged a day in decades. Haven't been sick that whole time."

"You're a pet and you accept it," Martin said as he loaded new cartridges into his rifle. "How much farther?"

"There's a sort of exam room up ahead."

Martin's eyes narrowed. "If they've touched her."

The frontiersman held up his hands. "You didn't give them much time."

~*~

Ana was naked on a table, the bright yellow light shining down on her.

Martin ran to her. He touched the smooth skin of her belly. It was tight and warm. She was alive and whole.

He tried to rouse her, but nothing worked.

"Where are her clothes?" Martin asked.

"I'll look," the frontiersman said.

Martin opened Ana's eyes with his fingertips. They were both there, but they were unseeing. They remained open even after he took his fingers away.

He sat her up. She moved with him and remained upright. It was as if the light hadn't put her to sleep but made her malleable as clay.

He turned her so that her legs dangled off the side of the table and then eased her down so she stood beside it. He pulled her a few steps away from the table, away from the center of the room, her gate a slow shuffle. Then he pulled his revolver and shot out the light.

Ana turned to look at him but did so without recognition for a moment. Then her brow furrowed and she said, "Martin?"

He holstered his gun and put a calloused hand to her cheek. "I've got you back," he said.

"What happened?"

"Lights took you."

"Like a sheep?"

He nodded. "But I've got you now."

The frontiersman returned with Ana's nightshirt.

"You must be worried they're all dead," Martin said, taking the garment from him. "I figured you'd run off for help."

The frontiersman shrugged, seemingly the only physical gesture he used, and said, "I'm more afraid of you just now."

Martin helped Ana dress.

The frontiersman lingered, waiting for them.

"I'm not going to kill you," Martin said. "I suspect time will do that to you now, if your keepers are no longer around to care for you. Get out of here."

"I have nowhere to go."

"Not my problem," Martin said. "You stand here much longer and I'll send you to hell with the others. Now get."

The frontiersman nodded and backed away a few steps. Then he turned and hurried deeper into the mine.

Ana moved slowly, as if her muscles were still not quite hers to command, but they were not bothered again as they made their way to the mouth of the mine.

Zaldi remained where Martin had left her, and he helped Ana up onto the saddle.

"I shouldn't…the baby," Ana said.

Martin nodded. "It'll be okay. Take it nice and slow, a gentle ride, but we need to get away from this place."

"Are they all gone, do you think?"

Martin exhaled. "I don't know. I know we're leaving. East or west, I don't care, but we're not staying here."

~*~

Once they'd settled in Oregon, Martin wrote to Jude Baker. They'd spoken before Martin and Ana left, and he wrote to Jude both to let the man know they'd reached a new home but also to ask if anything more had happened about the mine.

Enough time went by that Martin assumed a response would never come.

Then one did.

Dear Martin,

I fear you left just in time and those of us that remain have lingered too long. Whether, during your adventure in that cursed mine, you failed to kill them all or if others have since arrived, activity has hardly ceased. It would seem they learned something from their run in with you, Martin. They take whole families now, leaving no one to attempt rescue.

No one has turned up in the state you will recall from our sheep, thank heavens, nor has anyone disappeared entirely, but it seems we've all been losing bits of time. I myself experienced the uncanny sensation of sitting in the cool air and fading light after supper and then, as if only an instant had passed, waking in my bed the following morning. This was not owed to drink or illness. It has happened to many of us.

I think we are being taken into the glowing mine and returned with our memories of that time washed away. What they have done to us there, I am too afraid to speculate.

Nathaniel and Doris Jackson found new scars that seemed years old when they woke. Little Alan Davies wakes screaming in the night, every night. Sarah Matthews, Carl's girl, says she sees pictures in her mind that she does not understand; she draws them out on paper and I'll admit I don't understand them either: they appear to be unfamiliar constellations.

Do not write to me here again. You'll not reach me. I am leaving this place. I only wish I had done so sooner. I will send word to you once I am settled.

Sincerely, Jude Baker

Martin folded the letter and slid it into his pocket. He joined Ana at the table, where she sketched on a sheet of paper.

It was a design Martin recognized, though its significance remained unknown to him: A ladder, its rungs all straight but its side planks twisted so that it made a long, ribbed spiral.

One Shot, One Sin
Jason M Waltz

The sun ticked closer to its zenith, though its scorching heat already surpassed yesterday's apex. Silence reigned, at least on the dusty street. Workers of the two and four legged persuasions continued their labors behind the scene, unknowing or uncaring. Witnesses hugged the board and tarpaulin building fronts, fearful for their lives but not too much. Most were gunslingers just like the participants of this day's drama; some were not.

Some wore no guns at all. They were the ones who fed and clothed and buried those who lived and died by the gun. Some other few were gunfighters — like only one of the main street's occupants. The rest? They were the vultures, the promoters and profiteers of violence. They used all the others till there weren't nothing left to be used.

Except for The Taker. They couldn't use him. At least, none had figured out just how to do so yet. So now the vultures were trying to kill him, for that was the mantra of all vultures: what- or *whom*ever you cannot control, destroy. Oh, not by themselves directly; they were not brave enough to put their lives on the line. They sent their minions instead, as rats slipped into the caged serpent's pen.

The Taker, he didn't mind. It actually made his mission simpler. While a sinner were a sinner after all, he aimed for the bigger game, as it were. The killers, not the liars; the betrayers, not the drunks. Instead of him having to track and hunt prey, they came to find him. Taking the sins out of a man willing to kill another human for some trinkets did just fine by The Taker. He would have been much obliged if he felt any gratitude toward them vultures at all. He did not.

Fallen angels can't afford the luxury of gratitude.

If Fate — and by that he meant time and The Big Fella — allowed, he just might be able to earn his return to heaven. As a thirteenth-tier angel he hadn't even rated a name, not like Michael and Lucifer; just a number. He realized too late that 'just a number' in heaven beat by far any alternative, and he still hadn't received a name.

So he named himself. When he had finally hit upon how he was going to earn God's forgiveness and hopefully his position back, the name was obvious. 'The Taker' was exactly what he decided to do and be. He would buy his way back by taking the sins out of humans. Every sin if he had to…from every mortal if that's what it came to. Whether they lived or died in his doing of it.

The heat rose again, and the fiery ball on high moved closer to its target. The street audience seemed to hold its breath now, everyone intent more on watching death than living life. They licked their lips in anticipation, awaiting the fateful fade of the steeple's silhouetted shadow. Main street shootouts had become such a part of the norm here in Tombstone, folks had crafted a simple method of timeliness. High noon fell regular every day in a straight line along the east-west street with the sun rising behind the House of the Lord. Set dead center on Main was the new Tinhorn & Tenderfoot, largest saloon, gambling, and reputable ladies fine establishment in town. Thirteen paces east stood the sheriff's office and accompanying jail; thirteen west yawned the door of the first undertaker and coffin maker founded the day after Tombstone named itself.

Embedded in the middle of the street stood what appeared to be a hitching post, though on examination no ring provided a place to tie or loop. No sir, atop that post was a highly polished and overly large piece of fool's gold. Denizens of Tombstone knew it for what it was, but on occasion it had gone missing until visiting thieves discovered their mistake. Invariably it always found its way back. None were quite certain who kept it polished, but every morning its twinkling eye reassured all that someone had bent to the task through the darkness.

As said, folks here had come to regard their daily shooting deaths a required moment of silence and acknowledgement of the permanence of death and the impermanence of time, and they determined they were not leaving witnessing it to chance. Nor were they allowing it to have more than its singular moment, however. Tombstone was about the silver after all, and only thing almost as valuable as that ore was the time necessary to round it up by one method or another.

Which is another reason the 'decision makers' had instituted this more reasonable control of shootings. Past June, afore the officially recognized daily public street cleansing, The Taker had collected a few of his sinners inside the Arcade Saloon after a raucous night. In the ensuing festivities one of the dying fallen had dropped his cigar in an open whiskey barrel. Now mid-October and mostly rebuilt, Tombstone did not wish a repeat of that devastating night.

No sir, so the Earp Brothers, they did some talking, first amongst themselves and then with the establishment voices, which included them vultures referenced earlier. They all come to understand there was no encouraging The Taker to move along, and frankly, none of the plans to kill the man had come to fruition, so they agreed to work him into the solution. Then perhaps, once the solution ran smoothly, they would reevaluate and find a way to end or send The Taker.

As the newest establishment rebuilt upon the embers of the Arcade, the Tinhorn & Tenderfoot may have monopolized the center of the main thoroughfare and garnered its fair share of first timers, but it was distinctly third in the popularity of the general populace. The more respectable citizens went on up to Schieffelin Hall for their liquid lunches, while the majority headed to the Bird Cage. But such destinations and tables waited upon the steeple's shadow to send yet another soul, poor or not, on its dusty path to the afterlife.

The Taker waited patiently for that last shift of sun and shadow. He stood framed by the open doors of the church at the head of the street, watching for the moment the shadow of its steeple blinked out that sparkling piece of fool's gold. He did not mind the game these humans played. The risk to him was nil — time was immaterial to him and he could not miss, not with these 'bullets.'

Lady Luck had smiled on him when he had stumbled into his old right-side-even-numbered angel in Dodge City, he trying to drown his misery in rotgut (and failing), she trying to save yet another drunk (not him) from himself. She had expressed her sorrow at his fall and longing for his return; he then confessed his intention: to earn his way back by liberating humanity of sin, come death or high water.

Despite her dismay, she had solved the dilemma of how he was going to achieve this. In a blink she took them to a back-alley dive in the sordid slums of Chicago and introduced him to a prodigal devil. This impudent imp reveled in causing chaos, and spoiling the plans of both Lucifer and the Almighty did not faze him in the least. His 'apothecary' hawked all sorts of mischief to the multitude of miscreants, from peddlers to politicians to preachers. There was not a sin he did not know.

Together, angel and devil crafted special casings for The Taker's Colts they named sin-gatherers. Instead of black powder and lead slugs, these brass shells appeared almost empty. Close inspection could maybe discern the sheen of a spidery web outlined against an inky darkness in the base.

Close inspection by a knowing eye could maybe identify the angelic hair embedded in the demonic tar…for a more decorous word.

These sin-gatherers did not punch holes into their targets; they pulled holes out of them by snaring, ripping, and finally trapping their sins. A sinner's body riddled by The Taker looked like he had back-shot the victim with what appeared to be all the exit holes facing him. Which was another reason Tombstone's regulated shootouts worked well for him — no one could deny he faced his opponents fair and square. After a shootout, The Taker ejected filled rounds instead of empties. Casings now filled with the sins of his victims. His saved ones.

Most fellows in this Wild West were not singular or mild sinners, so it took several shots for The Taker to rid their mortal frames of all the filth inside. Hence his carrying two ivory-gripped six-shooters. Those humans, sadly, did not survive The Taker's salvation here on earth, though their souls did rise to heaven cleansed as babes.

On occasion, he did fire upon a wee or mostly innocent sinner and one suction of sin was all it took to scrub them clean. So long as the hole left in the body was not in a vital area, these humans survived redeemed. They turned their backs upon their former lives and walked the world itinerant evangelical preachers. Sadly, this did not prevent some of them from sinning anew.

The Taker kept a bag of the rounds filled with sins tied around his saddle horn. Roughly once a month or whenever he ran low of special empties, he would return to Chicago and meet the angel and the devil. The Taker would watch the duo extract each sin-gatherer and dump its contents into the narrow snout of a bulbous bladder-like container: his 'sin safe.' The safe was woven of angel hair and lined with demon scat, and the snout was a one-way entrance. The Taker had no idea how many sins were stuffed inside it, but it had been flat like an empty hot water bottle when they began his crusade. After he sealed the stopper with a drop of his once-holy-now-damned blood, he would take his new bag of sin-gatherers and return to his quest.

Today, as the sun shifted its final incremental tic, he knew he faced a dastardly desperado. He was confident it would require emptying at least one of his Colts into the man to redeem his soul. His hands dropped, drew, aimed, and sent searching rounds of sin-gatherers streaking downrange.

He was unprepared for the wallops that slammed into his own frame and knocked him backward once, twice, then a third time. Tremendous amounts of white smoke filled the street before him as he gasped for breath, adding to his choking and hampering visibility. The Taker heard the confusion among the willing but now worried witnesses and added his own to it as he squinted down the street.

Opposite him, The Man in Black laughed and turned his back, his sun-bleached charcoal duster flying wide like wings of a predator as he spun. The gleam of silver-heeled pistols, mother-of-pearl shirt buttons, and a dinner-plate-sized belt buckle briefly glinted and winked from the dark recesses before the long coat slammed closed and the man's black shadow stretched before him. The Taker shook his head to clear the ache setting in and brought his breathing back under control.

Ignoring the excited chatter along the street and mentally replaying events, he could swear in addition to the silver gleams on the man's clothes he had also seen the gleam of a large rapacious grin filled with teeth. Sharp, pointed teeth. And now that he thought of it, he knew he had seen things writhing in that long black shadow that moved before The Man in Black.

A hand grabbed his forearm and shook him. "What in blazing hells was that? Neither of you dropped! He hit you! You hit him!" The man's eyes widened as he looked at The Taker's chest then to the ground. "You…you're…you're buh-leeding!"

The Taker jerked in surprise and looked down at himself. Sure enough, the blue-silvery sheen of his blood leaked down his chest, slowly pulsing with the pumping of his heart. Shocked, The Taker did what all demons do when confronted and confounded — he involuntarily vanished.

~*~

He was not happy.

Once he regained his bearings, The Taker discovered he had rematerialized in Hell. The absolute last place he wanted to be and one that would prove a challenge to exit in a timely manner. In addition, apparently he had just disappeared from the dusty street before the eyes of dozens of witnesses. Returning to Tombstone might prove even more difficult than leaving Hell. Demons were only authorized to depart Hell when dispatched on missions. Which meant he must report to his squad leader and give an update on his current mission status. The Taker gnashed his teeth in frustration. This was not part of his grand plan.

A guttural voice ground behind him. "Whatchu doin' here, spittle-prick? Yous knows this area is off limits to yous."

The Taker dropped into a crouch and spun toward the threat, hands reaching to his twin Colts. Except they slapped empty air, and he found he was again as nude as every other devil in Hell. His eyes met the grotesque naked groin of one of the 'Heavies,' second-level demons that answered — defiantly, but answered — only to Lucifer and his handful of lieutenants. These were the fiends that Hell used as guardians and bodyguards. Dozens of them secured all the gates, the secrets, the dignitaries, and the supplies of Hell. Size-wise they were nowhere near as tall as the elites, but their girth was gargantuan and they outweighed every demon.

These were the angels that fell hardest. Unlike Lucifer and his co-planners who actually believed they were doing the right thing, these fallen exulted in rebelling and the opportunity to embrace their dark natures. Their rage and hate fueled insatiable appetites for the destruction of all the Almighty's creations from divine to mortal.

Also unlike Lucifer and the top-tier fallen angels, they were not beautiful. The figures of each were as ugly outside as inside, and each viler than another. This particular Heavy dwarfed The Taker into insignificance. He was surprised the thing's eyes could even pick his once-again red-mottled hide out against the rust-hued and shadow-strewn hellish terrain. The ground trembled and he realized the beast laughed at him.

Guffaws of deep baritone sounded high above. "Look at the wittle-prick! Been playin' cowboy, eh? Haw-haw-haw. Bang-bang, gotcha!"

Another voice, like tectonic plates shifting, chuckled, "'Wittle-prick' instead a spittle-prick, good one." And the ground shook more violently.

The first voice sounded again, much lower and closer. "I said, 'Whatchu doin' here,' bottom-feeder? Better answer up afore we stomp you. Then you can explain that to yer boss."

The Taker could not stop the gag that groped down his throat and pulled the contents of his stomach out after it. His searching eyes had located the speaker: the first Heavy's oversized sexual organ ended in an evilly grinning face. Its cruel laugh echoed like thunder from above.

"Oh-ho-ho, he's never seen a penis-head afore boys!" The freak stuck its tongue out while it flopped up and down with the giant laughter shaking its body.

The Taker saw the massive shape of a dark pyramid towering behind the behemoths. He had no idea where in Hell they were, but he had never heard of a pyramid. Then his eyes widened; the fiery orb of a great eye had just popped open against the black roof of Hell at the peak of the monument. He quickly ducked his head and turned to flee only to see a large mob of demons had gathered behind him. All of them were looking upward in awe. Even the Heavies' laughter was slowly silencing, though the little head spit at him before peering upward in anger.

A powerful voice sang out across the sky. It was the dulcet tones of Lucifer. "What have we here, my children? All the merriment garnered my attention. I do so love good times."

None answered. The Heavies did not take their eyes off their king, though all the other demonfolk averted their gaze, most even ducking their heads. The Taker slipped into a muddled mass of them, trying to lose himself in their flailing shadows.

"Uh-uh-uh, is that you there, Number thirty-two-million-eight-hundred-seventy-three thousand, twenty? I have not seen you in such a long time," The Morning Star gushed.

He may not have recalled it, but at the sound of his true name, The Taker froze in place. All the demons surrounding him scattered, leaving his immobile form starkly exposed.

Lucifer continued. "I am delighted you all are enjoying yourselves. I think I will take our little friend here along though, and leave you to continue on your own. I hope you don't mind."

A hand appeared above the crowd of demons. Thumb and forefinger speared down, snatching The Taker up even as all the others, including the Heavies, jumped and ran like hellfire chased them.

The Taker was definitely not very happy.

~*~

He found himself seated at a round table. Five paper playing cards lay face down before him. Raising his head, he discovered a man-sized Lucifer sat across from him. There were five cards face down before him as well, the remainder of the deck held in the claws of a green-visored imp. The dealer was dressed in long white sleeves, black bowtie, and black sleeve garters. A white Stetson perched atop Lucifer's head and a shining silver star reading 'Sheriff' stuck out on his chest.

The Taker continued eyeballing the room and found they were in a familiar western saloon filled with familiar faces. Right there at the next table sat Doc Holliday, one hand holding pairs of kings and queens, the other a Derringer in his belt. The back of an Earp's head rose from the bar, and in the far corner the Clanton brothers muttered together over drinks.

"Yes indeed, my little devil, this is the Tinhorn & Tenderfoot. The very same establishment you just vanished from in front of." Old Deuce's velvet timbre was intended to put him at ease.

The Taker noticed the saloon was silent, then realized everyone but the three of them was not moving. He looked back to his master and tentatively cleared his throat. He looked at his hands in his lap and found the familiar low-slung belt with the heels of his revolvers to either side. He tucked his head a bit further and saw the slight trickle of blood still oozing from the hole in his chest.

"What we have here, Number thirty… No, let us do away with that. I much prefer your chosen moniker: The Taker. Less cumbersome and my, does it have a ring to it.

"As I was saying, what we have here is an opportunity for the both of us." Suddenly Satan's hands were above the table and something shone dully between two fingers. The same fingers that so recently had pinched him up, The Taker uncomfortably thought.

"I just love these 'sin-gatherers' as you call them. Fascinating devices. I do love the creativity of all my children. It's why I leave you to your own devices, you know. All your little minds working tirelessly on new ways to be devious. Saves me an immense amount of labor, let me tell you.

"Anyway, I think you and I differ a wee little bit on their proper usage." The brass cartridge fell to the table where it desultorily spun while the Devil held both hands up and patted the air in a placating manner. "I have no desire to question the inventor's aims, no worries! What I see is a chance for both of us to benefit here." He picked up his cards and nodded at The Taker to do the same.

"One game of five card draw will decide it. Win or lose, I will return you to that street out there just before you so amazingly and disturbingly vanished before all those eyes. It will be as if you never left." Lucifer slid a finger along his nose and winked. "And your squad leader back home will never know you were in town, as it were. Everything will be as it was, my dear Taker. Though those Heavies, they will remember you, so best stay far away from them.

"It's only the one game, so we will turn our cards up and play everything in the open. I would not want anyone to suspect nefarious play. Winner," here Old Deuce paused and smiled, his lips friendly but his eyes betraying a predatory gleam, "takes all."

He nonchalantly picked up and overturned his cards. Two sixes, two aces, and a nine stared back. Lucifer whistled. The Taker thought he heard a faint chorus of devils chuckle.

He had no choice; he had to ask. "What are the stakes…sir?"

Lucifer feigned surprise. "Why, we never said? Oh, not much, really, just the ownership of your sin safe."

The Taker could not refrain from gasping. Panic assailed him and the crazy idea of trying to draw and fire and flee erupted in his mind. The Devil continued as if nothing were amiss.

"It is such a marvelous idea, I cannot believe none of your numerous siblings ever thought of it before." He shook his head in mock wonder. "Honestly, how I and my brothers never did is astounding. Yes, the prize before us is your sin safe. It really changes nothing for you. You can continue to make and fill and empty your sin-gatherers, heavens know I wouldn't want to halt that! And you will carry on filling that sin safe with all those many, many sins you are gathering. It will only be the owner of the safe that's at stake, and really, why would you want the responsibility of minding all those sins? Can you just imagine what would happen if such a vast amount of dirty, despicable, dangerous deeds were to suddenly be released? The potential devastation!"

The Devil beamed at The Taker. "I could never forgive myself the thought of you being responsible for such a calamity. The horror." He spread his fingers on the edge of the table and leaned forward. "Now turn your cards."

The Taker took a deep breath and hesitated. He recalled the gleam of The Man in Black's evil grin, saw again the black maw of the creature's shadow. "I want The Man in Black," he blurted.

Lucifer blinked. Then his brow furrowed and shadows gathered around him. Great wings seemed to grow behind him and he loomed above The Taker. Just when he opened his mouth a shimmering glare struck The Taker's eyes and he jerked his head aside. The lawman's star upon The Tempter's chest glinted in the glow of the rafter oil lamps it now was among. Abruptly the shadows fled and Lucifer regained his seat. He laughed.

"Well now little one. I am truly impressed." He nodded. "Agreed. You win, I will give you the path of The Man in Black. I will not give him to you — you will have to defeat him. But I will set you on his trail." He grinned again. "If you win. Now turn them."

The Taker nodded and turned his cards face up. A king, queen, jack, and ten of spades and a jack of hearts.

"My, my, we have a game!" Lucifer clapped his hands in delight. "Looks like I hold your ace though." Sure enough, the ace of spades lay before the Devil.

Lucifer took up his nine of clubs and tossed it to the dealer. "I'll take one card."

The imp slid the top card off the deck and dealt it to his left. Old Deuce snatched it off the table and brought it to his face. His delighted grin was unmistakable. With a gallant wave of his off-hand and tip of his head, he flipped his card to the table. The Taker held his breath, dreading what he knew would appear. A six.

"Full house, my Taker. Six-six-six over aces. I do worry for your chances. Instead of five cards, there is now only one card that can help you." That chorus of devils joined in again, the grating sound setting him on edge.

The Taker had stopped praying long ago when he finally understood he no longer held a relationship with the Almighty in Heaven. But he breathed a prayer now, and while it was to win, primarily on his mind was winning to keep the sin safe out of Lucifer's possession. Horrified at the possibility the Devil had explored, The Taker knew he could never allow it to happen.

"One," he croaked, and pushed the extra jack away.

Lucifer beckoned at the dealer, who turned toward The Taker. The top card of the deck flicked off the top and spun through the air, landing on his fingertips. A hush fell upon the devilish cacophony and The Taker realized he had scrunched his eyes shut. Slowly he lifted his lids.

First he saw the cowering dealer. Then he saw the inferno of fury on Lucifer's face. And then the nine of spades, highlighted by the brilliance of the sheriff's star.

A hiss escaped Lucifer's lips, echoed by the hellish chorus. Then one hand swiped out, morphing into a gigantic talon that took the dealer's head off with a snick. The imp's body vanished in a puff of plasmatic powder. The Morning Star rose from his seat and plucked the silver star off his chest with his normal hand. "No need for that any longer." He tossed it on the deck of cards. "Law and order always wins my ass." Sweeping the white Stetson off his head, he threw it high then viciously impaled it with his talon against the center beam that supported the peak of the roof.

"You win this time, Taker. You keep real close eye on that sin safe; never know who might hear about it and come a'looking." He sniffed. "Whenever you leave town, The Man in Black's trail will call you." He pointed with his human hand to the pinned hat. "You can explain this if you stick around. Now get out of my sight!" He twisted and savagely bent the talon. A loud snap sounded and everything went black.

~*~

"You…you're…you're buh-leeding!" a man cried in his face.

The Taker looked at his chest, again saw his silver-blue blood. "Why, so I am, stranger. So I am." A flash of light and the snap of wings caught his attention. He saw the briefest refraction of sunlight bend in the direction of the horse corrals. "I best get me to the doc."

Ignoring the hubbub rising all about, The Taker strode to the nearest corral to buy a horse. Pulling his vest closed to cover the slowing ooze of his blood, he bartered with the wrangler, then waited for the man to outfit the mustang with a full kit. He tipped his hat to the sign for the O.K. Corral and mused aloud, "All-in-all, things did turn out okay."

He smiled slightly to himself when he heard the snort and whisper of his favorite angel. "Good thing your Lady Luck just happened to come to town to warn you. Our Chicago prodigal told me the Devil himself had cottoned to your scheme and was planning a surprise for you. If I had not been near enough or it had been the dark of night rather than the bright day of Arizona desert…"

The Taker lifted his face to the sun and smiled wide. He could not see her, but he knew she could see him. "That's a good name. I will call you Lady Luck forever more."

He could hear the smile in her reply. "And your name is official now. Lucifer himself chose to accept your name. You are forever The Taker." He sensed her smile gone. "I will move the sin safe when I return to Chicago. Don't ask me where yet, I don't know. I'll find you in a month." A fresh bag of empty sin-gatherers plopped to the dirt. The Taker knew she was gone.

He would leave Tombstone to the Earps, let them clean up the sinners ranging its streets. There were plenty of other places to gather sins. Besides, he had The Man in Black to find and Old Deuce's hands to keep off his sin safe.

Final Words
B. L. Blankenship & L. B. Stimson

He lay there on the floor weeping and wailing, yet his faith had not flown. Folks tell that there's a sort of sadness that goes to the bone. A man eaten up with a thing like that could be freezing to death and wouldn't get himself a blanket. They say when something like that comes over a person, they kind of get a faraway look in their eye as though they're hoping to see something beyond this mortal veil; something removed by time and space. It's the kind of thing that can leave a hole in your heart. Generally, it's somebody; not a thing that can be bought and sold. The loss of the irreplaceable is what does a number like that on somebody's heart. Such was the case of Leon Montgomery Jefferson.

He met his darling wife and from there on, time never seemed to move as it had before. Oh, how they loved one another. There was almost a manner of music about it all. It seemed like everything in his life had led up to him meeting her. Her name was Opal, and in Leon's eyes never was there a gem so fair as she. Her eyes sparkled like diamonds. Her dark raven-black hair cascaded down her shoulders in pure perfection.

Leon couldn't remember a time when his dear, beloved Opal wasn't the very picture of perfection. Her only fault, if one could call it a fault, was that her womb seemed to be barren; or at least the two of them hadn't had any success in making any baby during their nearly eight years of marital bliss before the fever set in. His perfect little wife had been bitten by a tick. The tiny vampiric menace did more than draw her blood. Tragically for them, it was unto the death. In spite of his attempts to save her, there was nothing he could do.

Leon went down to the local church without her as she lay in bed ailing. Standing in the gap as an intercessor, he prayed. The poor man looked as though he were dying, too. Leon's face had a sunkenness to it. There was a hollowed-out, cavernous look to his eyes. Very clearly to all of the congregants, he was losing everything he loved. The feeling among some of the church members was that if Leon's dear Opal was to pass, his heart would die with her. They prayed what seemed to be all of the right words, saying all of the right things, and yet for weeks, her fever carried on — until one day a thick, quiet stillness came.

Leon wailed and he howled. He cried out into the nothingness which now filled the house that was once their home. Pleading and adjuring the Holy Spirit of God, he called out with desperation to please revive her again.

"My God. My God. I can't live without her. God, I've given you so much. I've always loved you. I've asked you to bless every meal. I've gone to church, been kind to my neighbor, and paid my tithes and offerings. Please, please, don't take her from me. God, please don't take her from me. God..."

Howbeit, it wasn't a short prayer. Leon's words continuously erupted into the night, transitioning from asking to demanding. Was God deaf so that He did not hear him? Was He asleep? Did He not care to at least give an answer as to why…why amid all of his prayers he'd been answered — or rather unanswered — in this harsh of a matter?

Tragically, he likely knew the answer the preacher would give, or for that matter what any church person would give to someone like him going through something like this. Doubtlessly, they'd quote the Apostle Paul's letter to the Corinthian Church in that we look through a glass darkly; and how in this mortal life, while things are unclear, once we've transcended into glory we'll understand all things like this that were indiscernible.

Still, imagining these words and this conversation with the preacher, particular church folk, and so forth, it did nothing to help Leon, nor his situation. He drowned in pools of sorrow that day and shed tears in such magnitude that they seemed to be without end.

Flipping through the Bible frantically, he sought for answers. He read how Jesus said to Mary and Martha that He was the resurrection and the life; and thereafter raised their brother Lazarus from the depths, back to the world of the living. Therewith determination for a miraculous work of the Lord God Almighty, the hysterical husband of the late Opal Louise Fitzpatrick-Jefferson decided that he would fast and pray. He'd fast until she came back to be with him or he'd go to be with her.

~*~

As the sun went down in the blueing crimson skies, her stench only grew worse, despite his tending to her. Opal's once fair skin had turned a deathly, lifeless gray. Her bowels had emptied out, and with buckets, rags, and water, the heavily grieving Leon — who'd held her so dear for the best years of his life — saw to cleaning her. He filled the house with wildflowers, laying them both around her and upon her in hopes to mask the stench, all the while getting a little weaker. His only nourishment came from drinking water, which kept him hydrated.

Additionally, he administered the Lord's Supper, the Holy Eucharist, to himself daily, with a pinch of bread and a minor swig of wine. Reading the passage aloud and praying at the appropriated times, in accordance to the scriptures, he read: "For I have received of the Lord that which also I delivered unto you, That the Lord Jesus the same night in which he was betrayed took bread: and when he had given thanks, he brake it, and said, Take, eat: this is my body, which is broken for you: this do in remembrance of me. After the same manner also he took the cup, when he had supped, saying, This cup is the new testament in my blood: this do ye, as oft as ye drink it, in remembrance of me. For as often as ye eat this bread, and drink this cup, ye do shew the Lord's death till he come." Thereafter followed an amen, though many an amen had been found amid the intermediary prayers he'd spoken before taking up the bread, the body of the Lord, and the wine, the blood of the new covenant.

Speaking no evil, no word of doubt or unbelief, he called those things that were not as though they were. Leon Jefferson remained faithful that God would raise his wife even as he had Lazarus, for there could be no other way. In his mind, this alone could free him of the darkness that had become his world. If not for the Lord, he would have no hope. His faith was secure, though others no doubt might come to dissuade him. Like the bitter cold that kills the trees — only for spring to bring new life to them again — so would the Author of Life resurrect his beloved. Praying again and again, he'd always finish by saying that there can be no other way.

All of these were happenings of the first few days and an open door for what was to come. Wholly Leon expected that just as Jesus Christ raised himself on the third day, so would the Lord do unto his wife; whom he felt that he could not live without. Lying upon the floor in a heap of ashes that he had gathered — as was the fashion of the Old Testament — he lamented her. Like Job, taking a razor he shaved his head and beard (a sign of intense mourning) and praised the Lord for this miracle that he knew would happen, for there was no other way.

Exhausted, as he finally went to rest, Leon was jarred by the feeling of his wife's hand pressing down gently upon his, so much so that he opened his eyes fully expecting to see her up and about as she had once been. Howbeit, no discernible figure was there. So great was his torment. The only consolation was that his faith was now greater, or so he said. Bitter tears rolled down his cheeks as Leon Montgomery Jefferson crept into a world of nightmares somewhat indistinct from the one that he seemed to be living.

~*~

As he lay there with eyes shut, her mortal shell stared off into the nothingness, as he'd not closed his wife's. Opal's mouth hung open so that her spirit might again return by way of it. That night was so dark and the air in their home foul, despite the flowers' attempt to completely cover up the smell of death. A rancidness perfumed the air.

A figure watched, hidden in the dimness of shadows that gathered in the corner of the room. It let loose a low, crackling chuckle as Leon continued offering murmured prayers for the raising of his beloved. *Such a pathetic creature*, it thought. *Lamenting and wailing and calling on his Lord to raise her from the dead. No, his Lord did not hear his cries.*

Leon jerked from his slumped position in the chair, his legs kicking out straight and steadying his body. He rubbed his eyes. A slight hiss and rustling rose from the corner. He held his breath. A shadow moved like a slithering creature of sorts before a shallow glow emerged. Leon let loose his breath; his prayers had been answered. It was an angel of light; a vision of divine Providence coming to ease his pain and restore the breath of life to his beloved Opal.

The shadowed figure continued in its emergence; a golden aura flickered, wrapping itself around the forming creature. Its features were that of the most delicate and beautiful woman Leon had ever laid his eyes upon. He remained still as it lowered its head, the voice a mere whisper.

"You seek a miracle."

Leon wiped at the tears streaming down his face.

"I do. My Opal."

"I shall offer you the blood of a new covenant, however you shall always be mine. Body and soul."

Leon once again held his breath. The Lord had sent him an angel of mercy. Both he and his beloved were being offered the opportunity to free themselves from purgatory. Leon nodded, his hands quivering as he gestured towards Opal's body.

Again, the odd creature let loose a slight, rattled chuckle. *Such a feeble, weak-minded being, this man of God. Blinded by his faith, so easily fooled.* It moved from Leon and swirled around Opal's body as it lay still on the altar. The dried petals from the assortment of wildflowers floated about as though being tossed from invisible hands, a confetti of sorts to celebrate the impending moment. Moving upon her body, the figure twisted and elongated, transforming into an ashen mist and streaking into Opal's mouth.

Leon gripped the seat of his chair. A flash of crimson eyes boring into his own caused a whimper to slip from his mouth. The creature rose before him; the golden aura was no longer. It was instead tattered, blackened, and layered with the rancidness of the perfumed air that was also no longer disguised by the supple, freshly cut scent of wildflowers.

On the table, Opal's head had turned, her eyes open, staring at Leon. Her pupils pulsed with the same crimson hue as that of the shadowed creature darting about the room. Leon felt his head begin to swoon from the dizzying array of movement. He tried to stand, however he stumbled and fell to the floor. His eyes locked on his beloved's eyes that were not her own. Her mouth closed and fell open, a pool of blackened tar-like spittle dripping from the corners of her mouth. She made a gagging sound as she expelled more of the sticky substance.

"There, there, my son. She has risen. Just like you requested. I have answered your prayers. I have resurrected your beloved," the creature's voice rattled and cooed as it extended an iridescent finger. The finger traced its way down Leon's temple, coming to a rest beneath his chin.

Leon held still. The touch of the creature's skin against his own made him quiver. How could he have been so wrong? This was not an angel of light. This was an angel of death. And he, a mere mortal of a man, consumed by grief to the point of blindness, had failed to uphold his faith. He had conjured not The Lord of Light. Not the miracle of life. He had conjured a demon; a monster; an immortal creature who now held both his and Opal's soul captive for all eternity.

"Rise now and go to her. There is much to be done."

Leon lifted his chin but not before a prickle from the creature's nail pierced his skin. He held back his revulsion as the creature sucked a droplet of blood from its fingertip. He stumbled to the altar where Opal now sat upright, her neck moving stiffly from left to right, her arms outstretched as though she were an alien being learning to use a new body. The completeness of sheer terror gripped every muscle in Leon's body. He stretched his hand out and let it rest upon Opal's. Again, with stiff movement, she raised her head, her crimson-hued eyes holding his gaze. A smile tugged at her mouth. Leon gulped as he noticed the flash of a snow-white pointed tooth protruding from her upper lip.

This was not his Opal, yet it was. His mind swirled in a chaotic haze of thoughts. This angel of death — what did it mean by there was work to be done? He was a servant of the Lord. The Lord of Light. Leon turned from Opal. The creature was darting, once again, around the room. With each movement, Leon noticed, the creature seemed to transform — from male to female to a mere wisp of solidity. It was evolving; it couldn't be, but yet it was. The room fell silent. A sudden rush of frigid air swept about the room and then, there it was.

"Behold, your master."

Its voice was masculine in tone. It was tall, but not so tall as to be considered peculiar. Its skin was fair, but not too pale. Broad shoulders rose upon a narrow and fit torso. The eyes were nearly black with flecks of crimson and, as it smiled, the pointed ends of snow-white teeth appeared.

How could this be? Leon questioned. The creature had done the unimaginable. It had transformed into a man. It now stood before him, clothed in the finest of tailored suits, donning a dark, oil-skinned duster. The threads of its shirt glistened in gold against the silken black hue of the fabric. Leon's eyes fell to the floor. It was all madness. It wasn't real. It was grief. It was the lack of sustenance. He stepped back to his chair and reached for the cask of wine set upon the nearby table. He took several long gulps and shook his head.

"That's right, now. Drink up, for tomorrow we ride," the creature's voice cooed and hissed.

Leon jerked around. The creature was hovering behind his Opal, raking its fingers through her long raven tresses. Opal's head swayed and fell back as though she were waiting for a lover to extend a trail of kisses. He wanted to lunge towards it — how dare it touch his Opal! He watched as the creature lifted several strands of hair to its face before pulling in a protracted breath of air through the nostrils of its slender nose.

"Oh so lovely. I feel your jealousy. I did what you requested, however I never promised she would be yours. She belongs to me, but I shall be inclined to share her. You are my servant and she is my new maiden. Now, we shall remain here, and tomorrow you and I shall take a ride about. So many souls in need of my tending. In need of answered prayers."

Leon's gut tightened as the flash of the creature's pointed teeth caught his eye. He looked at Opal; she was a mere empty vessel of the woman he had loved. The woman he had failed. His head fell; he squeezed his eyes shut to push back the onslaught of tears that threatened to burst forth.

"There's one thing I would like to ask, if I may?" Leon's voice hovered above a whisper.

"Certainly."

"What do I call you?" Leon need not ask for what the creature truly was; as he knew, it was a monster, a demon, and an ungodly creature, planning to unleash hellfire upon the land with both his and his beloved Opal's assistance.

Again, the creature chuckled with a smooth hiss of sorts.

"You may call me..." The accursed name was not one he could have pronounced or repeated, a blasphemous combination of the sacred and the demonic.

He hesitated, thinking what matter of maddened delusion this must be that stirred all around him. Yet the mark that this vile thing made upon his chin told another story. Its infectious burning was intense, as though he had been kissed by a hot iron rather than a clawed finger. Moreover, the odors of rot, death, and decay were ever present, though that in and of itself could merely mean that Opal's bowels had perhaps spilled out once more. Would that be odd, he pondered? And still, amidst all of the reasonable explanations that anyone might tell themselves, when set before this vile thing he knew that what stood before him was far too great of a nightmare to conjure up with his mind.

Seeking to calm himself and at the spirit's suggestion, he began to consume more wine. As unsettling as it was to look upon this shapeshifting abomination, this somehow seemed preferable to casting his eyes onto the empty shell where once dwelt the woman that he loved. Her eyes had become completely black, and with that single fang stemming down from her gums in front of her incisors, something about her looked like a sort of mosquito hybrid. Her face was pale and expressionless, not fully recovered from the mask of death, but seemingly more alive looking than she had been. That is, if you could even call her status alive. Truly, by any account, she was nothing more than a puppet version of herself; a doll possessed and forced to play the muse of this foul thing.

"I didn't call for you, spirit," said he of a sudden, his mind struggling with the possibilities.

Therein recalling to himself that he'd never even given this thing his name, he took another slug of wine and, being Biblically minded, began to recall scripture. He remembered the account with the would-be exorcists who were written of in the Acts of the Apostles. Being charlatans, the devils spoke from the demoniac, telling Sceva and his seven sons, "I know Jesus and I know Paul, but I don't know you."

Yessir, Leon Montgomery Jefferson might have been a broken man, but he was a man who had a sincere relationship with Jesus Christ and so found it important to read and meditate upon His Holy Word. With this rationale, he thereby knew that this was no devil, or it would have known his name.

His faith was not shipwrecked. His was not merely a song and a dance, but something that he lived every day. Thereby, he knew this was no devil that stood before him. Howbeit, it wasn't human either. This wretched creature, which thought itself clever, was not of the planting of God, and as it was in days of old when giants roamed the earth, it too ought to be devoured by the sword. Still, Leon didn't mean to show his hand.

God knew that he had fasted before, and oft times when a Christian person fasts — or at least, in his own personal case — they become keenly aware of things. Hashing and rehashing all of this, he again thought how he'd not shared his own name. It was an issue that brought his mind to the imposter wife sitting still and looking strangely. Could it access her memories? Did the thing living inside of her know who he was? He pondered it all and whether this shape before him — of whose true form he did not know — knew his name was Leon Montgomery Jefferson.

Taking more drink, he pressed the being with riddles asking why it would have the three of them wait till the morrow, adding, "Do you think it is wise for my deceased wife to traverse through an area where she is known?" There were many other things he said or thought he said, but they all became jumbled and strung together in the nonsensical way that things happen in dreams. Certainly, he'd not had this much alcohol, he told himself. As he rubbed the scar that the creature's fingernail had made, the thought then occurred to him that this had somehow poisoned him. Leon Jefferson was fading fast.

~*~

Before his eyes a gate opened to the world of dreams. They took him back to when he was happy. He fell in love with Opal all over again. It was like a sort of Heaven, freeing him from the Hell that he'd just encountered. Everything in it felt so real because it was real. All of the places, things, and people in it had actually happened. He danced through a memory of sheer bliss with his dear, sweet Opal. There the two of them walked hand in hand and side by side, for there could be no other way. It was all that he'd ever wanted. It was all that he'd ever dreamed or known, or at least it felt that way.

In its own way, it was a perfect dream. It was the sort where you forget all of the misfortunes in your life, all of the years spent and occurrences that might trouble you. It's like they were blocked somehow, so that all you might know for the time is sweet peace. Together, the two of them talked about the nicest things.

When he first awoke from it, the dream held to him so well that for several minutes thereafter he remembered it perfectly, then less and less. He had to let the realization come to him slowly of where he was and what was happening.

Recalling something about a scar, he rubbed his chin but felt nothing unusual; no blood graced his finger when he pulled it from his face. He glanced around; the house was not unkempt or dirty. Everything was as clean swept as it had been during the days when his beloved Opal was with him. Then he asked himself if that was just a passing thought. How wonderful it'd be for it to be true. Could his Opal still be with him? Had the Rocky Mountain Spotted Fever been a figment of his imagination? Had it all been merely a dream?

"Opal," he called.

"Yes, dear," replied his beloved wife's sweet voice as tenderly as ever.

Leaping to his feet, Leon dashed to meet her. Declaring how much he loved her, he clasped her precious hand. She looked just as youthful as she had before the supposed sickness took her. Her hand felt just as tender, her eyes looked as natural, and even her smile was there just like normal. There was no central mosquito-like fang protruding from her upper gum. He kissed her, and thereafter she continued making breakfast.

"Do you think that Dark Lords ask questions they know the answers to?" she asked.

"Why," he replied, finding it an odd question to ask while preparing breakfast.

"Do you think that Dark Lords only ask questions about things they don't know, or do you think they might prefer to test people?" she said, ever so casually.

With that, a terrible feeling came over him. *Perhaps I had been scratched after all,* he thought. Impetuously he asked her what she meant by those questions, raising his voice and looking for some otherness about her to surface. Despite this, she seemed perfectly calm and said no more of it, acting as though these were perfectly normal questions one minute and almost acting as though they'd not been asked in the next.

Racing to the bedroom, Leon took his revolver from the nightstand drawer. While it was in its usual place, it felt light, or at least that was the reason he gave himself when checking to see if it was loaded like always. It wasn't. A deep foreboding consumed him. Inwardly, this affirmed to Leon that he must have been right about all of the nightmarish things he'd seen before, as well as this creature being killable, and yet, the question was raised on how to kill it.

Leon tucked the revolver into his coat pocket and searched through the drawers. A single bullet rolled towards his trembling fingers. He pushed the extractor pin. The cylinder fell open with a sharp clack. His fingers continued to tremble. He pinched the bullet and pushed it into the awaiting chamber. He had one shot; one opportunity to end the madness.

From across the house, he heard Opal's sweet voice calling him to come to breakfast. The song of her voice interspersed with the sizzle of steak and eggs cooking on the woodstove. Leon stared into the oval mirror hung above his dresser. His eyes were empty, sullen, dull. Was it the madness that had overcome him to lend to such an expression? Had he been drugged? He straightened his spine, ran his fingers through his hair, and returned to the kitchen to take his seat at the table.

As he watched her place his meal onto the metal plate, he noticed the creature watching from the corner. It was different now, though, the duster jacket now pale. Leon's eyes darted from the woman — whom he no longer recognized as his Opal — back to the creature. It was all wrong. This place. It was similar but yet, no. This was not his home; it was a mere reflection of time and place. A duplicate.

His head hung heavy with a mass of thoughts. Beyond him, their voices murmured with a serious tone. He stabbed the slab of steak with his fork and reached for a non-existent knife. He raised the fork; his teeth tearing into the thin layer of pink flesh. He kept tearing away and swallowing at a frantic pace. His meal. His last meal.

"Now, Mr. Jefferson," the voice hissed as the creature glided closer. "There's no need to rush. Take your time. We are in no hurry. In fact, it is I who was able to secure you additional time. It is I who explained the importance of monitoring you; studying you; and quite possibly saving you."

Leon dropped the torn remains of the steak onto his plate.

"What do you mean? Saving me? My life is of no value; it has no meaning without my Opal," he quaked.

"But yet, you decided her fate."

"I?"

"Leon, for you to proceed, you must accept your actions and ask for forgiveness, otherwise, I cannot save you."

He mulled over the creature's words. What was he talking about? Accept my actions? Determined her fate? What sort of purgatory had he been swept into?

"Leon, I am capable of many things, but you must be the one to make the decision. I have shown you all that is good and evil. Now, you must choose. It is time to make your decision."

No. He had to kill it, end it now. His hand dropped into his lap; his fingers fumbled to cock the hammer. In a rushed movement, he jerked his arm upwards. His chin fell atop the barrel. A flash filled the room, a mist rose and settled.

His final words, left unspoken, flitted through his mind before he reached his end.

How did this monster know my name?

And then Leon Jefferson Montgomery was no more.

Afterword & Acknowledgments

First of all, thank you, Reader, for purchasing this anthology. My obvious desire is that you will have enjoyed each of these fifteen tales of the Odd Wild West. I'm super proud to showcase every author and story, all with a different mix of horror and the macabre.

A project like this is a collaboration, of sorts. It takes the authors, of course, but also readers like you, and an editor (or 'project manager') like me to bring us all together. So again, you have my gratitude for being part of the 'Monster Fight' team.

Special thanks go out to our Kickstarter Backers! Without your interest and support this anthology would not have gotten off the ground. I want to especially recognize the following 'super backers' who provided a bulk of the funding to pay our authors and illustrators for their creativity.

Alicia T. Stoesser/Kiwri/Nattwinged and Thomas Helm, along with Brittani Maddoux, Dark Owl Publishing, Elizabeth Fuller-Nicoll, Frank Lewis, Howard Blakeslee, Kerri 'Banshee' Abrahams, Marc Sorondo, Michael T. Burke, Michael Hickman, Phillip Miracle, Rose Prickett, Shawn Phelps, and a few others who wished to remain anonymous. Thank you!

Fans like you keep the world of weird westerns filled with monsters, ghouls, ghosts, and cryptids. Over the next few pages you'll read a few short biographies of the authors involved in this volume. Please track down some of their stories, novels, and other projects. Support them if you can or drop them a note and let them know you enjoyed their contribution to this anthology. As an author, I can tell you, those notes are super encouraging!

Finally, if you do social media, check out The Weird West Facebook Group. (Link: https://www.facebook.com/groups/1399320000228965) It's a pretty cool community where fans can share the latest updates and new releases relating to western horror and adjacent genres.

Oh, and any review of this book would be very much appreciated!

Once More, Thank you!
Lyndon Perry

Monster Fight Contributors

Thanks to all who contributed to Volume Two of *Monster Fight at the O.K. Corral*. (Authors, your check's in the mail or in the ether, as the case may be.) Let me introduce each of these fine writers to you.

Aaron Smith is an avid reader who decided to write the sort of stories he wanted to read. He does that now, in between doting on his wife playing with their two sons. A family law attorney, he has found much material in real life to help him create fictional monsters. He has been published in *Microhorror.com*, *Liberty Island*, and the anthologies *California Screamin'*, *Trump Utopias and Dystopias*, *MCSI: Magical Crime Scene Investigation*, *Ye Olde Magick Shoppe* and *Beyond Ballyhoo*. Follow Aaron on X at @AaronCSmith1 and Facebook at facebook.com/aaronsmithauthor.

Since 2020, B. L. Blankenship has notably been regarded as one of the major flag bearers for the popular subgenre of Western Horror. The extremely violent literary stylings that he has published under this name have stood in complete contrast to the theological and leadership titles that he has otherwise published as Benjamin Blankenship. In real life, he's a Holy Ghost-filled minister who has held different licenses and ordinations through multiple denominations. He likewise holds various degrees and certificates in different fields. He's a historian, a demonologist, an authority on the occult, a theologian, and so forth. For more, find him online here: linktr.ee/WesternHorror.

David Powell has taught school, directed plays, and portrayed zombies, but now he writes full-time, seeking out the pockets of chaos brewing in the corners of the grid. You can find his writings in magazines such as *Calliope* and *First Line Literary Journal*, and anthologies such as *Shattered Veil* and *Georgia Gothic*. You'll find a complete list, as well as free reads, on his website, davidlpowell.net.

Gregory Nicoll is an author and journalist whose work has been honored over the decades in both *The Year's Best Horror* and *The Year's Best Music Writing*. During 2021 he was able to memorably combine both of his specialties for a story in *Gabba Gabba Hey: An Anthology of Fiction Inspired by the Music of The Ramones*. Greg's enduringly popular short-short "Beer Run" (about the difficulty of shopping for barley pop during the zombie apocalypse) was recently reprinted in *Horror for the Throne: One-Sitting Reads*, and his mystical western "From Camelot to Deadwood" appeared in the July 2022 issue of *Frontier Tales Magazine*.

Gustavo Bondoni is a novelist and short story writer with over three hundred stories published in fifteen countries, in seven languages. He is a member of Codex and an Active Member of SFWA. His latest novel is a dark historic fantasy entitled *The Swords of Rasna* (2022). He has also published five science fiction novels, four monster books, and a thriller entitled *Timeless*. His short fiction is collected in *Pale Reflection* (2020), *Off the Beaten Path* (2019), *Tenth Orbit and Other Faraway Places* (2010) and *Virtuoso and Other Stories* (2011). In 2019, Gustavo was awarded second place in the Jim Baen Memorial Contest; in 2018 he received a Judges Commendation (and second place) in The James White Award. He was also a 2019 finalist in the Writers of the Future Contest. You can find out more at his website gustavobondoni.com.

Henry Herz's speculative fiction short stories include "Out, Damned Virus" (*Daily Science Fiction*), "Bar Mitzvah on Planet Latke" (*Coming of Age, Albert Whitman & Co.*), "The Magic Backpack" (*Metastellar*), "Unbreakable" (*Musing of the Muses,* Brigid's Gate Press), "The Case of the Murderous Alien" (*Spirit Machine,* Air and Nothingness Press), "The Ghosts of Enerhodar" (*Literally Dead,* Alienhead Press), "Maria & Maslow" (*Highlights for Children*), and "A Proper Party" (*Ladybug Magazine*). He's edited five anthologies and written twelve picture books, including the critically acclaimed *I Am Smoke*.

Jason M Waltz believes in storytelling heroes. Not only does he write them, he publishes them through Rogue Blades Entertainment, he promotes them with Rogue Blades Foundation, and he teaches writing them on The Write Side of the Road. For more information on all these endeavors, visit: rogue-blades.com.

John M. Floyd's work has appeared in more than 350 different publications, including *Alfred Hitchcock's Mystery Magazine, Ellery Queen's Mystery Magazine,*

Strand Magazine, The Saturday Evening Post, and four editions of Otto Penzler's best-mysteries-of-the-year anthologies. A former Air Force captain and IBM systems engineer, John is also an Edgar finalist, a Shamus Award winner, a five-time Derringer Award winner, a three-time Pushcart Prize nominee, and the author of nine books. Visit him at johnmfloyd.com.

Jonah Buck wanted to study eldritch knowledge and commune with pale, semi-human creatures that flit across the sunless landscape to terrorize the living, so he became an attorney in Oregon. His interests include history, professional stage magic, paleontology, and exotic poultry. He is the author of *Carrion Safari, Substratum,* and *100 Dark Horror Stories.*

L.B. Stimson has an extensive professional communications background in business and education. In 2015, she decided to renew her love of fiction and set to writing her first Gothic Horror novel. Since then, she has published six more books in the Gothic Horror Ghost genre, all of which are now available in audio format. Her books are inspired by her travels and her interest and experience in dealing with the paranormal. Most recently she was an expert witness for an episode of *Ghost Hunters*. Her experiences in the Philip Williams' House has inspired her to begin her first historical fiction book. *What Shall Remain* is due to release in 2024. While L.B. grew up in a rural community in central Idaho, she now resides in Virginia and enjoys exploring the vast history that continues to inspire her Southern Gothic books. You can learn more at www.lbstimson.com.

Lyndon Perry is a writer, editor, coffee drinker, and cat wrangler. He and his wife just moved to Puerto Rico with their 19-year-old orange and white tabby, who seems to be adjusting to beach life. He releases his projects, and those of a few others, through his indie publishing venture, Tule Fog Press at www.TuleFogPress.com.

Marc Sorondo lives with his wife and children in New York. He loves to read, and his interests range from fiction to comic books, physics to history, oceanography to cryptozoology, and just about everything in between. He's a perpetual student and occasional teacher. For more information, go to MarcSorondo.com.

Shawn Phelps studied anthropology at the University of Chicago. After leading a series of expeditions in the Amazon, he was elected to membership in The Explorers Club. He has been published in *The Watsonian, Penumbra,* and *Vastarien.*

Stoney M. Setzer lives south of Atlanta, GA. He has a beautiful wife, three wonderful children, and one crazy dog; and he is also a diehard Atlanta Braves fan. He has written a trilogy of novels about small-town amateur sleuth Wesley Winter (*Dead of Winter, Valley of the Shadow,* and *Day of Reckoning*). He has also written a short story anthology, *Zero Hour,* featuring Twilight Zone-like stories with Christian themes. He has also written short stories for *Ye Olde Dragons* anthologies, *Residential Aliens,* and *Fear and Trembling.* He is currently working on a novel about the residents of fictional Sardis County, Tennessee, and the strange events that happen there.

About his anthology contribution, Setzer writes: The inspiration for this story came from an exhibit at the Creation Museum in Petersburg, KY. The exhibit chronicles sightings of dinosaur-like creatures seen by humans. One display, entitled 'Cowboys and Dragons,' shares an article from the April 26, 1890 edition of the *Tombstone Epitath.* The article tells of two ranchers seeing and shooting at a creature described as "a winged monster, resembling a huge alligator with an extremely elongated tail and an immense pair of wings." That, along with the fact that Rodan has always been my favorite kaiju movie monster, helped spark the idea for 'Birds of Prey.'

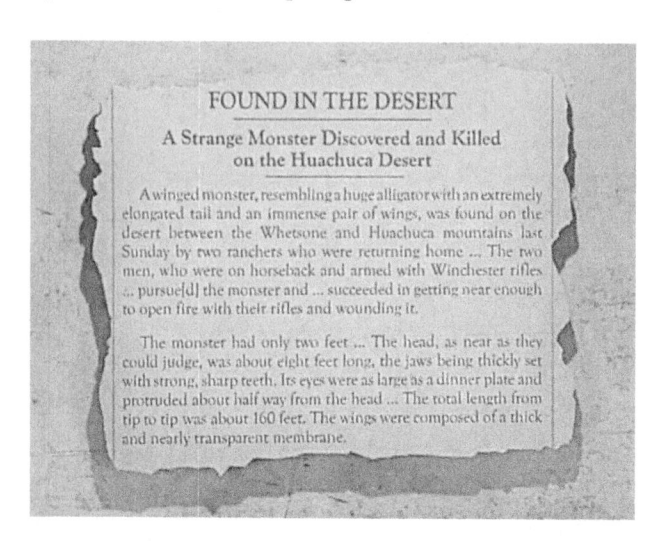

FOUND IN THE DESERT

A Strange Monster Discovered and Killed on the Huachuca Desert

A winged monster, resembling a huge alligator with an extremely elongated tail and an immense pair of wings, was found on the desert between the Whetsone and Huachuca mountains last Sunday by two ranchers who were returning home ... The two men, who were on horseback and armed with Winchester rifles ... pursue[d] the monster and ... succeeded in getting near enough to open fire with their rifles and wounding it.

The monster had only two feet ... The head, as near as they could judge, was about eight feet long, the jaws being thickly set with strong, sharp teeth. Its eyes were as large as a dinner plate and protruded about half way from the head ... The total length from tip to tip was about 160 feet. The wings were composed of a thick and nearly transparent membrane.

Su Haddrell lives in a quiet and picturesque corner of Worcester, UK, that's been cleverly disguised as a noisy council estate. She has had stories published by Fox Spirit, Grimbold Books, Phrenic Press and others. Her other interests include drumming, painting and organizing Lawless Comic Con. She loves rum, her cat, her boyfriend, and movies where things explode within the first fourteen seconds.

Tim Hanlon has been a history teacher since the dawn of time. He tries to follow the tenets of Stoic philosophy but generally fails. Since he began submitting stories during the great lockdown of 2020 he has had some success with tales selected for anthologies by Specul8 Publishing, Sundial Magazine, 18th Wall Productions, DMR Books, and Wicked Shadow Press. When not writing or reading, Tim enjoys banging on about craft beer with friends, boxing, and getting caught in the rain.

Trevor Denning is a freelance writer in middle-of-nowhere Michigan. When he's not writing, he's working out or feeding his cat scrambled eggs. You can find him on Locals at meanwhilewithtrevor.locals.com

Copyrights and Illustrations

Monster Fight at the O.K. Corral – Volume Two © 2023 by Tule Fog Press. All rights reserved. Lyndon Perry, Editor and Publisher, Vega Baja, Puerto Rico

The individual stories in this collection are copyrighted by their respective authors. These stories are fictitious; any resemblance to actual events, locales, or persons, living or dead, is entirely coincidental.

Water Talks to Water © 2023 by David Powell
Riding Out With a Dead Man © 2023 by Shawn Phelps
Only One Color Matters © 2023 by Aaron C. Smith
Silverlake © 2023 by John M. Floyd
The Watch © 2023 by Jonah Buck
Trail of the Black Coach © 2023 by Tim Hanlon
Entrails West © 2023 by Gregory Nicoll
The Cost of Gold © 2023 by Henry Herz
A Day's Ride from Tarabuco © 2023 by Gustavo Bondoni
The Hills Had a Heartbeat © 2023 by Trevor Denning
Birds of Prey © 2023 by Stoney M. Setzer
The Price of Gold © 2023 by Su Haddrell
Light in the Mine © 2023 by Marc Sorondo
One Shot, One Sin © 2023 by Jason M Waltz
Final Words © 2023 by B. L. Blankenship and L. B. Stimson

All illustrations in this anthology are used by permission. The copyright of each image belongs to its respective creator. The artwork portrays fictitious scenes; any resemblance to actual events, locales, or persons, living or dead, is coincidental.

Monster Fight, Volume 1 ~ cover design copyright by B. L. Blankenship
Monster Fight, Volume 2 ~ cover design copyright by B. L. Blankenship
A Witch's Brew ~ image by SquareFrog and licensed via Pixabay
The Gunman ~ image by SquareFrog and licensed via Pixabay
Double Helix ~ image by Erzebet Prikel and licensed via Pixaby

No part of this publication may be reproduced, stored in a retrieval system, or transmitted in any form or by any means without prior written permission from the publisher, except in brief quotations in printed or online reviews. Email TuleFogPress@gmail.com for information.

Monster Fight ~ Volume 1

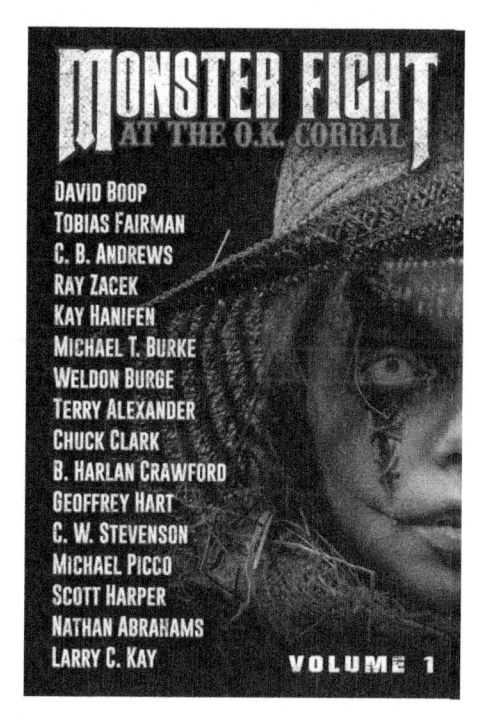

Of Trains and Tentacles by David Boop and Tobias Fairman
They're Bitin' Down at Bonita Creek by B. Harlan Crawford
Montague and the Return of Don Villanova by Scott Harper
At Dusk, Ye Shall Eat Flesh by Michael Picco
Eric Stone's Stallion by Terry Alexander
Not Forgotten by Nathan Abrahams
Nanimwé by Weldon Burge
Lucky by Chuck Clark
The Pilgrim by Ray Zacek
The Hungry Dead by Kay Hanifen
Gone Hunting by C. W. Stevenson
None Shall Be Lonely by Larry C. Kay
Under a Blood Moon by C. B. Andrews
Debate at the O.K. Corral by Geoffrey Hart
The Valley of Yellow Death by Michael T. Burke

Available on Amazon

Please Support our Authors and Sponsors

More About B. L. Blankenship...

 Prior to writing horror, Blakenship had a footprint in music as a lyricist, singer, and drummer — much of which was through his very Pentecostal band/group BEN*JAM. Beyond all of this, he is a full-time graphic artist and loves to create. In early 2023, Blankenship announced his departure from writing secular horror to shift his focus toward other endeavors. His books and music both continue to draw money. There are also video games, comic strips, and other mediums that he has been involved with.

 In 2024, a few more books have been announced to come out, two of them are within the subgenre of Christian Horror. Their titles are: *Give 'Em Hell: Christian Horror Anthology* and *Holy Ghost Exorcist*. While he has been very open about his wife's complete disdain for him writing horror, she (Victoria) has expressed enthusiasm toward the two Christian Horror books. Notably, she's stated that *The Confederado: A Western Horror Tale of MesoAmerican Gore* has no right to exist. Blankenship describes the book as total depravity, and horrotica, and says that it is what the world and life look like devoid of GOD. It stands to contrast the extremely comprehensive world of his series *God Walks The Dark Hills* where a full display of the intricacies of religion, culture, politics, and authentic history are utilized as a backdrop to tether these ultra-violent and demonic tales of terror to the real world.

 In the Summer of 2023, he re-released his book which was originally titled *Josey Wales Rides Again* as *Jodie Walls Rides Again* to avoid copyright issues. It is a late straight Western and coming-of-age novella that a lot of people love. He also released an illustrated book entitled *Chronicles of The Velveteen Preacher: The Dark City & World of Sin and Other Woeful Tales*. It comes off in a very Dr. Seuss meets Tim Burton sort of way. It's dark, dismal, and disparaging. The book is sort of like a narrative poem storybook for adults and maybe kids who aren't super sensitive or sheltered. While he said that he didn't necessarily think it'd sell super well, but put it out to pull this thing from him — Blankenship adds that he hopes that people enjoy the melancholy little ragdoll based on himself and his earlier life. If it goes well, more Velveteen Preacher stuff will surely arise, as he wrote a lot of it nearly a decade ago — only to have it sit in the shadows until now.

 For more, visit: linktr.ee/WesternHorror.

More from L. B. Stimson…

The Redwood Trilogy
A Pale Shade of Winter
The Farmhouse at Peace & Plenty
Gaston Hall: A Southern Gothic Horror Tale
The Haunting of Noyo Bay: A Gothic Ghost Story

www.lbstimson.com

REACH FOR THE SKY
Rogue Blades Entertainment

GUSTAVO BONDONI

PALE REFLECTION

A COLLECTION OF DARK FANTASY

Dark Owl Publishing

Novels, collections, and anthologies for adults and young readers

And lots more!

Follow us online on our website and social media!

Dark Owl Publishing, LLC
Where quality fiction comes to nest.
www.darkowlpublishing.com

ZERO HOUR

SHORT STORIES

STONEY M. SETZER

Are you ready for tales that carry you through the farthest reaches of imagination and lead you face-to-face with timeless truths? From the deck of the Titanic to the distant future, from carnival sideshows to secret laboratories, author Stoney M. Setzer presents this anthology of short stories that explore the shadowlands of imagination through the lens of faith. 350 pages. Available in e-book and paperback on Amazon.